The Couple Upstairs

Ann Girdharry

First published August 2021

Chapter One

At the river

Terror spurs me on. If I stumble or if I fall, they've got me. Then I'm dead.

I've discovered their secret and now they're coming to get me.

It's been pouring for days and I can hear the swollen river up ahead. My breath comes quick and sharp as I suck in rain and cold air.

Get to the water. Don't look behind. A vicious cramp stabs and I clutch my side and stumble on. I'm slipping and sliding on the muddy ground. The local radio said the banks have been breached and the bridge is unsafe but I've no choice.

The rain comes hard as hail and as the path heads downhill I struggle to keep my balance. Though I can't hear them I know they're not far behind. That's the problem with secrets – once you know other people's there's no going back.

I push through the trees and branches slap my face. *Not far now. You can make it.* If I cross the river I've got a fighting chance. Crowded with houses, the streets on the other side will make it impossible for them to follow me. I can get a car or find my way to the train station or to Brighton or hitch a lift to London and then I'll be away. It's them or me – a question of survival.

When I hear a shout coming from behind, my chest constricts. They're closing in. *Faster come on, go faster.* I'm jogging and my foot skids as the path takes a turn and then the river is in front of me. Swollen to a monstrous size, it's brown and churning with the force of the water.

'Stop!' Their shouts are full of rage.

The bridge is close and I'm out in the open now as I put on a spurt, pushing to my limit. The police have erected barriers to prevent cars accessing the crossing.

I can sense the river's threatening power. Hair plasters across my forehead and into my eyes as I skirt the barrier and in the corner of my vision I catch sight of a flash of movement. They're coming my way fast. *Hurry. Get across before it's too late.*

As I step onto the bridge my foot sinks into water as deep as my knee. *Oh no.* The flood has risen in record time.

'Come back! We can keep it secret.'

It's a lie.

I take another step and their shouting is drowned out by the roar of the current.

Clenching my teeth, I wade forward into the icy water. There's a stone wall and I cling to it, making my way cautiously as the force pushes against my legs. Three more strides and the level is over my knees. Oh god, I'll be washed away. I grab the wall with both hands as my left leg loses purchase.

If I turn back now I'm dead. And if I try to advance, I'm finished. Who could survive being swept away in this torrent?

'No! Come back.'

A quick glance behind and I see them standing at the barrier.

One more step, come on keep going. You deserve to live.

And if not, better at my hand than at theirs.

As I lift a foot, I feel the greedy suck of the current. I scrabble madly for safety, panic overwhelming me and the last thing I hear is the roar of the water as the river drags me under.

Chapter Two

Ellie wanted to throw something at her husband's head. Rob was such an idiot. Why had he agreed? When they'd already decided – no children.

'We discussed it and I said no children in the apartment,' Ellie said. 'You shouldn't have told the agent he could bring one here.'

'He sort of got under my guard,' Rob said.

'Did he?'

Rob ran a hand through his hair. 'You know what Adam's like.'

Ellie understood how their agent, Adam, who was also their neighbour, could be very persuasive. That wasn't the issue. The problem was Rob giving in.

'You know how convincing Adam can be,' Rob said. 'You said so yourself last time we saw him – Adam is full of charm and it's what makes him good at his job. Besides, Sabrina Gibson sounds like a good prospect.'

Ellie felt tears prickling the back of her eyes and she blinked them away. 'The child is a complication and I don't want her here.'

'Give it a chance.'

Rob came up and put his arms around her waist. He pulled her close and ran his hands up and down her back and massaged her shoulders. Wow, her husband was irresistible.

He always could get her to do what he wanted. That was the madness of being in love and it made you weak and stupid.

'What's the harm in meeting her?' Rob said, brushing his lips down her neck.

Ellie snuggled close. 'Stop trying to win me round, Rob Mitchell. I'm not falling for any of it. One adult, female, and no children, that's what we wanted.' Her voice sounded muffled against his shoulder. She wiped quickly at her eyes and hoped he didn't notice.

It was hard for Ellie to believe how much her life had changed in the last twelve months. Before their whirlwind romance she had been in London, living the life of a single woman fast approaching middle age. She worked long hours writing her novels and, for relaxation, spent time at the gym or with women friends. Men friends had been sparse and boyfriends even rarer.

Though no one she knew was aware of it, she had been living her life one day to the next, with no plan other than to survive. Every morning she had allowed herself a few secret moments - of despair for what she had to endure - before heading to her laptop to start work.

Then, one rainy night in the little Sussex town of Lewes, everything had changed because Ellie met Rob Mitchell. Several months later he proposed to her and she decided to sell her London property because she said she fell in love not only with Rob but also with the quaint town of Lewes.

It had been Ellie who searched for a new house to suit them both, and she had pounced on this grand old place on the hill. They had it renovated from top to bottom and it was perfect with a loft room for Ellie to do her writing, and the ground floor already had a self-contained apartment which they decided to keep.

It had been her idea to rent the apartment out. The houses on the hill were set in their own grounds which meant the nearest neighbour was several minutes' walk away. She was used to being in a city surrounded by apartments. It might be nice to have someone downstairs when Rob was at work. Rob had been happy about the idea.

'Of course you're in charge, darling,' Rob said. 'Look, it's too late to cancel now. They'll be here any minute so let's make them welcome and just see how it goes. Remember the first two prospects have been no-goers so if Ms Gibson is as good as she seems…' Rob was giving her a winning smile.

'Let me decide if she's right or not.' *And I really don't think she will be.*

Why was married life so complicated.

Chapter Three

Rob Mitchell watched his wife as she plumped the cushions on the sofa. Well, Ellie was bashing them rather than plumping them. With long dark hair and wearing a chocolate-coloured dress, she was beautiful to him. He knew she didn't think that way about herself. In fact, she had confided in him that men rarely looked her way and how at school she had been taunted for being ugly. At the very best, Ellie considered herself to be plain. Rob was making it his job to persuade her otherwise.

Ellie turned her hazel eyes on him. She seemed upset he hadn't discussed it with her. *Uh-oh*. Rob prepared to defend his corner. After so many years on his own, married life was turning out to be quite a challenge.

'We discussed it. I said no children in the apartment,' Ellie said. 'You shouldn't have told the agent he could bring one here.'

Rob put his arms around his wife. He pulled her close and ran his hands up and down to melt away the tension. His wife's skin was silky smooth and smelled of vanilla. The scent tickled his nose.

'What's the harm in meeting her?' he said, brushing his lips down her neck.

In their short marriage Rob had learned Ellie wasn't very good at standing her ground. He waited and could feel her leaning into him and softening under his touch. With luck, her resistance to the idea of a single mother as a tenant would fade away. And why not? Having a child downstairs didn't pose any extra difficulty. Actually, as far as he was concerned, it could speed along his plans.

Rob put on his softest expression. The problem was he had been on his own for so long it was difficult to do things as a couple. He was still learning how to compromise. Twenty long years he had lived alone and then along came Ellie like a miracle just in the nick of time. It was true, they had agreed no children in the apartment but couldn't she be a bit flexible?

Before they met, Rob had been living in a place down by the river. He never admitted to others how lonely he was and instead he filled his life with work and with play. He had been expecting to reach his fifties and still be a widower. Meeting Ellie had been the best thing to happen to him in the last two decades and when she married him, he couldn't believe his luck.

He had agreed they rent out the downstairs apartment because he wanted to do everything he could to make her happy.

'Let me decide if she's right or not,' Ellie said.

Rob kept his mouth shut. The agent had already sent a file on Sabrina Gibson. Sabrina was moving down to Lewes to escape a messy divorce. It made it sound as if she'd be isolated, and isolated and vulnerable was just about perfect. As far as Rob was concerned, she sounded the ideal person.

Chapter Four

Sabrina's stomach was scrunched into a knot. *Get a grip,* she told herself, *a woman your age should be able to keep it together*. All she had to do was give a good impression but being an almost-forty mother of one wasn't a recipe for having nerves of steel. Sabrina's hands were anxious and sweaty as she gripped the seat belt.

They were driving along Lewes town high street. The lettings agent had his concentration on the traffic and she hoped he didn't notice the state she was in.

As the houses went by, fear swirled around Sabrina's insides making her glad she'd not eaten breakfast. To be honest, she felt right on the edge a lot of the time. It got worse when she left the house and peaked whenever she was in a car. People said you learned how to live with the aftermath of trauma and most survivors learned how to control overwhelming feelings. She knew it wasn't true.

The lettings agent, Adam, indicated to turn right and he took his eyes off the road to give her a smile.

'I've squeezed you in for this appointment and we're lucky because it's a great apartment. The sort to get snapped up fast,' Adam said.

Adam, young and with a light-hearted way about him, was the type of person who reminded Sabrina there were still good people in the world.

'Don't be worried,' he said. 'The Mitchells are keen to rent it out as soon as possible. They requested no children except it was easy to persuade the husband to let you come for a viewing. A mature renter makes all the difference. The Mitchells want to meet you.'

Sabrina twisted her hands in her lap. 'You really think I've got a chance?'

'Of course you have. When renters say no children they usually mean toddlers. Your daughter, Maddy, is five years old and she's a model child and like I said your maturity will swing it. Trust me.'

He was kind. He was trying to calm her nerves because he knew that being a single mum, Sabrina didn't feel optimistic about finding somewhere decent to rent even if she was as he diplomatically said, a mature woman.

Adam was right about one thing – Maddy was an easy child. It was probably because she lived in an imaginary world of her own most of the time. There had not been a day when Sabrina didn't thank her lucky stars for her daughter's ability to cut off the outside. Without it, how could Maddy have survived their past?

The Sussex town of Lewes was picturesque, with a high street lined with quirky-looking shops. They passed a bookshop in a building which was so old, timber beams showed in the walls. Lewes was a lot different to the place Sabrina had come from.

'What do you know about the owners?' she asked.

'Believe it or not they're my neighbours. I rent a place in the big house down the hill from them.' Adam smiled. 'The Mitchells are both late thirties and professionally successful. Rob Mitchell is a doctor and Ellie is an author. Our office administrator was at school with the landlord and I know I shouldn't gossip but she says Rob Mitchell was known as the perfect catch. Apparently there was a terrible tragedy and his first wife died. After that, he stayed a confirmed bachelor and he remained single right up until he met his current wife, Ellie, only last year.'

'You said she's a writer?'

'Yeah she writes romance novels which is not my thing at all. Seems like Mr and Mrs Mitchell had a whirlwind romance themselves.' He laughed. 'Ellie's really nice. She and I get on well.'

Once they crossed a little bridge, Lewes high street narrowed into a pedestrian area. The road turned a corner and they started to climb a hill.

Adam waved his hand. 'That's the river Ouse. It goes all the way to the south coast. At the top of this hill there's a golf course and the South Downs which is a great if you like walking and the view is stunning. The Mitchells' house is about half-way up and I've got to tell you it's a fabulous location. I love it.'

The road wound its way upwards. The area had an exclusive air with big houses set in their own grounds. The apartment they were going to was on the ground floor of the Mitchells' house. Both modern and affordable, Sabrina had spotted it in the online announcements. She'd thought it sounded too good to be true.

'Not far now,' Adam said.

Strapped in at the back, Maddy gave a small burp.

'Mummy, I feel sick.'

Oh no. Sabrina felt her own stomach flipping. She imagined turning up with a kid covered in vomit and she could see her hopes draining away.

'Should we stop?' Adam asked.

He was early-twenties. He didn't have children, she was sure of it, and he was full of sunny good vibes.

Twisting in her seat, she assessed her daughter. Maddy was fast going green at the gills.

'Sorry, I think we'd better pull over right now,' Sabrina said.

'No problem.'

It was a single lane road and they parked as soon as they got to a passing place. Sabrina helped her daughter out and Maddy was promptly sick into the grass verge.

'Looks like we made it in time. You did good to hold it in, kiddo,' Adam said.

'I feel better now,' Maddy said.

Sabrina fumbled for tissues in her bag and did her best at mopping up. Luckily, Maddy's hair had been tied back and she was glad to see most of the damage had avoided her daughter's clothes.

'Gosh I'm sorry, Adam.'

'Please don't keep apologising. Tell you what, why don't we walk from here? It's only a couple of minutes. That house down there is where I live, do you see it? The one covered with ivy. The Mitchells' place is up the hill but it isn't far. Think you can make it kiddo?'

Maddy grinned at Adam as he tucked his laptop case under his arm and pretended to get ready to sprint.

'Bet I can beat you there,' he said.

Though Maddy rolled her eyes, he had hooked her. 'Bet you can't,' Maddy replied.

Sabrina watched as Adam and Maddy laughed and set off together with her daughter's blonde hair swishing across her back. If only she could be as carefree as them only that went out the window many years ago.

It was a lovely day and the sun was hot on her shoulders. It looked like it was going to be a nice summer. As she slipped off her jacket, Sabrina felt a sudden tingling at the back of her neck. She swivelled and scanned around her, suddenly cold. Was someone watching? Was someone spying? Her gaze settled on the ivy-covered house and she shivered. *Stop that,* she told herself. *No one can be watching you here.*

She made herself take a few deep breaths as she rubbed away the goosebumps. From close by came the sound of a lawn mower. A strong scent of cut grass wafted her way. Sussex was a lovely rural area, full of people who lived normal lives, who did normal things behind their doors and outside their doors. *You can do this. There's no danger here.*

Shaking her hair and then smoothing it down, she stuck out her chin. This was a new start. *Come on,* she said to herself, *you know what you want and nothing and no one can stop you.*

Chapter Five

A while later, Sabrina sat with her hands clasped firmly between her knees. Beyond the formalities of introducing herself she was scared to speak. What if she said the wrong thing? What if she put Rob and Ellie Mitchell off?

Adam had already taken her on a tour of the apartment and the place was lovely. It took up most of the ground floor with the rest being the Mitchells' double garage. Since the house was on a hill, the main room of the apartment had a wonderful view of the sky and then of the rooftops of the town below. She had her own entrance tucked into the corner, which led into the apartment's kitchen. There were two bedrooms, an open plan lounge with a dining area, and a bathroom tiled in oyster grey with a bathtub set into an alcove like something she had seen in a film. She could imagine what it would be like lying back in that tub – it would be heaven. The Mitchells must have spent a ton refurbishing the place. If this was anything to go by, their own house, above the apartment, must be absolutely luxurious.

Adam was doing a brilliant job showcasing Sabrina's good references from her time as a hotel receptionist. As usual, Maddy was behaving, sitting quietly on the carpet engrossed in playing with her plastic farm animals and Sabrina thanked her lucky stars for the millionth time for how blessed she was to have her.

'You're new to this area aren't you? What are your plans, Ms Gibson?' Ellie Mitchell asked.

Rob and Ellie were a stylish couple. Sabrina found it difficult to take her attention away from Rob, with his golden brown curls and an unmistakable air of success. He wore smart trousers and an open neck shirt. A specialist in heart surgery, Rob Mitchell worked at Brighton General Hospital, which was about half an hour's drive away. She was sure his patients must adore him – especially the women.

Then there was Ellie. It was difficult to understand what a man like Rob would see in such an ordinary looking woman. She wore a nice dress with her dark hair tied over one shoulder, although she had no striking features. In fact, Sabrina had to admit Ellie looked very plain. Ellie didn't look like an author either, then again, how did Sabrina know because she'd never met one before.

Rob's hand languidly draped across the back of the sofa, his fingertips teasing the back of his wife's neck. Sabrina could not help feeling a twinge of jealousy.

As far as ages were concerned, she guessed all three of them were similar. Smoothing her skirt, she suddenly noticed a stain she had missed, made by Maddy heaving up her lunch. She quickly covered it with her hand.

'Oh you mean will I be working? Well, I'll only start looking once I've got Maddy settled at school and I'll want something part-time.'

Adam had already explained Sabrina had significant funds from the settlement of her divorce and was financially self-sufficient.

'Do you like the apartment?' Ellie asked.

Only someone with brain cells missing wouldn't like it. The place was perfect. Just like its owners.

'Oh yes, it's ideal and I can promise you my daughter won't be a nuisance.'

Everyone's attention turned to Maddy and Sabrina cursed her own clumsiness because she and Adam already agreed Maddy was supposed to stay in the background.

'What I mean is she's very well behaved,' she added quickly, realising she was digging herself in deeper.

'We can see that,' Rob said. 'She's absorbed. If we had children I'd hope they'd be as content as Maddy.' Rob Mitchell reached out and squeezed his wife's hand.

Ellie seemed to freeze. There was a small silence as Ellie Mitchell's hand fluttered to her chest. It was as if there was something wrong with her. Ideal husband, flawless house – yet perhaps the woman's life wasn't so perfect after all. Adam smiled at everyone and especially at Ellie until Ellie relaxed.

Attention drifted back to the little girl. Maddy didn't notice them inspecting her and Sabrina held her breath and braced herself for a rejection. How could they want her and Maddy in their immaculate flat? She almost wished she had never seen it because it would make it so much harder to know what she had missed out on. Down on the floor, her daughter played with a cow and a horse making them talk silently to each other.

'She's adorable,' Rob whispered.

'Is there any particular reason you've decided to move to Lewes?' Ellie asked.

'I want a fresh start. There's no point going into details but our lives haven't been easy since the divorce and we needed to get away.'

'Oh dear,' Ellie said, her brow puckering. 'That doesn't sound very nice. Divorce can leave women so… vulnerable.'

Ah, so Ellie Mitchell had a kind heart. Sabrina hoped it could be turned to her advantage. Nodding, she bit at her bottom lip.

'I don't like to think of women struggling because they've been left in a difficult situation,' Ellie said.

Sabrina shrugged. 'It's tough being on my own.'

'You mean you don't know anyone in this part of the country?' Rob said.

'Not a soul.' Sabrina tucked her hair behind her ear. 'My family are in the Midlands except I didn't want to move back there. Maddy and I stuck a pin in the map and it landed in Lewes. A centimetre more and we'd have been in the Channel.'

Rob's sudden chuckle took her by surprise. She clenched her hands and gave a nervous smile.

'What will you do if you don't find a place to stay?' Ellie asked.

'I'll just have to keep looking.' She glanced at her daughter. 'Though, as you can imagine, it's not easy.'

'Let me have a quick word with my husband.'

Rob and Ellie stepped out of the room and Adam gave Sabrina a grin.

'It's going well,' Adam said. 'I'm getting good vibes.'

'Let's hope so.'

It seemed an age before the couple came back. *Take it on the chin and for goodness sake don't let your disappointment show. No tears!*

'I'm glad you decided to come today,' Ellie said. 'We think you sound perfect. When can you move in?'

Chapter Six

Every time Ellie looked at Rob it reminded her how lucky she was. She felt so grateful because he was handsome and alluring and special. In her quiet, secret moments, Ellie knew he was The One. The person she had been waiting for her whole life. It helped to silence the little voice that whispered in her head, that said things like – How can he be in love with somebody like *you*? What if he finds out what you've done? And he realises he's made a terrible mistake?

At the kitchen sink, Rob was washing salad for supper, his wedding ring glistening on his finger.

Ellie went to the vase of roses on the counter. Rearranging them, she inhaled. She loved their sweet scent as much as their gorgeous colours. At the cupboard, she took out supper plates and put them on the table. The days were lengthening and getting hotter. Soon they would be able to eat outside on the terrace and she was so looking forward to lazy summer evenings. Then a cold sliver of reality slipped in to shatter her dreams. She was living on borrowed time and the longer she left it, the worse it would be when the truth came out. How could Rob ever forgive her?

Staring at the cutlery in her hand, she gripped it over tight. *Tell him, just tell him*. But it was too late for that now.

'You're very thoughtful,' Rob said. 'Sometimes I catch a certain look on your face and it's like you've gone off to another place.'

She laughed it off. 'Hmm, well I got a feeling you took a liking to Sabrina,' she said, deftly changing the subject.

'You know I'm a sucker for a sad story.'

Placing down the forks, she watched her husband carefully. The tone of his voice didn't change and neither did his posture. There was no defensiveness in him yet she knew women were his weakness. *Come on Ellie, loosen up - you can't suspect him of being drawn to every attractive woman who comes into his orbit. Besides, you're the one who felt sorry for Sabrina and it's too late to change your mind now.*

It was silly of her to feel suspicious yet she couldn't help it – the nurses Rob worked with, the female doctors, the patients – they all adored him. Ellie told herself off. She had nothing to worry about. Rob was one hundred per cent hers and he was always telling her so. Besides, Sabrina Gibson wasn't the sort of woman who might attract his attention. Sabrina wore clothes which didn't do much for her and, basically, she had let herself go. Though no one could blame her after a separation and with a little one to look after.

Ellie sighed. She should stop looking for a threat where there wasn't one. The last twelve months were the happiest she had been for a long time. Rob Mitchell was the catch of the year if not the decade, and if she had not realised that already, then she soon did once she moved down to Lewes because everyone kept telling her so.

Lewes was a small town full of small-town gossips and Ellie constantly met people who told her how woman after woman had gone after Rob and failed. She had heard it at the dentist, at her yoga class, even at the goddam bank. It turned out half of Lewes wanted to gossip about how, when Rob's first wife who was his childhood sweetheart, died, he had been heartbroken. He had been a bachelor ever since.

Against all the odds, Ellie had been the one to change him.

The elderly neighbour down the hill, Kath, who was Adam's landlady and Ellie's friend, had said it to her face as soon as they met. Ellie had worked a miracle on Rob Mitchell.

And why shouldn't I be happy? Why shouldn't I be in love and find someone who loves me? Except she could think of a very good reason why.

Pouring the sauce over the pasta, she gave it a stir and breathed in the rich cream and parmesan. Guilt for the secret she kept welled up and she pushed it away. Her mind drifted back to when she and Rob first met.

A local art gallery had invited her to give a talk on being an author. It had been pouring with rain and she had driven down to Lewes from London. The motorway had been nose to tail and the spray had been blinding. In the dark it had taken her ages to find the venue and it was still chucking it down when she arrived outside the gallery. She was muttering and swearing when she parked and grabbed a box of books from the back. It felt like it weighed two tonnes and the car park was riddled with puddles. Then the bottom of the box collapsed. As her novels splattered into the wet she had desperately tried to save them.

It was Rob who came to her rescue. Together they salvaged as many as they could. It was only once they were in the dry she got a good look at him. She noticed Rob's curls and his warm eyes and the spark between them had been almost tangible.

Though she wrote about romance she had never been lucky in love until that night. Rob Mitchell had stayed for her talk, joining the twenty-or-so avid book readers who had ventured out on a rainy night. It turned out Rob's sister, who was the art gallery manager, had arranged the session.

Much later Ellie discovered Rob hated reading novels, especially romance, which had given them both a good laugh. He sat in the front row and Ellie had found it hard to not stare in his direction and whenever she did she found Rob Mitchell's attention riveted on her. It had given her tingles. She thought of herself as mostly invisible to men and it had been like that all her life.

After the talk Rob asked her to dinner. It turned out the spark between them wasn't only from her side which had seemed like a goddam miracle. Twelve months later they were married and the rest, as they say, was history.

He placed his hand over hers. 'After we've eaten I was wondering about an early night – what do you think?'

'Lovely idea.'

That was the other amazing thing because Rob clearly liked sex with her and he wanted it often, and desirable was the last word she would have used to describe herself.

Twenty minutes later, she pushed away her supper and led the way up the stairs. Sex was something she had not had any of for years and now they couldn't get enough. How could life be this good? Especially for someone like her who didn't deserve a second chance?

Rob wanted children and Ellie pretended she did too, except she knew she could never have one. It wasn't right to keep secrets from Rob though she knew he could never withstand the truth. It would destroy them. She should have told him right at the beginning and she had been too much of a coward to, sensing how it would push him away. And now she carried on blindly going forwards – a lemming heading for the cliff, except this one knew it was on a course for disaster.

Chapter Seven

On her way down into town, Ellie called by her neighbour's house. It was their regular coffee slot and she enjoyed chatting to Kath Nettle. Kath was retired and she had lived in Lewes all her life. She knew everyone and she knew everything about them too. When Ellie first arrived in Lewes, Kath had been very welcoming. As editor of the Lewes Blog, Kath published articles of local interest, all masterminded from her own computer. Ellie had already written a couple of pieces for the blog about being an author and she'd given an interview.

'Hello my dear,' Kath said, as she ushered Ellie into the lounge. 'I've been looking forward to seeing you.'

Ellie laughed. 'Is it because of our new tenant?'

'Of course not, well, I've got to admit she's piqued my curiosity. Adam is so discreet, he refuses to give much away. When does she move in?'

Early on, Rob had warned Ellie how Kath had a terrible reputation as a local gossip. He didn't like Kath, though it seemed Kath didn't have a bad word to say about Rob.

'Next week, and all I can tell you is she's very nice and she's recently divorced.'

Kath took the lid off the teapot and peered inside. 'Oh. I guess we'll have to wait and see then.'

Ellie kept a diplomatic silence. Ellie was convinced Kath's acceptance of her had helped along insertion into Lewes social life. Rob had scoffed at the idea, saying Kath Nettle didn't have that kind of influence, she simply thought she did, but Ellie wasn't so sure.

'How's your new manuscript coming together?' Kath asked.

'Slowly. I've got the plot in my mind and now I'm concentrating on the people. I'm thinking of having a French woman as my main character.'

'Ooh, maybe you can get a trip to France in to do some research,' Kath said. 'Wouldn't that be exciting.'

'It would be if I had a chance to travel.' Ellie wafted her hand. 'We said we wouldn't let being married get in the way of our careers although the truth is, Rob goes away on his weekend doctors' conferences but he prefers me to be a homebird. Since I like making him happy it means…'

'Ah, it means no long weekend in Paris for you.'

'Not at the moment. Maybe later, once we're more used to living together.'

'Hmm. In my experience, it's best to start out how you mean to go on. Don't give too much up for him, otherwise Rob, even though he's such a lovely man, might get to rely on it.'

Kath often complimented Rob. It had been embarrassing at first. Kath had been a primary school teacher, and apparently, Rob had been one of her favourite pupils. She had predicted his success early on and didn't miss an opportunity to say great things about his achievements. *A heart surgeon, no less. How wonderful.*

'Why don't you tell me about your new plot?' Kath said. 'I'd love to hear the beginning of the story. Do you share them with Rob?'

'Are you kidding me. He hates romance.'

'Well, he's too busy saving lives, I suppose. He's a very talented man. Did I tell you he operated on my late husband?'

Kath had told Ellie several times. What made it more awkward was how Rob pretended to like Kath to her face and behind her back made nasty comments about her. He was always complaining about her gossiping and he liked to spread the word Kath was getting confused, though Ellie knew this was a frank lie. Ellie didn't like it because, as a local boy turned successful surgeon, Rob had a lot of influence in the town. She tried to turn a blind eye. Weekly chats with Kath were something Ellie looked forward to and she counted her neighbour as a good friend. She stirred her tea and sat back, recounting the beginning of her new novel and liking Kath's little smile as she quietly listened.

Chapter Eight

It was an exciting day. Sabrina was moving in and Ellie was looking forward to welcoming their new tenant and getting to know her. She put on jeans and an old sweatshirt. Standing at the kitchen window, she tapped her nails on the countertop.

When they refurbished the house they hadn't held back on the money – with luxury fittings throughout, Ellie had a top of the range kitchen with granite worksurfaces and an oyster grey theme, a white stone fireplace in the main room and polished floorboards with Persian rugs, four huge bedrooms two of which had ensuite bathrooms, and her own loft room sanctuary. It was a dream house. Rob had a good job and having inherited money from his late wife, he was wealthy. Ellie had a comfortable income from her books. She had insisted on going fifty-fifty with him on the renovations though he had offered to pay for it all.

Her husband was a generous man and he willingly shared his money with her. Ellie was more cautious, and she preferred to keep her earnings separate because she had learned the hard way to protect herself. All Rob said was that one day he hoped she would trust him. It had made her feel guilty because she realised that day might never come. The good thing was, Rob hadn't pushed her on it.

She loved the wonderful view across the rooftops of Lewes. Today there was blue sky to the horizon, with a few wispy clouds here and there. The skylarks were singing and it was going to be glorious.

Not long after, Rob came downstairs, buttoning his cuffs.

'I've a heart bypass surgery to perform this morning.'

He liked to make grand announcements and his expectation was she would then shower him with compliments about how wonderful he was. Ellie had learned to go along with it because without her adoration Rob was prone to bad moods. Well, he was a heart surgeon after all, so didn't he deserve it? What he did was pretty awe-inspiring.

She patted his chest and smiled into his eyes. 'Oh gosh darling, I hope it goes well.'

He drank it in. It was a small price to pay for Rob Mitchell's love and she followed up with a kiss. 'Love you,' she said.

'Sorry darling, it means I can't be here to welcome Sabrina and Maddy.'

'Don't worry about it. I've decided to give myself the day off.' She brushed the curls back from his face. 'Helping out will be a great way to get to know our new guest.'

Rob kissed her. 'Remember don't ask too many questions, we don't want to put the poor woman off. Let's ease our way into this.'

'No worries. You know you can trust me.'

'Can I?'

She laughed and popped some bread in the toaster. Rob was getting to know her habits. If there was one thing she could not resist, it was a good story. Sabrina Gibson was divorced and her bowed shoulders spoke of someone who dragged around a mountain of baggage. There was definitely a story to be had about Sabrina's ex-husband and why it went wrong. Curiosity made Ellie a good writer yet it sometimes meant she found it difficult to hold back on the questions, however hard she tried.

She passed the time by doing a little bit of gardening, not that she was a pro with plants, far from it, she was a novice, but having been restricted in London to a balcony and a few pots, having her own outside space felt like paradise.

On one side of the house, they had a terraced garden with a huge main lawn on the top terrace, and trees and shrubs on the lower terrace. She had the whole thing landscaped when they moved in, keeping the old trees along the bottom wall of the garden and creating the terraces and changing the layout of the rest. She had flower beds along both sides of the lawn, and there were cosy places to sit, like where they put the hammock or the barbecue area with a roof for shade. Ellie also had her own herb garden close to the house and the main lawn was overlooked by her kitchen and the first-floor terrace.

A fence partitioned off a strip along the side of the lawn for the apartment. On the opposite side of the house was the driveway and Ellie had added two banks of flowering shrubs. Right outside Ellie's front door, which was at ground floor level on the driveway side due to the incline of the hill, she had kept a lovely bank of roses which had been planted by the previous owner. They were either side of the front door and currently in full bloom. Ellie adored them, breathing in their sweet scent every time she passed. When she took a break from her writing, she had a habit of making a drink and then going outside to admire them.

While she waited for their new tenant, Ellie spent the time snipping off the dead heads.

An hour or so later, Sabrina drove into the courtyard in a battered looking hatchback.

'hi Sabrina, pull in here. As close to the house as you can and then you can park further down the drive once you've finished unloading.'

Their driveway led past the house to a lower parking area which was separated from the terraces by a thick hedge.

'Okay, thanks,' Sabrina said.

Maddy was in the front seat and the car was stuffed with boxes. Gosh, when Ellie moved in she needed to hire a huge moving van and three men to do the lifting. Where was the rest of Sabrina's belongings? This couldn't be all they had. What had happened to mean Sabrina had to leave so much behind? Ellie's inquisitiveness jumped up a notch.

'I thought I'd give you a hand moving in your stuff,' she said, taking off her gardening gloves.

'You really don't need to. I can manage.'

'Not on your own you can't.'

'I can smell those roses from here, how lovely. When I came here with Adam I remember thinking how beautiful they were.'

'I know, wasn't I really lucky to inherit them? The previous owner must have been a rose lover because they've been so well looked after and I just hope I can do as good a job.' She smiled. 'Come on, why don't we get started.'

'Gosh thanks, that's really kind.'

Sabrina opened up the boot which was crammed full.

'You should have asked and we'd have recommended a moving company,' Ellie said.

Sabrina wafted a hand. 'Just for this lot? It wouldn't be worth it and I didn't fancy a whole load of strange men tramping through the place.'

'Right.'

To Ellie's relief, Maddy didn't speak to her. The child hung around the car for a while and then her mother led her through the apartment and out into the garden on the other side. Ellie swallowed hard as a feeling of terrible loss welled up. Closing her eyes, she did her best to squeeze it away. At least it's a girl, she thought, a boy would have been even worse.

An hour or so later, the boxes had been stacked inside.

'This is really kind of you,' Sabrina said.

'Don't be silly it's only a few boxes and I want us to be friends. I don't know many people here and it would be nice if we get on. Why don't we have a cup of tea and then I can help you unpack?'

Ellie took Sabrina up to her kitchen and out onto the first-floor terrace. The terrace was her pride and joy.

'What a fantastic view,' Sabrina said.

'Isn't it. It's what made me choose the house in the first place and can you see that chalk cliff at the edge of the South Downs? Would you believe it's the site of a historic 1800s avalanche. They say it was the worst ever recorded in England.'

'Cool. There's a castle in Lewes too, isn't there? And a priory named after one of the wives of Henry the Eighth? Lewes has got a lot of history for such a small town.'

'Yes it has and you probably mean Anne of Cleves Priory and it's really nice. Then there's Southover Grange with lovely gardens and the tea shop will be open there soon. We should go sometime.'

They chatted about the history of the town and Ellie talked about giving her place up in London and deciding to move to Lewes. She told Sabrina how they had made the attic into a room where she did her writing. It would have been natural for Sabrina to share a little about her own background, except she didn't. Ellie stopped herself from prying though she was dying to know more. She reminded herself Rob wanted them to go slow.

Maddy came up to the terrace carrying palms full of daisies she'd picked from the lawn.

'Are you going to make a daisy chain?' Sabrina said.

'Uh-huh. Can I have some juice please?' Maddy asked.

With the child so close Ellie found it difficult to act normally and not hold her breath. All she could do was hope Maddy would go away soon.

'Of course you can,' Ellie said, hoping they couldn't hear the wobble in her voice. *Come on Ellie, you can do this.*

'Do you and Rob have plans to have children?' Sabrina asked.

It took her completely off guard and she almost dropped the jug, slopping juice over the table.

'Opps, how silly of me.' She grabbed some paper roll and dabbed at the mess. 'Oh, w-we're not in any rush. It's been a crazy year. We met and fell in love and got married and bought a house. My feet haven't touched the ground for twelve months. That's enough of a miracle for the time being.'

'Sure,' Sabrina nodded. 'I understand.'

Did she? Ellie doubted it.

'Anyway what about you?' Ellie said, her good intentions forgotten. 'You said you were divorced so I'm guessing you've left Maddy's father?

'That's right and the least said about him the better. You should probably know I never mention him to my daughter because she gets upset. He was an unpleasant man and things were pretty bad when we parted.' Sabrina leant towards Ellie and spoke softly. 'He became aggressive.'

'That's terrible.'

'It doesn't matter because it's in the past, trust me, you don't know how vindictive people can be until you've experienced it. My ex must have been one of the worst.'

'Shit.'

'Exactly, why do you think I'm a nervous wreck? It was years of being ground down by a bastard and then struggling to get free.'

Poor thing, she must have been through the wringer.

'Anyway, maybe I should make a start on the unpacking and if I'm lucky I can finish it by the end of the day.'

'Why don't I give you a hand?'

'You really don't have to, Ellie. You've done plenty already.'

'Nonsense. Tell you what, how about if I do the kitchen?'

Wooden stairs led from the terrace to the garden and they went back down and into Sabrina's kitchen. Not all of the boxes had been labelled. The ones which were, they dragged into the correct rooms and the few unmarked cartons they left in the hallway.

Ellie started on filling the kitchen cupboards while Sabrina was in the main room, and since it was an open plan area they carried on chatting.

'Tell me about your husband,' Sabrina said. 'He seems really nice.'

'He is. What do you want to know? Rob's one of the best and pretty good in bed too.'

She didn't know how that had slipped out because it really wasn't like her to be indiscreet. They giggled like teenagers.

'Lucky you. My ex was a disaster in that area,' Sabrina said. 'So at least I don't miss that side of things.'

'And to think I wrote books and books about all that stuff and I never had it myself.'

That gave them another good laugh.

'It must be so exciting being an author. How did you get to be one?'

'By chance. I had a dead-end job in an office and I wrote romance stories in my spare time. It was the only thing which kept me sane and then one of my friends persuaded me to send one to a women's magazine. I thought the editors would laugh their heads off when they read it. Instead, they serialised it.'

'Wow.'

'I couldn't believe it. My writing snowballed from there because the confidence boost from the magazine pushed me to write my first novel. After that, I juggled work and writing and I found a publisher. I didn't give up my job until six years later and by then I could earn a living from my books.'

Ellie could not believe her own good luck. She had been stuck in a boring job with a horrible boss who disliked her as much as she disliked him and having to jump to his demands and then another doorway had opened. She would never have imagined it possible.

'I've got to read one of your books.'

'I can give you a copy of my last one if you like though don't feel obliged. Romance isn't everyone's favourite.' Ellie smiled. 'Tell you what, Rob and I are having a barbecue soon, just with a few friends. Why don't you come along?'

'I'm not sure. Meeting people isn't my thing at the moment, what I really need to do is get my head together and that means lying low.'

'You can't be a hermit and besides, it'll be pretty disruptive with it in the garden, and noisy for you too. Please think about it. We'd love you to come.'

Sabrina glanced towards her daughter.

'Oh and Maddy too, of course.'

'Thanks. I'll let you know.'

A while later and the kitchen was finished. Ellie went into the hallway to deal with the three remaining boxes.

'Shall I just slit the tops of these stragglers so we know where to put them?'

'Yes please,' Sabrina called from the bedroom.

Using the cutter, Ellie sliced through the tape and ripped open the one nearest to her. It was full of books.

'Hey you didn't tell me you liked crime. Where do you want the books?'

'Main room please.'

Ellie dragged them through and went back to the hallway to open up the next in the row. This one contained photographs. *Curiosity killed the cat*, she told herself, *don't snoop*. She carefully folded the top back down.

'Photographs in this one,' she called out.

'The lounge too, please.'

She dragged it through and came back for the last carton. This one contained more novels and she was about to pull it into the lounge when something twinkly caught her eye. It was lying across the top layer of books – a delicate, silvery chain.

Hooking in her finger, she pulled it out. It was a necklace and on the end was a Celtic shamrock design, also in silver, unusual, and very pretty. As she held it up, she had an odd feeling.

Sabrina was chatting to Maddy in the bedroom. Light glinted off silver as the shamrock twirled on the chain. Something about it seemed familiar. Had she seen one before? Ellie wasn't sure and she didn't know why but she didn't want Sabrina to see her with it. Quickly, she slipped the necklace back, hiding it amongst the books.

Chapter Nine

From her window, Sabrina saw Ellie heading off to her yoga class.

The last few weeks she had been watching carefully and she was getting to know the Mitchells' routine. Rob drove off early in the morning and didn't come home until late. Ellie spent most days writing in her loft room. She told Sabrina the mornings were the time of day when she produced her best work. Around lunchtime Ellie often went out for a long walk. Twice a week, she went to a yoga class in town. Then every Monday and Friday, she drove off before midday and didn't come back until just before Rob got home. When she got back on a Friday the car was full of groceries although Ellie for sure didn't spend six hours food shopping. So far, she had not let those Monday and Friday appointments slip in conversation.

She and Ellie had had coffee together a few times up on Ellie's terrace and her new landlady seemed to be genuinely friendly.

She knew the Mitchells liked to order take-aways, they quite often went out for dinner on a Saturday evening, and so far, they had not invited anyone to their house either during the evenings or at the weekends.

Rob and Ellie had proven themselves to be creatures of habit. Tapping her pencil on the pad, Sabrina tucked away her notebook, slipping it amongst her recipe books. She reminded herself she was keeping notes for her own safety and for Maddy's – just to be careful.

Maddy was settling in and Sabrina had decorated her little room with pictures of flowers. Since Maddy's birth, it had been difficult for Sabrina to let her daughter go. Although she knew being kept too much by a mother's side wasn't healthy for a small one, Sabrina could not kick the compulsion.

The Mitchells' garden was on a slope and fashioned into two terraces. The bottom terrace was full of shrubs and trees. It was bordered by a wall which backed onto the garden of the ivy-covered house. The top terrace was a huge lawn, the side of which had been partitioned off to belong to the downstairs apartment.

Sabrina was glad her daughter was loving playing in the garden. She had bought plants which Maddy was looking after, watering them with a little green watering can they had picked out at the garden centre. Their patch was private because the Mitchells had cleverly put an L-shaped wicker fence between Sabrina's area and the main lawn.

She loved to watch her little girl digging in the earth and constructing miniature play pens and grazing areas for her plastic animals. They had one tree and it was an apple tree at the angle of the wicker fence. Some days, Maddy would sit under the apple tree with her animals spending the whole day there and Sabrina liked it because she had a view straight from the kitchen door.

Today, Sabrina decided to bake a cake. She watched Maddy get settled under the apple tree, leaving the kitchen door open so she could keep an eye on her daughter. Cooking was one of Sabrina's passions and though she had left a lot of her things behind, she had been sure to bring the essentials for baking. Today she would make one of Maddy's favourites with orange flavouring and a layer of pineapple at the bottom.

She soon became engrossed. It was only when she was ready to put the cake in the oven she looked up to check. Maddy wasn't there.

The metal container slipped from Sabrina's fingers, landing with a thump. She rushed outside. Empty grass. Empty garden.

She could hardly breathe. Grabbing at the fence, she smelled an overpowering scent of male eau de cologne. The musk and sandalwood made her gag. She choked, trying to scream Maddy's name but all that came out was a whisper.

No, no, please. Not Maddy.

Forcing herself to move, Sabrina ran inside. She stumbled from room to room almost falling over the lounge rug. Snatching her phone from the counter she punched at the pad and couldn't work out why it wasn't functioning. It took a few moments to realise it had no battery. Ellie had suggested a landline, only it hadn't been installed yet.

The panic felt black and suffocating. The Mitchells were out. The next nearest house was down the hill. What if Maddy had got out onto the road? What if someone had snatched her?

Sabrina ran blindly back outside and she staggered along the drive. It was a few minutes run to the neighbour's ivy-covered house and by the time she arrived she was sobbing. Hammering on the front door, she screeched like a mad woman.

'Help me!'

What seemed like hours later, the door creaked open and she found herself face to face with an elderly woman who had grey frizzy hair and clear blue eyes.

'Please help me! My daughter is *gone*.'

The woman nodded and smiled and Sabrina wondered if maybe the woman had dementia or was too confused to understand this was an emergency. She wanted to grab the woman's shoulders and shake her.

'You must be Maddy's mother. Don't worry your daughter is with me.'

To stop herself collapsing, Sabrina hung on to the door frame. 'Maddy!' she screamed.

'She can't hear you dear because she's right out the back in the garden. What a terrible shock it must have been for you. Why don't you come through?'

Sabrina didn't know if the grey-haired woman was lying. Or crazy. She rudely pushed past and ran down the hallway. She could see a patch of green lawn through a far doorway and she flew outside. Maddy was in the garden, throwing pebbles into a fishpond.

'Hello Mummy.'

Sabrina screeched and threw her arms around her daughter's neck.

'Ouch, Mummy you're hurting me.'

Sabrina was panting and it was impossible for her to let go. 'Don't you dare run off like that again.'

'I didn't run off I walked.'

Sabrina's legs skittered out from under her and she plonked down on the grass, clutching her child to her chest.

She kept going over and over what might have happened. Maddy could have been hurt. Maddy could have been dead. Mutilated. She might have lost her daughter forever to some mad man.

'It's all right,' the elderly neighbour said. 'Your child is safe.'

But she might not have been! Sabrina wanted to scream it. *She might have been taken!*

It took a lot of deep breathing for her to calm down.

The old woman was very patient. She waited for Sabrina to come back to her senses. She offered a drink of water, and she prattled on about a path and the river over and over again until the words started making sense. Sabrina's head stopped swimming and she got a grip. She let Maddy go and dragged herself into a chair.

Her hair was falling in her face and she tied it back with trembling fingers. There were grass stains on her clothes and Maddy had a small graze on her neck where Sabrina had grabbed at her.

It turned out the elderly woman was called Kath Nettle. Oh, thought Sabrina, Adam's landlady. Kath brought antiseptic spray and cotton balls for the mark on Maddy and Sabrina guiltily dabbed at the sore patch. She hadn't meant to hurt her.

Kath Nettle lived one property down the hill from the Mitchells.

'Your little one got out of Ellie's garden and in to mine,' Kath repeated patiently. 'Didn't they tell you there's a connecting gate? Running between my house and theirs is a public footpath, and I've only got bushes and shrubbery on my side between my garden and the path, whereas on the Mitchells' they put a wall with a single gate. The path is a much faster way of getting down the hill into town if you're walking. Mind you, it leads to the river so you need to be careful with little ones.'

Maddy had simply wandered out of their garden and into Kath's? And there was a connecting gate and it seemed as if it can't have been locked? How could that be possible and why hadn't the Mitchells mentioned it? And why hadn't the Agency told her about the footpath? She had never seen Ellie heading that way.

What if her daughter had made it to the river? What if she'd drowned? What if… The panic threatened to surge again.

'I can see it threw you when she went missing,' Kath said. 'I'm surprised they didn't warn you about the gate.'

Sabrina wasn't surprised she was shocked. She should have been told about it, especially because of the path leading to the river because it was dangerous. Why hadn't Ellie told her? And what about Adam? Or else they should have made sure the gate was locked. Then again, the Mitchells didn't have children so perhaps they hadn't realised how important it was. And Maddy had somehow found her way from their part of the garden into the Mitchells' which Sabrina hadn't anticipated and maybe they hadn't either. How had she got around the L-shaped fence?

'Goodness, you're still shaking,' Kath said. 'Why don't I make us a nice pot of tea?'

Maddy was happily poking at the pond with a stick and humming to herself. At five years old it was normal for children to get more independent. Her daughter wasn't tiny anymore.

She tried to shake off the panic. It wasn't right for her to keep Maddy close all the time but she couldn't help it. When you've lost one, the survivor becomes too precious. Maddy had never had friends. She seemed happy with her plastic animals and her books. Yet one day, Sabrina would have to loosen her hold. The thought made her sick with fear.

Kath came back a few minutes later carrying a tray with cups. She was kind and concerned and as the neighbour poured out the tea, Sabrina started to feel foolish.

'What must you think of me screeching like that? And I'm really sorry I barged my way in, I couldn't stop myself.'

'Oh don't worry I've two grown-up children and grandchildren a similar age to Maddy, so of course I understand you panicked. Little ones are precious and we can't help our emotions.' Kath patted Sabrina's knee. 'You must be the new lodger.'

'That's right. I moved in a few weeks ago.'

'Well whenever you want to pop in, feel free. I like having company and you and your daughter are welcome anytime.'

Kath chatted about her grandchildren, who lived in America and Scotland, while Maddy prodded at the pond weed.

'Be careful with the pond,' Sabrina said. 'It's not ours.'

'I'm searching for tadpoles.'

Kath sipped at her tea. 'It's not the season for tadpoles which means you'll have to wait for next spring.'

Kath was a nice person and she let them stay until Sabrina felt she was back to normal. Sabrina could tell Maddy liked Kath and Kath liked Maddy and her daughter was often a better judge of character than Sabrina, because Sabrina tended to regard everyone with suspicion. Her daughter being relaxed made Sabrina feel as if they might be safe here in Kath's garden.

When it was time to leave, Sabrina waved a fond farewell and so did Maddy. As she crossed Kath's garden she realised how nice it would be to have someone trustworthy to talk to, especially if trouble came knocking at her door.

It was so overgrown with shrubbery, they had to push their way out of the end of Kath's garden. It led to a nicely kept, narrow footpath, hemmed in by Kath's bushes and the Mitchells' wall, and in the wall was a small gate. How Maddy had found the gate Sabrina didn't know because it was well hidden behind bushes on the Mitchells' side.

She made sure the gate was closed firmly behind her and there was a bolt on their side and no lock.

'This bolt is very stiff. How did you manage to wriggle it free?'

Maddy's eyes went big. 'I didn't.'

'You mean it was already open?'

'I think so but I can't really remember.'

'Hmm.'

'You're not angry are you?' Maddy said, her lip quivering.

'Of course I'm not. Let's forget about it.'

She didn't want to blame her daughter nor did she want to find fault with the Mitchells. The best thing would be to ask them to put a child-proof latch at the top of the gate and leave it at that.

Back in her own garden, Sabrina inspected the wicker fence, realising there was a small gap at the intersection of the L. It had been hidden by the apple tree.

'Gosh darling, you must have made yourself very small to squeeze through this space.'

'Sort of. I didn't do it on purpose.'

'I get that but do you realise how worried I get when I don't know where you are?'

Maddy nodded.

When they got home, the door was wide open and cake mixture was splattered across the tiles. It had completely slipped her mind. Thank goodness she hadn't put it in the oven otherwise she might have burned the place to the ground by now.

'Oh no Mummy, what happened?'

'Don't worry. I'll make us another one.'

She cleaned up the mess. Then she washed out the bowl and began measuring her ingredients again. It was calming going through the routine of it and it was just what she needed to make her feel better.

A while later, Sabrina heard Ellie's car pulling into the drive. She jotted the time down in her notebook, tucked it away and got on with beating the mixture. It was a few minutes after this that Ellie knocked on the kitchen door. When Sabrina looked up, Ellie was standing in the open doorway, waving a white envelope.

'Go and play in your room, darling,' Sabrina said. 'I'll call you when the cake is ready.'

Maddy obediently trotted off.

'Hi Ellie.'

'Hi, wow, that looks nice. This was put through my door by mistake. It's for you.' Ellie held out the letter.

She wiped her hands. 'It's a bit early for a utility bill, isn't it?'

She took the envelope and ripped it open. Inside was a white oblong card. Pulling it out, she slowly turned it over. When she read what was written on the other side, she started to hyperventilate. Black dots danced in front of her eyes. Cupping her hands, Sabrina breathed into them, drawing in the carbon dioxide which was supposed to help calm her down. She could hear the voice of her therapist, telling her what to do as she fought off the panic attack.

'Sabrina!'

With her back to the cabinet, Sabrina slid to the floor.

'Sabrina! What's wrong?'

She tried to speak but she couldn't. Instead, with a trembling hand she showed Ellie the five black words written on the card.

I know where you are

Chapter Ten

Ellie stared at the words. 'What on earth is this?'

Sabrina was biting her lip and wisps of her hair trembled.

'It's okay, everything is okay,' Ellie said, and she tried to make it sound convincing. *I know where you are.* What kind of maniac would send a note like that? Poor Sabrina looked on the verge of a panic attack.

Sabrina nodded, fighting to control her breathing, so Ellie kept up a stream of soothing words. She wondered if she should call an ambulance but Sabrina had taken a firm grasp of Ellie's hands.

'Th-thank you,' Sabrina said. 'I'll be all right.'

Ellie wasn't so sure about that, though after a few moments Sabrina took some huge gulps of air. Then she started crying.

'Sabrina, what's going on? What is this note? Do you know who sent it?' Ellie reached for a box of tissues on the countertop and pulled out a bunch, pushing them into Sabrina's hands. 'Please don't be upset.'

'I can't help it. It m-must be from m-my ex.'

'It's a threat? He's threatening you, isn't he! What a pile of shit.'

'When I left he got nasty. He couldn't stand how I got away from him.'

'Jesus.'

Sabrina gulped. 'He's not allowed to see Maddy because he's been violent.'

Oh my god. 'That's terrible. I'm calling the police.'

'No! Please, you can't. He's a senior police officer and he knows police personnel all over the country. If I report it I'm sure he'll know and it will only make him crazy mad.'

More tears came and Ellie grabbed another fistful of tissues. *What the hell. It sounded like a nightmare.* 'I am so sorry. Thank goodness you got away. But wait a minute, how did he know you came to Lewes?'

Sabrina blew her nose. 'He probably used his contacts.'

Ellie stared at the card lying on the floor and tried to come up with some ideas. If they couldn't involve the police then what options did it leave? 'What are we going to do?'

'I don't know. There's nothing I can do is there?'

Sabrina started crying again and when Ellie pulled her into a hug, she could feel her shaking.

Later, Ellie had her hair tied over one shoulder and her yoga mat tucked under her arm as she hurried through the pedestrian area of Lewes. She had stayed a long time trying to help Sabrina to feel better.

Should they go to the police? Should Ellie tell Rob? Sabrina had begged her to do neither and in the end Ellie had agreed because Sabrina was getting even more upset about everyone knowing her problems. Ellie hoped she would not regret agreeing to keep quiet. Sabrina's ex sounded like a monster. A nasty note dropped through your front door? That didn't sound like a man who had let go of the past. Sabrina needed protection.

Ellie needed a yoga class to de-stress and she hoped to be there in time for the beginning of the session.

Her new best friend, Lian, was already installed in the front row and she gave a little wave as Ellie took her usual spot at the end of the second line. Ellie settled herself. It was difficult to concentrate but by the end of the class she felt better.

She and Lian had a routine of going for tea and cake at a little café around the corner. As newcomers to Lewes, they had struck up a natural friendship probably because so many locals already knew each other or knew each other's families. Like Ellie, Lian had moved down to Lewes from London.

'That was a wonderful class,' Lian said. 'I feel rejuvenated.'

'I really needed it.'

Lian raised an eyebrow. 'Manuscript not behaving itself?'

'Something like that.'

The café they liked was only a short walk away and the bell tinged as they entered. They headed for their favourite table at the window.

Lian managed to be both laid back and chic in her yoga pants, with a colourful headband holding back her dark hair and with not a trace of makeup and a body to die for. It was a style Ellie wished she could pull off, though never in a million years would she ever look an iota as good as Lian. Lian did a ton of meditation too which was probably why she was so unfazed even though she was a teacher at the local school and managed a class of six-year-olds, which was something Ellie admired her tons for.

They clinked mugs.

'I bet you're looking forward to the end of term,' Ellie said.

'Yes but it's been a fabulous first year and I'm so glad I left London. This town is really growing on me.'

'Yeah. Me too.'

'I hear you landed someone nice for your apartment.'

'News sure travels fast.'

'You're telling me. I heard a couple of the parents talking about it which goes to remind us there are no secrets around here.'

Ellie laughed. 'Her name's Sabrina and she's lovely though she's a bit ruffled at the moment. Something horrible happened today.'

Lian took a sip of her juice. 'What's going on?'

'I can't tell you because I promised. All I can say is Sabrina's divorced and she's having a hard time of it.'

'Oh no.'

'I feel really sorry for her.' Ellie took a bite of cake. 'But I'm not sure she's ready to accept help. It's too raw.'

'I can't stand hearing about women suffering, sometimes life just isn't fair, I mean why should we keep getting the shitty deal. Tell you what, why don't you invite her to the yoga class? It's a nice way to get out and meet people.'

'I guess, though I'm not sure she's much into exercise and then there's her daughter to think of because she'd need childcare.'

'You know, sometimes kids play quietly at the back when childcare goes south. Maybe you could check with the teacher.'

'I'd forgotten about that.' Of course she had. Just like Ellie always blocked out anything to do with children.

'Listen, when you meet her, don't let on you know anything, okay? She's super-sensitive,' Ellie said.

They moved on to updating each other about stuff going on in their lives – the launch of Ellie's new book, Lian's partner who was a musician and was starting to record his own songs, and Rob's ideas for the barbecue. Ellie always avoided talking about Lian's two boys who were about the same age as Maddy. Lian didn't mention them either, probably because she knew Ellie always froze up. In fact the first time Lian had talked about them, Ellie's plate smashed to splinters on the café floor. Although she tried to pass it off as a slip of the fingers, she suspected Lian knew there was more to it and was too diplomatic to ask. From then on, Lian barely mentioned her boys.

When they said goodbye, she really wished she'd been able to tell Lian about Sabrina's panic attack and the horrible threatening note. Ellie decided she would do everything she could to draw the new tenant into her own circle of friends because it really seemed as if Sabrina needed support.

Chapter Eleven

That evening Ellie and Rob had a quiet supper. The heart bypass had gone well and Rob was in a satisfied mood. She was learning how to tell as soon as he came through the door when he'd had a good day. As usual, Rob gave her a blow-by-blow account of how wonderful he had been and how grateful the family were, and she supplied the expected oohs and aahs. He positively glowed. Wasn't it amazing how he was so won over by flattery?

After supper they went upstairs for an early night.

'I almost forgot. Sabrina has asked if we can fix a child lock on the garden gate.' The reason she'd forgotten was because the gate had been eclipsed by the anonymous note. But she wasn't supposed to be talking about that.

They were getting ready for bed and Rob was putting out his clothes for the following day. He liked to lay the items side by side along the top of his dresser. Some people might have found it obsessive compulsive but Ellie preferred to see it as him not wanting to disturb her in the mornings, which was something she thought of as endearing.

'Right, we should probably have thought about that before,' Rob said.

'We should have because Maddy found her way down to Kath's place.'

'Uh-oh that old mad woman. Was Sabrina okay with it?'

'Firstly, Kath is not mad and she's my friend. I wish you'd stop talking about her like that.'

'You haven't known Kath Nettle as long as I have. She's always been a troublemaker and it got a lot worse when she started that damn blog of hers. God knows why people read it.'

'Well, it seems to be extremely popular. Anyway, to get back to the gate, Sabrina sort of pretended she was okay with it though I got the idea she was spooked as hell.'

Rob was unbuttoning his shirt. 'Sounds like you and Sabrina are getting on well. That's nice. You know it didn't even occur to me to get a lock and it should have done with Maddy being so young. I guess we're going to go through a steep learning curve once we've a little one of our own.'

Ellie tensed. She had been moisturising her legs with her favourite vanilla balm and a giant sticky blob plopped onto the bedcovers. She quickly screwed the lid back on.

'Hmm, that stuff smells good.' He smiled and nodded absently and she knew he was thinking about a baby.

Avoiding Rob's gaze, she slipped into the bathroom.

Standing at the sink, she turned on the tap, trying to still her shaky hands. She started to cleanse her face, hoping Rob would not continue the thread of the conversation.

'Since we're talking about it, I bumped into my colleague Tim Greenwood the other day, you know, the one I told you about who specialises in fertility issues.'

Oh shit. Fertility. Of course, it had been inevitable it would come up again. Staring at the mirror, she felt her pulse accelerating. She willed herself to stay in control. Squirting more cleanser onto the pad, she held it mid-air, telling herself to keep the charade going whatever Rob said next.

'I had a bit of an informal chat with him and anyway in the end I made an appointment. He said it makes sense to get myself checked out. You know to actually make sure I'm capable of being a father.'

He left a long pause. He was waiting for her reaction. Her arm had not moved and her throat was so constricted, words would not come out.

'Though where there are problems, Tim said he prefers to work with both partners…'

The suggestion hung like something dead between them. Rob came to the doorway and she started cleansing her face doing her best to not drag savagely at her own cheeks. Would he notice fear in her eyes? Know she was hiding something? She closed them and wiped at her lids. A fertility check had been bound to come up. They'd been together for a year, with sex frequently, and nothing had happened.

'What's your thoughts on it?' Rob asked, giving it another little push.

This is it. It's the moment. Now or never – be courageous and tell him the truth. She hesitated as she'd done so many times during their relationship. The truth would destroy her new life. She wanted her husband to know, she really did but when she tried to force out the words, they wouldn't come. She gripped the sink.

'Tim's a really nice guy,' Rob said. 'I think you'd like him.'

'D-does Greenwood know how old I am?' Ellie asked.

'Yeah.'

'From what I've read, once women get close to forty their fertility plummets and a lot of experts recommend waiting two years before seeking help.'

'I know darling and I don't want you to feel I'm putting on pressure, it's just I so want to be a dad.' He ran a hand through his hair. 'You know how badly I want us to have a baby.'

'I know you do and I want a baby too,' she lied. 'Let's try to be patient. Everyone says once you get professional help all the fun goes out of it and I really don't want that to happen.' She stared at herself in the mirror and saw a scared woman who had trapped herself with no way out.

Rob came up behind and placed his hands on her waist. 'With the chemistry we've got that's impossible. Listen, Tim said it's best not to put it off too long.'

She threw the makeup pad into the bin. 'You mean you want me to come with you to the appointment?' She hoped he couldn't detect the wobble in her voice.

'Only if you want to.'

'Not yet. I'm not ready for procedures and tests. I want it to happen naturally.'

He was disappointed, which sliced her in two, and there was a flash of something behind his eyes. Impatience? Anger? It made her tighten up even more. Why was he so obsessed about having a child? Why couldn't he be content with just the two of them?

'Then how about joining me in the shower,' Rob said, as he turned away.

'Sure, give me a moment and I will.'

She went back into the bedroom and waited until she heard the water and then the glass cubicle sliding closed. Ellie had her own walk-in closet and she tiptoed inside. Slipping her hand down the back of a drawer, she took out her pack of contraceptive pills and popped one into her mouth. How she wished she'd had a sterilisation except she had never expected to meet anyone – she'd resigned herself to being single for the rest of her life. No one would understand the choices she had made in the past and it was far too late for regrets. The further she went lying to Rob the more impossible it became to tell him, though it didn't matter how much she wanted to make her husband happy she could never allow herself to have another baby.

Chapter Twelve

Sabrina put on heat-proof gloves and took the tray of cupcakes from the oven. Nicely risen and golden brown, they smelled delicious and with a little icing they would be perfect. Maddy couldn't wait to decorate them and then they could take a batch down to Kath Nettle. Sabrina hoped Kath would appreciate the baking because she needed someone to talk to.

'Once they're cooled you can put on the topping. I tell you what, why don't we start mixing it up.'

Maddy ran to the drawer to fetch the bag of icing sugar.

'At Kath's, can I feed the fish?'

'We'll have to see,' she said, knowing full well that Kath would let Maddy do it. 'Remember she told us she doesn't like them being overfed?'

Maddy put on her most serious expression. 'She says it's bad for them.'

'Exactly.'

A while later and they fitted some pink cakes into a plastic container. The lid closed with a snap.

Sabrina had had a sleepless night. She needed to press ahead with her whole reason for moving to Lewes. With Maddy occupied by the pond it would be the ideal moment to talk without the risk of upsetting her daughter. She planned to show Kath the anonymous note and she was sure Kath would be supportive and then Sabrina would have someone else on her side. Kath could be another independent witness if it ever came down to it.

'Run and get your shoes and we'll walk down.'

'Can I carry the cakes?'

She couldn't help smiling. Maddy was becoming more and more independent. 'If you hold them carefully, then yes.'

Sitting in Kath's garden, Sabrina admired the roses. They flanked both sides of the lawn.

'I so love English roses,' Sabrina said. "Especially these red ones.'

'My husband did too,' Kath said. 'He's the one who planted them, God rest his soul.'

Sabrina doubted Kath was able to maintain the outside herself, she must have someone who came to take care of it.

'Your garden is in great shape.'

'I'm so lucky. You wouldn't believe it, but Adam is the one who looks after it for me.'

'You're kidding.'

Kath shook her head. 'He doesn't look the type, does he?'

'Not at all.'

Kath laughed. 'He said he grew up in a house with a lovely garden. Adam is a dark horse.' She carried the tea tray with a plate of Sabrina's cakes neatly nestled in the middle. Her hair was tied back today with only a few grey strands escaping to stubbornly stick out. She didn't like to ask how old Kath was but by Sabrina's reckoning, Kath must be at least in her seventies.

Sinking into a garden chair, Kath opened the tea pot and gave it a stir. 'How is it going with your landlord? I don't suppose Rob is in a very good mood at the moment, is he? I don't blame him.'

What a curious thing to say. As Sabrina shifted, the chair creaked and she tried not to look too eager. Kath liked to talk and having lived in Lewes forever she knew all the local gossip as she had already proved during their previous chat. If her elderly host was keen to recount stories about Rob and Ellie, that suited Sabrina just fine because it was time to start filling in the blanks about the Mitchells.

'I didn't catch sight of Rob this morning, though yesterday he seemed his usual self,' she said, as a way of kicking Kath off.

This was not true. As she did each day, Sabrina had been watching every move, making sure she remained hidden from view by the side of her window. She had noted the time Rob left – it had been before seven o'clock and was a break from his routine of leaving exactly at seven thirty.

'Well my dear there's a reason it might be a difficult day for him. You see, I know a thing or two about that young man and today is the anniversary of the death of his first wife.'

'Gosh.'

'Every year he visits her grave,' Kath said. 'Her name was Hayley.'

'How do you know he visits her grave?'

'Because I'm friends with the vicar and it seems Rob only goes once a year and that's once a year for the last twenty years.'

It was quite a tale and Sabrina made sure to leave a significant pause, as if she had never heard the story before.

'Hayley is a very pretty name. Was she local?'

'Oh yes, and as I think I mentioned before, I was a teacher at Lewes primary school and I taught the reception intake. Hayley started with Rob's sister, Rebecca, and then Rob started the following year. Hayley and Rebecca were great friends and then, a long while after, Rob took a liking to Hayley. I can tell you it was no surprise to me to learn, many years later, they got engaged. I always enjoyed keeping track of my pupils and Rob was one I took particular interest in.'

'Why him?' Sabrina said with a laugh, 'I thought teachers didn't have favourites.'

Kath offered the plate of cakes and then helped herself. 'Just one of those things. You can't help getting attached to some children and he was always a bright boy. Here Maddy, come and get one of your mum's lovely treats.'

Maddy skittered over and then retired to her spot by the pond.

'I can't remember who told me, yes I heard they were childhood sweethearts,' Sabrina said as she bit into pink icing.

'Childhood sweethearts and then they married young and then there was the terrible accident.' Kath tutted and shook her head. 'It was a tragedy and the whole town went into mourning.'

In between mouthfuls of cupcake, Kath described Rob and Hayley's wedding at the local church and then how they had taken off on their honeymoon.

'They both had such a bright future ahead of them and they were perfect for each other. Hayley was a nature lover and they went on a walking holiday in Scotland for their honeymoon. It was a bit unconventional – but why not do what you want to, when you're young and in love. I can still remember her smiling on the church step, with confetti raining down.' Kath sighed. 'They were hiking in a remote area when Hayley slipped and fell. The newspapers reported it as a drop of several metres down a scree slope. Hayley broke her neck.'

Sabrina listened, rapt, her own cake discarded on her plate.

'Rob was training to be a doctor and of course there weren't all these satellite antennas and all of that then. They were too remote and he had no way to call for assistance so after she fell Rob took the decision to go for help. He said when he left her, Hayley was unconscious though still alive and he believed she would survive. But by the time the rescue team got to her, Hayley was dead.'

'That's dreadful.'

'Isn't it.'

'If she died from a broken neck surely he realised that before he went for help?'

'There was no proper explanation. He swore she was not terminally injured after she slipped and they think she might have fallen further after Rob left her.'

Sabrina tipped her head on one side. 'Why do I get the feeling there was more to it.'

'Everyone had their suspicions and especially the Scottish newspapers but I've always believed Rob had no blame for it. Of course, with Hayley's family being so well known around here it was a big shock.'

'Poor Rob.' Sabrina imagined him stopping by the cemetery on his way to the hospital and laying flowers on Hayley's grave.

'No wonder the man never recovered. As the last person to see her alive, Rob was investigated by the police and it didn't help how Hayley's family were so wealthy. Her ancestors owned Southover Grange, you know the huge manor house down the other end of Lewes. That was before it was donated to the local council.'

'You mean the one with the beautiful gardens?'

'That's the one and it's lovely in the summer when the flowers are in full bloom. Well, Hayley's family were rich and her parents had both died several years earlier. The estate had been split in two, between Hayley and her brother, but even so, Rob Mitchell inherited a lot of money. That's why the police had him under suspicion. It was ridiculous because everyone here knew how devoted he was to her. If you ask me, that's why he was never the same again, it wasn't just because he couldn't save her, it was the way the Scottish police kept questioning him. It went on for ages and I've no idea what they had against him.'

'And they didn't identify anyone else who might have been involved?'

'Never.'

Sabrina shivered and edged her chair into the sunlight.

'Don't let your tea get cold, dear,' Kath said, helping herself to another cake. 'These are delicious.'

How much money had Rob inherited? It sounded like it was substantial.

'Are you sure Rob had nothing to do with it?'

'Absolutely. Of course there was a lot of speculation. Hayley's brother, Christian, was six years old when Hayley died and he was devoted to her. He pelted Rob's windows and his car with eggs. Sprayed Rob's garden with weed killer, killing absolutely everything in it. In the end, some distant relatives took over care of Christian and he left Lewes to go to boarding school. No one heard from him after that.'

Sabrina couldn't help thinking a hiking holiday in a remote part of Scotland was definitely a strange choice as a honeymoon and it would be an ideal way of getting rid of an unwanted partner. Especially if you were the one to inherit a fortune on their death.

Sitting back, Kath sipped at her tea and her blue eyes regarded Sabrina over the rim of the cup. 'Poor Hayley. It was a horrible ending to a promising life.'

'It sounds like you cared for her,' Sabrina said.

'The whole town did and it took a long time for us to come to terms with it, though that's enough of my silly memories. What have you and your little girl been up to?'

'I think it's an interesting story and not at all silly, but since you ask, we've not been up to much. We've done a bit of gardening and there are some first flowers on Maddy's plants which is pretty exciting.' Sabrina took a deep breath and put her hand in her bag. 'And then yesterday this came and knocked my feet from under me. I've been worried sick ever since.'

She handed over the envelope and Kath took out the card and stared at it for a good few seconds.

'"I know where you are" Goodness what is this? Is it a threat?'

Sabrina clamped her hands between her knees. 'I think so.'

'It came through your door? And it's got a local postmark. Do you have any idea who sent it?'

Kath's concern was coming over loud and clear and she obviously believed every word Sabrina said.

'Actually it came through Ellie's door. It's got to be from my ex-husband. He's nasty.'

'But that's dreadful. Has he threatened you before?'

She nodded. 'He's not allowed to see Maddy because he's aggressive. The bigger problem is he's a senior police officer which is why I can't go to the police because if I do he'll find out and it will make him mad. He's got contacts all over the country.'

Kath was frowning. 'That's not logical Sabrina, you know that don't you? The police are here to protect us. If you don't inform them of problems how can they do their job?'

'I don't know what to do. In the past, after I moved out, he threatened me except he never actually *did* anything. Then when I went to the police, he turned up at the house and... it went very badly. He completely lost control accusing me of running him down to his colleagues. It was the only time he was violent. Before, he threatened it but he didn't *do* anything.'

She gulped back the tears and Kath passed over a box of tissues.

'This all sounds horribly nasty. I'm so sorry my dear.' Kath glanced over to check Maddy was not listening. 'I don't know what advice to give you. But you can't handle this on your own.'

Sabrina blew her nose. 'To be honest, it's a relief being able to talk about it.'

'We probably shouldn't have handled this note like we have because now it's got our fingerprints all over it.' Kath pushed away the card with her fingernail. 'Keeping quiet about it doesn't sound like a good decision to me. What if he turns up on your doorstep? What are you going to do? And what about Maddy? You both need protection.'

'The police can't save me if he drops in out of the blue can they? Honestly, I think he's playing a game. He knows I've escaped and he wants to get mental control back over me. He wants to scare me.'

'Hmmm and he's managed it. If you don't want to involve the police then perhaps I should speak to my daughter, she works in social services and I'm sure she might have some ideas about how to handle this.'

'Please don't. I don't want anyone else to know and playing mind games was always his thing. He knew how to get me frightened.'

'My goodness, what a nasty piece of work.'

Sabrina sniffed. 'He is.'

'Then there's the question of how did he find out where you were?'

'I've no idea. I went to so much trouble to cover my tracks, really I'd say it was impossible except if he somehow used his connections. Him being in the police makes it so difficult to disappear. All I want is for him to leave us alone.'

They both glanced across to where the little girl was playing with rose petals.

'Women don't have to put up with abusive partners,' Kath said firmly. 'Times have changed and you're brave to have got away.'

'Thank you and thanks for being a friend. Please, no police. I know I can trust you to keep it secret.'

Kath didn't look convinced. 'All right. I don't think it's the right decision but who am I to say? You know this maniac better than anyone although you must promise to let me know if anything else happens and if you ever need somewhere safe to go, you can always come to me.'

Sabrina nodded and wrapped her arms around herself. Kath was such a lovely trusting person. It was going to be useful having her as a neighbour.

Chapter Thirteen

Sabrina made herself another cup of coffee. The mornings were bad and coffee helped her to get through them. If she were honest with herself the worst moment was actually waking up because at the delicate point of leaving sleep she often felt a momentary happiness as if she were carefree again and facing a whole and happy life. Then she opened her eyes and remembered how half of her had been cut away. Reality came crashing in and she would curl up in bed. Did Maddy wonder why her mother's eyes were always red in the mornings? Why she felt as if she walked around with a gaping hole in her soul?

Maddy made it all worthwhile. Without her daughter she wouldn't have been able to continue.

Then there were the evenings. They held their own horrors. Every creak of the apartment, every noise outside, made her nerves light up as if she faced a full-blown life or death situation. Post-traumatic stress disorder, that's what her therapist called it. PTSD left survivors of devastating events in a state of hypervigilance. Deep down inside, Sabrina felt as if any moment disaster could strike.

The panic attacks, the wafts of eau de cologne which no one else could smell, and the anxiety she felt about letting Maddy out of her sight were all part of it. Lewes was her chance of breaking free.

She sat on a stool at her kitchen counter and inhaled the aroma of coffee. She downed another one. Two things helped get her through – Maddy and baking, and caffeine was a big support as well. Without her daughter she would probably have gone mad by now, whereas baking kept her mind and her hands busy. The only problem with it was packing on the weight from all the homemade goodies. She'd been paying more attention to the calories recently because now she had a very important reason to want to look alluring – Rob Mitchell.

Today was a big day because it was the Mitchells' barbecue. This would be her chance to meet Ellie's friends and she must be sure to make a good impression.

It looked like the weather would be perfect. There were a few fluffy clouds and the sky was blue. After her third cup of coffee, she heard the Mitchells come down their wooden stairs to the garden. The couple talked for a while and then one of them got the mower out of the garage and began cutting the grass. It was Rob. Sneaking outside, she could see him through the slats of the fence. Rob was wearing shorts and a t-shirt. Ellie had told her how he liked to play squash and it showed in the muscles in his arms and legs. He was an attractive man. Sabrina made sure no one saw her watching.

Later, Ellie came to help her husband and they set out tables and chairs.

'For next time let's buy plenty of chairs of our own. We've got storage space in the garage,' Rob said.

Ellie laughed. 'Shouldn't we see how our first barbecue goes before we plan more?'

'I know it will be a huge success.' Rob picked up his wife and kissed her.

Crouching behind the fence, Sabrina felt a stab of jealousy so intense it made her want to shred the hem of her shirt. She slunk back indoors.

Ellie had it all – a handsome wealthy husband, a man every other woman had wanted and not managed to get, she was a published author, successful and happy, living in a beautiful house in a lovely place. It made Sabrina gag.

What should she wear this afternoon? After all, she couldn't make a good impression on Ellie's friends looking like something the cat dragged in. And wouldn't it be nice if she could make Rob's attention flick in her direction? That shouldn't be too difficult when Ellie was the competition.

In the bedroom, she flung open her wardrobe and skimmed the hangers. What would make her stand out? She'd been observant of Ellie's taste in clothes and Ellie often picked blues and greens. Most days Ellie wore dresses or a skirt and Sabrina felt sure Ellie would look extra nice for the barbecue. Well, it was time to notch up the game.

Before coming to Lewes, Sabrina had invested in several new outfits – dresses, some lingerie and some skimpy summer items. She chose a dress and held it against herself. Yes, this one would do nicely.

In the oyster-coloured bathroom, she ran hot water in the tub, put on a face mask, and reclined for a long soak. This afternoon she intended to make an impact. It was time to burrow deeper into Ellie's life.

Chapter Fourteen

Whenever Ellie met with Rob's friends it made her nervous because it pushed all her insecurity buttons. Top of the list was Rob's older sister, Rebecca, who was fiercely protective of her brother. When Ellie first met Rob it had taken her ages to gain Rebecca's confidence, in fact, she still wasn't sure she'd completely won the woman over. As far as Rebecca was concerned, nothing and no one was good enough for her wonderful brother.

This wasn't unusual. At the beginning, most people in Rob's life had viewed Ellie with suspicion or jealousy, or both. She was the woman who bagged the catch of a lifetime, and look what she did for a living – she wrote smutty books. Ellie knew that was what plenty of people thought, even though her books were not smutty. But how could they know because they'd never read a word of them. Most of them weren't even sure they'd heard of her pen name. She knew romance lovers were a niche market, but it didn't help to boost her credibility with Rob's entourage.

Rob's doctor friends were the real nightmare. They were all so damn clever and educated up to their eyebrows. Just glancing in their direction made her feel inadequate. She could sense the questions they were too polite to ask - *A romance writer? What do you write about then, is it all about sex?*

Ellie didn't dare let on she'd left school with a slew of low grades which led her to secretarial jobs she found hard to stomach. Without her break into writing, she would have settled for a life of answering to people she didn't like, in offices she hated. Which is why her best seller status hadn't fitted comfortably back when her first novel made it big and if she was honest she'd never completely grown into it.

Choosing her clothes for the barbecue, she laid them out on the bed. Then she slipped on jeans and a blouse. At least she didn't need to worry about the guests flirting with her husband because when they had discussed the guest list, Ellie said straight out she didn't want to invite any of the nurses from the cardiac unit. She'd been talking about the female ones. Some of them flirted with Rob like crazy. She had seen it at the hospital Christmas party where she had been reduced to hanging on his arm for most of the evening, even though that really wasn't her style. She'd needed to get the message over loud and clear – Rob was totally in love. With her. If the nurses had not understood by the end of the evening they were blind. Rob didn't reject the flirtation and there was something about his attitude which made her uncomfortable because it was obvious he enjoyed lapping up their adoration.

Rob had given in about the guest list and he had only invited a couple of women – the ward sister and his boss.

When Ellie came downstairs, Rob grinned at her like a schoolboy.

'Our first time as hosts,' he said. 'Are you excited?'

Rob looked like he was bursting with it. Of course, it meant he'd be super picky about every detail. Everything would have to be perfect, otherwise he'd fall into a bad mood later.

'Kind of.'

'Do you think we've bought enough drinks?' he said. 'What about for the burner – I was thinking we should get more chicken and more things for the veggies.'

'Babes, probably half the food is going to end up in the freezer. We've got enough to last for ten barbecues.'

'The ones I've been to, I've eaten until I burst.'

'Our guests can do that if they want to and we'll still have tons left over. Listen, this is going to be great.'

'I want it to be the talk of Lewes.'

'It will be.'

Rob pushed a carton of wine glasses with his foot. 'At least the deliveries and alcohol came like they should, oh yes and I need to put out the table tennis. Do you think it should go alongside the hedge or over by the fence?'

'It doesn't matter much. Both would be okay.'

'Come and give me a kiss first.'

She did more than that. She pushed up his shirt and Rob was quick to move her against the counter and slip his hand inside her panties.

'Have we got time?' Ellie said, laughing.

'Always.'

'What about the table tennis?' she said, teasing him. Then she leant backwards, arching herself against him.

A while later there was a ring on the doorbell and it was Rob's sister, Rebecca. Ellie tried to stay relaxed. Trust Rebecca to turn up early. Any moment now and Rebecca would be swanning in trying to take over from her, as if she wasn't up to organising her own barbecue.

She heard Rob's voice in the hallway. 'Hi sis.'

'Hi,' Rebecca replied. 'What the hell happened to Ellie's roses? They caught the plague or something?'

'What?' Ellie hurried to the hallway, quickly greeting her sister-in-law and rushing past. Outside, she stared in dismay at the drooping flower heads and brown leaves of her beloved bank of roses. Every single bush looked as if it was on the verge of death.

'Oh my god.'

'What's wrong with them?' Rob asked.

He stroked a few leaves and as his hand contacted flower heads, the petals fell off. Ellie gave a shriek.

'That's plants for you,' Rebecca said. 'It's why I can't stand them because they always die on me.'

'But they were fine yesterday! Thirty-two rose bushes! How can this have happened, it's impossible.' She knelt and scooped a handful of browned petals, holding them up for everyone's inspection, and for answers.

Rob shrugged. 'Don't ask me. I don't know anything about the poor things but Bec is right, they don't look very salvageable, are you sure they didn't get some kind of rose disease? Do those exist?'

Ellie felt like crying. Her pride and joy ruined. Destroyed.

Though they inspected the roses and the ground around them and everyone was sympathetic, no one had an explanation.

'I'm contacting Adam to come over and take a look. He's Kath's expert on roses,' Ellie said. 'In case there's a chance.' She meant, of saving them.

Rob raised an eyebrow and Rebecca snorted.

'Waste of time if you ask me,' Rebecca said. 'They're well gone. Just chuck them on the compost heap and put grass here instead, or better still gravel.'

Ellie felt shaky for quite a while and she left a desperate message for Adam, hoping she'd hear back soon.

'We can get new ones,' Rob whispered in her ear as he rubbed her back.

It wasn't the same at all. Ellie locked herself in the toilet and quietly cried. When she came out, she put on a brave face for her husband and tried to focus on the preparations.

Brother and sister were soon chatting and Rebecca gave her brother an indulgent smile. When he was single, Rob had often gone on holiday with his sister and her family. He was generous with Rebecca and he spoiled her children, and Ellie got the impression Rebecca took full advantage of it. And why not? Rob hadn't had anyone else to splurge his time and money on. Naturally, when Ellie came along this meant Rebecca got less of her brother's attention. Ellie knew she would never be able to make that right.

'You picked a great day for it,' Rebecca said. 'Whenever we plan a garden event it pours with rain.'

'We got lucky,' Rob said.

'Sorry about the rose bushes you guys,' Rebecca's husband said as he came into the kitchen. 'Weren't they your favourites, Ellie?' When she gulped, he carried on quickly. 'Hey listen I've got the trestle tables in the car. Where do you want them?'

'Show them it, darling,' Rebecca said to her husband.

Rob put down the box of beers he was carrying. 'Show us what?'

Rebecca's husband pushed up his sleeve.

Ellie stared at the flashy watch. 'Is that a Rolex?'

'Sure is,' Rebecca said. 'It's a birthday present from me.'

'Looks great,' Rob said. 'Nice choice.'

Wow. How on earth did Rebecca manage it on her art gallery manager salary, Ellie thought. Plus they both drove expensive cars and went on luxury vacations, which was a bit odd given they had average sort of jobs.

A couple of moments later, Rebecca's two children dashed into the kitchen.

'Uh-oh come on out you two Auntie Ellie doesn't like you making a mess.'

Rebecca had a boy and a girl, with the girl, who was the oldest, being ten years old. Quickly, Ellie grabbed a giant packet of crisps and offered it before they ran into the garden. She always kept a cupboard stuffed full of treats and handed them out whenever the kids came by. It was her way of fending them off and it helped her to cope.

Rob went outside with his brother-in-law and she was left in the kitchen with Rebecca.

'I'm going to make a start on the salads and garlic bread.'

'Oh, I always do that the night before.'

She winced. Rebecca could be very critical without even realising it.

'I can help if you like,' Rebecca said.

'That would be great.'

'A barbecue is such a wonderful idea.'

'It was your brother's. He's wanted to have a big housewarming for ages.'

'All those years a bachelor and he couldn't wait to play host? I'd never have thought it,' Rebecca said. 'You're bringing out the best in him.'

It was a rare compliment and she appreciated it, even though she didn't feel it was really deserved.

'So, what's your new tenant like?'

'Her name's Sabrina and you'll meet her later. She's nice and er,'

'What?'

Ellie carefully told Rebecca a little about Sabrina's ex-husband though she didn't mention the threatening note. 'So it's a bit complicated for her, but like I said she's really nice and so is her daughter Maddy.'

Rebecca raised an eyebrow. 'A pain-in-the-arse husband doesn't sound good, and yeah, I was surprised when Rob told me about the daughter. I thought you didn't like kids?'

'It's not I don't like them I just... don't feel comfortable around children. My friends in London were like me – working women who led single lifestyles and I've never had to get used to the company of little ones.'

Ellie had gone over this a few times with Rebecca. She knew Rebecca had her children when she was young and all the people Rebecca knew seemed to have several kids. To her sister-in-law, single women with no children, especially Ellie's age, were like aliens.

'Mine aren't so little now,' Rebecca said. 'I'd like to have a third except I'm not sure we can afford it.'

Ellie didn't comment. She doubted money was a problem since Rebecca and her husband always seemed to have plenty of it. The Rolex was a good example.

'Don't worry Ellie, when you've got your own it will all come naturally.'

'I suppose you're right.' She mixed crushed garlic with butter and spread it onto baguettes.

'Do you mind if I open a bottle?' Rebecca said, waving her hand towards the wine. 'I could do with one and after the hectic week I've had at the art gallery I think I deserve it. The boss is away again and she left me in charge. Want a glass?'

She shook her head. 'I'm sticking to juice.'

'Oh?' Rebecca said, her eyes drifting to Ellie's belly.

'No, it's not that. It's because otherwise I'll be cross eyed by the time the guests arrive.'

She got on with slicing the tomatoes, hoping Rebecca didn't go all dreamy and start another of her monologues about the joys of pregnancy.

'I still remember the time I realised I was pregnant for the first time,' Rebecca said. 'Did I tell you? I was going for a bike ride and I got this weird feeling in my...'

Oh no, not again. Ellie sighed inwardly. Rebecca had recounted the same thing several times. Ellie did her best to block it out and carried on making the food. It was bad enough having Rob talking about babies constantly without her sister-in-law joining in and really those two could be quite a double act. Why was Rob so adamant he wanted an heir? Why couldn't he be satisfied with what they had between them? But it was true wasn't it, as Ellie knew from bitter experience – people didn't appreciate what they'd got until they lost it.

Chapter Fifteen

With all the dashing backwards and forwards, Ellie felt she hadn't had a moment to breathe properly for hours. The afternoon was going with a swing and Rob was in great spirits. He had decided he was in charge of their new gas-fired barbecue.

'Good luck,' she whispered in his ear as she left him to start it up.

In the kitchen, there were several cases of cooling beer and plenty of wine, and a heap of goodies waiting to be cooked on the burner. A local shop had delivered two huge desserts. The salads had been laid out and everything looked top notch. She wiped her hand across her brow. If this thing didn't go with a bang it wouldn't be from lack of effort. Let's hope it lived up to Rob's high expectations.

She was dying for a swig of wine although it would be dangerous for her with so many children around. She could not risk breaking down or freaking out. What the hell would Rob's friends think of her then?

Scanning the guests dotted about the lawn, everyone seemed to be enjoying themselves. It wasn't long before a wonderful charred scent drifted across from the burner. She liked the *chink* of glasses amidst the chatter. Popping a few strawberries into her mouth, Ellie poured another glass of juice. *Get back out there and mingle.*

She was strolling across the lawn when one of Rob's colleagues came through the gate. Ellie's confidence wavered. *Oh no, not her.* It was Ishtar Khan. Ellie could never begin to compete with Ishtar. A fellow cardiac surgeon, and technically, Rob's boss, Ishtar was the head of the cardiac unit, and Rob was next in line. They were on call on alternate days, which meant they had to spend a lot of time together for coordinating aftercare and patient consultation. If anyone pushed Ellie's insecure buttons, it was her husband's boss.

Ishtar was wearing flip flops, a drab shirt and a pair of shorts which hung baggy at the back, and she still managed to look stunning.

Ellie nervously smoothed her hair. She knew it was stupid yet she couldn't help feeling jittery around her. It didn't help that Ishtar was dark and strikingly attractive and the type of woman to turn any man's head. Worse, Ishtar's husband had pancreatic cancer and it brought Rob's protective side out big time. Ishtar's husband was nowhere in sight which meant Zachary had stayed at home. Ellie hurried across the lawn. Rob got there slightly before her and she heard his lips land lushly on Ishtar's cheek.

'Hi,' Rob said. 'Thanks for coming.'

'I'm so pleased you could make it,' she said, trying for her smile to not wobble at the corners.

'I can only stay for a little but I wanted to wish you both all the best in your new home.'

Ishtar pushed a gift into Ellie's hands. It was a box of chocolates, and not only that, they were Ellie's preferred ones. She flushed with shame for her ungenerous thoughts.

'We're really happy you're here,' Rob said.

'Yes, we're glad you came and these are my absolute favourites thank you. How's Zachary doing?'

'A little better today which is why I was able to pop out.' Ishtar bit her lip. 'Only I can't stay long.'

'I want you to relax and take it easy. Let me get you a drink, what would you like?' Rob said. 'Why don't you take a seat in the shade and I'll bring it over.'

What he said was normal for a host but his fawning manner took Ellie by surprise. Had he always been so grovelling around his boss?

'Oh and I wanted to let you know Rebecca is organising a fundraiser at the gallery for the hospice.' He gave Ishtar a charming smile.

That was news to Ellie.

'She's been really kind, popping over with takeaways and doing my shopping,' Ishtar said.

Ellie could hardly believe her ears because Rebecca really wasn't the type. She couldn't imagine her sister-in-law doing her own chores let alone for anyone else.

Rob put his arm around Ishtar's shoulders and Ellie watched as Ishtar leant against him. Or was it Rob who pulled her close? Being jealous when someone else's husband was dying really was the pits and she told herself off. She really should get over this insecurity thing.

'And a fundraiser for the hospice.' Ishtar wiped at her eyes. 'I don't know what to say.'

'Bec's good at that kind of thing and she's gone over and above to get the gallery manager on board with the idea. She's thinking of a show of new works, with wine and a buffet.'

'How lovely,' Ishtar said.

Ellie almost shook her head in bewilderment. Was there a charitable side to Rebecca she didn't know about?

'Don't let me drag you away from the burner,' Ishtar said.

'It's under control. Someone's keeping an eye on it for me.'

When Rob led Ishtar to the loungers, Ellie left them to it. She grabbed a bottle and went around offering top ups. Lian's boys were playing table tennis and Ellie looked the other way when she passed them. Another group of children were over by the fence and she skirted them too, her heart beating hard at the sound of their laughter.

Glancing back towards her husband, she saw Rebecca was there too and the three of them were chatting enthusiastically which probably meant they were talking about the fundraiser. Brother and sister were on either side of Ishtar and Rob was plying his boss with snacks. Ellie shrugged. Rob had wanted to be careful not to favour any of the guests over the others and he'd commented on how important it was for them both to keep circulating and not get waylaid. Still, if he wanted to treat Ishtar like the guest of honour, that was his business.

As she topped up glasses, lots of people sympathised about the demise of the rose bushes and every time it happened, Ellie felt a new wave of sadness. They were trying to be kind, saying how temperamental roses were and prone to sicknesses but she wasn't convinced because the flowers had been absolutely fine the day before, she was sure of it and she should know because she gazed at them every day. There was no way she would have missed signs of a problem.

When the wine bottle was empty, she poured herself another glass of fruit juice. Then she suddenly realised Sabrina wasn't there. Shit, she'd forgotten all about her. Sighing, she tossed the rest of her drink in the hedge. Time to bring Sabrina to the party.

Chapter Sixteen

Sabrina could hear the laughter and music drifting in from the garden. She had put her daughter into a little skirt and flowery top.

'You look lovely,' Sabrina said, kissing the top of her daughter's head.

'You too,' Maddy said.

Sabrina straightened her dress and flicked back her hair. This was it. This was her chance to infiltrate. She used to be good at socialising before her life fell apart. Well, it was time to get back into the groove. What she needed was for Ellie to come and find her, and promise to look after her, and she was betting that's exactly what her kind-hearted landlady would do. It would give Sabrina the best chance of Ellie's friends seeing her as being in need of protection. She would give it another twenty minutes and if she'd misjudged and Ellie hadn't turned up by then, she'd have to head out on her own.

When there was a knock at the door, Sabrina realised she had been staring at herself in the mirror, frozen in place for goodness knows how long, lost in the past. Maddy sat at her feet, playing with a hair ribbon. Sabrina shook her shoulders and fluffed her hair. PTSD. She must have blanked out for a bit.

'Are you coming?' Ellie called. 'My friend Lian's arrived and she's dying to meet you.'

Good. It looked like she'd been spot on about Ellie.

'On my way,' she called.

Squeezing Maddy's hand, she opened the door.

'Hi Ellie, I wasn't quite ready I was just…'

Ellie grabbed Sabrina's free hand. 'No need to explain, come on, there are lots of nice people and there's plenty of wine and there'll be loads of food. I want you to enjoy yourself.'

Sabrina's heels sank into the grass as she walked across the lawn. She held on to Ellie's arm and allowed herself to be dragged towards the throng clustered around the drinks table.

A glass of wine later and she felt ready for anything. Under Ellie's wing, everyone treated her nicely and Sabrina made sure to play the part of the wounded bird. Ellie introduced her to the teacher, Lian, who was very friendly and when Ellie needed to be hostess and greet new arrivals, it was Lian Sabrina stayed talking to. Lian's husband was entertaining their two boys who were a similar age to Maddy and Maddy shyly joined in.

'Lian,' Ellie said, as she left them. 'Sabrina is looking for a school for her daughter and I was wondering if maybe you could give her a few pointers?'

'Of course I can.'

Lian smiled. 'Look at your little girl joining in with mine. At that age, it doesn't take them long to make friends, does it?'

They chatted about their children.

'I don't know if Ellie mentioned it, but my ex has caused me some problems.'

Despite the way she blurted it out, Lian's face stayed neutral. Ah, so Ellie had been true to her word and not told anyone about the threatening letter. That was useful to know.

'Oh, that doesn't sound very nice. What's been happening?'

Sabrina shrugged. 'It's a long story and I don't want to bother you with it. Anyway, we're planning on staying here long term so my daughter will need to start school in September.'

'Uh huh. How old is she then, five? We've a couple of children leaving at the end of term and my school is in your catchment area so it's likely Maddy will get a place where I teach.'

'Oh gosh, that would be nice.'

'I'll look into it and let you know and I really like how she's having fun with my two. Leave her with my husband, he'll take care of her and then we can relax.'

'Oh no Maddy's not used to it. She's with me most of the time, she's not comfortable being left with other people.'

'My husband loves playing with children. You don't need to worry and she looks okay to me.'

'Are you sure? I wouldn't like to impose…'

'You're not and us mums need to look after ourselves. We deserve it.'

'Gosh I've not had a break for ages.' *Better not say, ever.* In fact, the only situation she had allowed herself to separate from Maddy was when Sabrina went out at night to work. It had been about a year ago and at that time she had hired a sleep-in nanny and only managed to force herself to leave her daughter because, one, Maddy was asleep, and two, Sabrina absolutely needed to work at The Grosvenor Hotel.

'Then treat yourself to time off now. Besides, she knows you're close,' Lian said.

They sank into comfy chairs. Sipping her drink, Sabrina congratulated herself. She had easily won Lian's sympathy. Maddy was giggling and chasing the others around and around their chairs – one blonde girl running after two dark haired children. Sabrina had the sudden thought there should have been two blonde ones running in the circle. A deep sense of loss welled up. Closing her eyes, she pushed it down. She was here for a reason and she must stay focused.

'Welcome to Lewes,' Lian said.

They clinked glasses.

'I hope you get to like it as much as I do.'

'Thanks. I get the feeling I will.'

Chapter Seventeen

By the time Ellie got back to Sabrina and Lian, the two of them seemed to be getting on well.

'Sabrina has an interest in craft work,' Lian said. 'She's been very generous and offered to help me set up the craft space at school.'

'Hey, that's a surprise,' Ellie said. 'Just what you need.'

Sabrina looked more attractive and curvaceous than usual. She was wearing a rather stunning red dress with a low neckline. It was an amazing transformation and with make up on, the woman looked lovely. Ellie didn't know how she'd not noticed before, and was it the drinks having an effect because Sabrina was coming across as having a bubbly personality too.

Rebecca wandered over. 'The barbecue smells so wonderful it's making my mouth water.'

Ellie introduced Sabrina.

'Hi, and pleased to meet you,' Rebecca said. 'Hey look at Rob, acting like he knows what he's doing. I think he's been dying to be in charge of a grill all these years.'

Ellie laughed.

'Then what stopped him?' Sabrina said.

It was a bit abrupt and Rebecca frowned. 'Rob was a widower. His first wife died and he never got over it.'

'Gosh I'm sorry, the agent mentioned it and I'd forgotten. I didn't mean to upset anyone.'

'You haven't,' Rebecca said. 'It's funny but I'm often the person being accused of being too blunt, so don't worry about it.'

Rebecca was making light of losing Hayley but the dark shadow that swept over her face had said differently. Rob's first wife had been Rebecca's best friend. Apparently, when Hayley had her accident, it had left both Rob and his sister in tatters.

'Is that your daughter?' Rebecca asked. 'She's lively.'

Sabrina gulped from her glass. 'I know. She needs to mix more with other children and not hang around the house with me all the time. It's what's best for her, isn't it?'

'You're right, young kids need to socialise. It's not good for them to be isolated from their peers,' Lian said.

'You couldn't stop my two when they were Maddy's age,' Rebecca said.

Ellie was glad the conversation had moved on and she made encouraging noises. Poor Sabrina, she was obviously torn about being separated from Maddy and her face was flushed after a glass or two of wine as well as the likely embarrassment of putting her foot in it.

A shout went up from over by the barbecue. 'First serving,' Rob called. 'Come and help yourselves.'

'Yum I don't mind if I do,' Rebecca said.

As they went over to the grill, Sabrina linked her arm in Ellie's. 'Thanks so much for inviting me. I've not felt at ease like this for ages.'

Over the top of Sabrina's head, Rebecca cast Ellie a look. *Poor thing,* she mouthed.

'Come on Sabrina, let's get you something to eat,' Rebecca said. 'It sounds like you need to get out more.'

'Gosh, you're probably right.'

Ellie was pleased. Lian liked Sabrina and Rebecca was being surprisingly kind towards her. If Sabrina carried on like this, she would soon become part of the gang.

Chapter Eighteen

Sabrina hummed a little tune to herself. As the sun sank low, the guests became merrier. The wine had gone to her head and she felt a rare sense of contentment as she swung in the Mitchells' hammock. A while before midnight, Maddy fell asleep in her mother's arms. Sabrina sighed. Time to tuck her daughter up in bed though how she hated the idea of leaving the party. Rebecca and her husband were still laughing and joking and about half the other guests were hanging around. She didn't want to be left out.

Rob was drunk and he was all over Ellie. Seeing him like that made Sabrina angry. Once or twice he had glanced her way and she felt certain Rob appreciated how alluring she looked although he hadn't approached her. She had been hoping he would find a moment to speak to her on her own. The thought of stealing a kiss or stroking his leg made her weak at the knees.

Was she going too fast? Had the drink gone to her head? The problem was the more she thought about Rob and Ellie getting intimate, the more it ate her up.

Sabrina stared at the back of Rob's head. He hadn't even noticed she was preparing to leave. Bastard. Why not shake him up?

The vanilla scent from his wife's body drifted over Rob. The last of the guests, which was Rebecca and her family, didn't go home until one o'clock in the morning.

'Let's clear up the mess tomorrow,' Ellie said.

'It was great wasn't it?' He imagined his own epithets. *He's the one to watch. We were lucky to get an invite. A social event to die for.*

'Hmm, wonderful, and I'm shattered.'

'Tell you what, maybe we should spend tomorrow in bed to make up for it.'

She giggled. 'I like the way your mind works.'

Laughing, they climbed the steps to their terrace. Downstairs, a light was on in Sabrina's kitchen.

'I hope we didn't keep Maddy awake,' Rob said.

'I don't think so. She was asleep at the end. Look at the sky, aren't the stars lovely?'

Rob didn't care about the stars. Dragging her into the kitchen, he unbuttoned his shirt then got impatient and ripped it off, pushing her against the cabinet. Ellie made a low noise which sent his blood pounding. He lifted her onto the counter and ran his hands up the inside of her thighs.

If Ellie knew why he went at it so much with her, she would be mortified. Rob smiled to himself. No need to tell her, was there. All he had to do was close his eyes and think of being with someone else. If only Ellie would get on with it and produce an offspring, then she could sort out a trust fund for her preciously guarded money and he would be all set.

Rob lost himself in the moment, moving in time to his wife's soft moans. The next thing he knew the night was shattered by crashing and splintering. *Breaking glass*. Ellie went rigid. Then a woman screamed.

Ellie gripped his shoulders, her nails digging in. 'Rob! What the hell!'

Scrambling to pull on his underwear Rob tripped over his own feet. 'Downstairs,' he gasped. 'It sounded like breaking glass and it came from downstairs.'

He was the first outside, his bare feet swift on the wooden steps leading down to the garden.

'Sabrina,' he shouted.

He found her lying on the kitchen floor. The tiles were covered with glass and traces of blood. She was surrounded by shards.

'Sabrina! Listen to me. I need you to calm down.'

She stopped screaming.

It looked as if a whole pane of the kitchen window had dropped out and Sabrina had been cut. How the hell could that have happened?

Pushing herself up to half sitting, her face was white as she stared at him.

'H-help.'

'Stay where you are,' he said. 'Everything is going to be okay and I'm going to help you. Listen, keep still, I'm coming back. I need to get the first aid kit.' *And shoes otherwise I'll rip myself to pieces.*

'My foot. I think there's something stuck in it.'

'Everything will be fine. Just don't move.'

He was about to rush upstairs when the little girl appeared at the far end of the kitchen. *Oh shit.*

'Stop right there, Maddy! Don't come close to your mum or you'll hurt yourself.'

'Mummy,' Maddy said.

The child hesitated. Wearing her nightdress, she took a tentative step into the kitchen.

'No darling! You must wait there,' Sabrina whispered. 'I'm okay I promise I'm okay.'

'But there's b-blood.' She started crying.

'Your mum will be all right. Don't move, Maddy. It's dangerous,' he said.

Ellie came up behind him. 'Oh my goodness what's happened? I'll get our shoes.'

'And the first aid stuff too.'

Rob kept his eye on Maddy, watching as well, the trail of red running from Sabrina. How extensive was the cut? And how deep? Would he be able to stop the bleeding? She might need stitches. Sabrina would have to go to hospital.

It seemed like ages before his wife reappeared. She was wearing trainers and she tiptoed to the other side of the kitchen until she got to Maddy. Then she knelt and put her arms around the child. Rob barely registered it though later he would remember how it seemed a natural gesture, even though his wife professed to know no children and was usually so uncomfortable around them.

Forcing his own shoes onto his feet, he went to Sabrina's side. When he saw the damage to her foot, he breathed a sigh of relief. The amount of blood looked serious but it certainly wasn't life threatening. She had been lucky because it could have been so much worse. The sole of her foot was lacerated and one cut was particularly nasty with a shard sticking out.

'How bad is it?' Sabrina asked.

'One piece of glass has gone in. We're going to have to get you to the hospital and they'll take it out safely.'

'Oh no please, I don't want to go there. Just pull it out.'

'It's not advisable. They can give you an anaesthetic and make sure none stays inside.'

'If you don't do it for me I'll do it myself!'

Rob was shocked by the edge in her voice which very much sounded on the verge of hysteria. He put his hand on her arm.

'There's no need to be scared. Everything is going to be okay.'

'It won't be if you don't help me! I hate hospitals.'

She wasn't thinking straight. Rob pursed his lips and carefully inspected the sole of her foot again.

'I don't know if I can grip it firmly and if it snaps off that's really going to cause a problem.'

'I don't care!' Sabrina screeched. 'Get it out. Or I'll do it myself I swear I will.'

Ellie gave him a frown. 'Can you give it a go?'

This really was a bad idea for Sabrina and for him. He could cut his own goddam hand trying to help her and then how would he carry out surgeries? Didn't Ellie understand how precious his hands were?

'Rob?' Ellie said.

'No way,' he said.

Sabrina's hand moved towards her foot.

'No no no, you mustn't.'

'You can't stop me.'

'For god's sake darling, help her,' Ellie said.

He swore under his breath. Taking a wad of gauze from the first aid kit, he wrapped it into a pad. Then he took out the tweezers.

'Okay, but if it doesn't come I'm not going to force it.'

Sabrina nodded and he took a firm grasp of the protruding shard. It slid out easily, bringing with it a flood of blood.

'I need to keep your leg elevated and I'm going to put pressure on it and if it doesn't stop bleeding, then we'll absolutely need to get you to the hospital and they'll fix you up with a couple of stitches.'

'Please no, I don't want to go there.'

'We'll see,' he said.

A while later, when he had the bleeding under control, Rob helped Sabrina to the living room sofa. They tucked her in with a blanket and Maddy cuddled up close to her mother. He thoroughly cleaned both her feet though the other one was not damaged.

He pushed his hair out of his face. 'What on earth happened?'

'I was standing with my back to the window when something crashed to the floor. There was glass everywhere and I panicked. It was the window pane that dropped out and I think I slipped or maybe it pushed me over when it fell.'

Rob was aghast. He didn't understand – how on earth could it have happened? The house had been renovated to the highest standards, including the apartment.

'How are you feeling now?' he asked.

'Cold.'

'Any light headedness?'

'A bit though maybe it's from the wine.'

It was possible she was also in shock. What a horrible end to a lovely evening.

'I'm going to check back on you in a couple of minutes. You stay here with Maddy, and Maddy, you call me if your mum needs me okay?'

Rob pulled Ellie away.

'This is awful,' Ellie whispered. 'She could have damn well bled to death.'

'That's a bit dramatic. It's not as bad as it looks though she was lucky and so are we because as landlords it's our liability.'

'What if she'd cut an artery or something?'

'Don't talk like that.' Rob ran a hand through his hair. 'I don't understand how it could have happened.'

'Like she said, it was an accident and we'd better start on a clean-up. Maybe it was a mistake to keep some of the old windows,' Ellie said.

'Too bloody right.'

He didn't want to tell Ellie it couldn't have been an accident because he had made absolutely sure the house was top notch. The builder was a friend of a friend and he had told Rob some of the old windows were sound and didn't require changing. All the rest had been replaced with pvc.

Ellie dragged the hoover out of the cupboard and she found a broom. Rob plugged in the machine.

'I just don't get it. Do you mind starting with this? I want to inspect the frame,' he said.

When they bought the house, the original windows had wooden frames. All the windows facing north had needed replacing whereas the ones on the south side were still in good shape and they had decided to have them renovated. The company who did the renovation had been a father and son outfit and Rob had trusted their work.

A cool breeze was blowing through the gaping hole where the pane should have been. He'd better find some panelling and board the damn thing up.

Checking the frame, he studied the edge where the glass should meet the wood. Bloody hell, the pane seemed to have fallen out in one piece because there were no ragged bits along the edges. Also, there were no missiles on the kitchen floor, meaning it had not broken from an object being thrown in. One explanation was it had been faulty in the first place and the pane had not been secure in the frame – which was something he found hard to believe. He peered closer. Was the torch playing tricks with his eyes or were there gouge marks along the top edge of the frame?

Rob's back was covered in sweat. What the bloody hell was going on? Could someone have tampered with it?

Chapter Nineteen

As they cleared up the mess, Rob's head was too full of alcohol to think properly. None of this made sense. Why had the glass fallen? And had Sabrina been drunk because how on earth had she managed to cut herself like that even if the pane landed on the floor? Or was it like she said, and she had lost her balance and somehow got the glass in her foot when she fell?

They cleared it up, with Rob going periodically to check on Sabrina. She was still pale not from blood loss, he thought, but from the shock of it. For a while, Maddy clung to her mother like a limpet, and then the next time he looked she had fallen asleep.

'Everything is clean and safe,' he whispered to Sabrina. 'I'm really sorry about this. I'll get someone out to fix it up properly first thing Monday morning.'

'Thank you,' Sabrina said, and her voice sounded shaky.

'Ellie and I are going to get some rest.'

'Could you pop Maddy to bed please? I don't think I can manage it.'

'Of course and you need to keep as much weight as possible off your foot. I don't want it to start bleeding again.'

Scooping up the little girl, he carried her to the bedroom. As he tucked her in, he heard Ellie explaining to Sabrina how they had boarded up the gap.

'I'd better just check your blood pressure one last time,' Rob said, as he returned to the lounge.

Sabrina's bottom lip trembled as he put the cuff on her arm. 'I know this sounds silly only I don't feel safe with the window broken. Someone could get in.'

'Who would want to?' he said. 'We're too isolated and it's not as if there are passers-by who are going to notice.'

'I'm being ridiculous, aren't I?' Sabrina said, and she started to cry.

Ellie sat on the arm of the sofa. 'It's all right. You don't need to worry.'

He ran his hands through his hair. 'Tell you what, why don't I stay down here? I can take the sofa and we can get you to bed.' He shrugged at Ellie. 'It's the safest thing and then I can be on hand… in case.' Out of Sabrina's view he pointed in the direction of her foot.

'Oh would you? That's so kind.' Sabrina started to edge off the cushions.

'Let me help you,' he said, putting his shoulder under her arm. She was small in comparison to him and he practically lifted her off her feet.

Ellie followed them into the bedroom and she pulled back the bedcovers.

'I can manage. Thank you both so much.'

'If you're sure,' Ellie said. 'Are you certain you don't need anything else?'

'No, I'm fine now.'

They left Sabrina and went to the lounge where they kissed goodnight, and then Ellie returned back upstairs.

A few minutes later, Rob was taking off his shoes when he heard a muffled cry coming from the bedroom. Sabrina was sitting where he had deposited her on the bed. She was in pain, wincing as her foot brushed the carpet. Looking up at him, her eyes were two dark pools in the muted light from her bedside lamp.

'Whenever I move, it hurts.'

He checked the time. 'I can't give you any more painkillers for a while.'

'Please, if you could just stay with me.'

'You know I can't do that.'

'I don't mean… I mean just to be close.'

The room was dark and smelled of Sabrina's citrusy perfume. There was an awkward moment as Rob stood in front of her, acutely aware he was in a woman's bedroom.

'Sorry if I worried you,' Sabrina said. 'It really was an accident.'

He didn't know what to say because it seemed so unlikely.

Sabrina gave him a warm smile. 'Goodnight, and thank you for helping me.' And she flicked off the lamp.

He headed for the door. 'Yeah sure, see you in the morning and give a shout if you need anything during the night. I mean, a drink or something like that,' he added hurriedly.

Going back to the lounge, Rob turned off the lights. He could not be bothered to go home to get more comfortable clothes so he lay on the sofa fully dressed. As he piled the cushions at one end, Sabrina flicked the lamp back on in her bedroom. He could see through her doorway and Sabrina was lit up by the pool of light. Slowly unbuttoning the front of her dress, she slipped it off her shoulders. *Don't watch,* he told himself. *She doesn't know you can see her.*

It was impossible to tear his eyes away. Underneath, Sabrina was wearing a lacy bra. Her fingers swept one strap away and her movements were languid. Then the second strap fell. He licked his lips. As she undid the clip on her bra she bent to extinguish the light and he caught a quick sight of her full breasts. It could not have been more erotic. He swallowed and took a deep breath then blew it out slowly waiting for the wave of lust to ebb. My god, she was gorgeous.

Lying down, he tried to get comfortable. There was no doubt Sabrina was a very sexy woman. What would he do if she called him in the night? Would he be able to resist? With Ellie so close by, he would be a fool if he didn't.

He closed his eyes, knowing he wouldn't be getting much sleep.

Ellie got herself a big drink of water and then grabbed a duvet to take downstairs to Rob. She hadn't told him about the threatening note. Now she wondered if she should have done. Had Sabrina's ex been responsible for breaking the window? How else could it have happened? And if it was him, shouldn't they be getting the police involved?

Slowly, she descended the wooden staircase, the duvet bundled in her arms. She shivered. From the bottom she could see into the dark kitchen of the apartment and from beyond all she could see were lights coming from the lounge. *No need to be suspicious,* she told herself, *nothing is going to happen between them.*

Putting down the duvet, she tiptoed around the house until she reached the windows along the side. From here she could see into the lounge but her husband was nowhere in sight. Where was he? She hid to the side of the bushes, careful not to make noise on the gravel of the drive.

Wrapping her arms across her chest, she tried to get herself to stay calm. *You're reading too much into it. He's probably just gone to the toilet.*

When Rob came back into the lounge, she let out a sigh of relief. He turned off the lights and she could make out his silhouette as he threw the cushions to one end to form a headrest. Then a lamp flicked on further inside the apartment. Ellie knew it came from Sabrina's room because she had a view of her husband on the sofa and beyond, the open doorway into Sabrina's bedroom.

She felt herself going hot. Damn, why the hell had the door of Sabrina's room been left wide like that? The woman was undressing and Rob was staring at her. Ellie had a clear view of the racy underwear lit by a pool of light and the way in which the dress and underwear were discarded. She couldn't help thinking it was as if Sabrina knew she had an audience. As if she knew Rob could see her and she did it especially for him. *Get a grip,* she told herself. *The woman just cut a chunk out of her own foot. Of course she's not putting on a show for Rob. You're imagining things.*

How she wished she had said she would be the one to stay with Sabrina, but it was too late for that. Now she was stuck outside. And Rob had been the proper choice because he was a doctor. She didn't want to act like the insecure wife and barge in. Did she trust her husband? If she went in there now would he guess she'd seen him ogling their tenant? *Don't be stupid, what man in their right mind would have turned away*? Yet she wished Rob had.

Ellie tried not to let her fears surface. Her romance with Rob had happened so fast. They barely knew each other. And what about Sabrina? Had she deliberately been seductive? That could not be possible. Or could it? At the barbecue Sabrina was showing her curves in a flattering dress, not at all like her usual self, slobbing around in baggy clothes. So what? Ellie told herself. Why shouldn't she look nice?

Rob was the knight in shining armour and Sabrina was the damsel in distress which was the perfect recipe for a wayward fuck. Ellie should know because she wrote about it in her novels. *You're the one Rob loves. He would never be tempted. You're being silly.* But as everything went dark downstairs she found it hard to move away. When she finally returned to her house clutching the duvet, she realised a little seed of distrust had been sown.

Chapter Twenty

Ellie lay in her double bed with her arm outstretched across the space beside her. Rob's absence cut like a knife and all she could think about was him with Sabrina. *You're being ridiculous. Neither Rob nor Sabrina are like that.* But how could she be sure? Except by going down to spy again. At one point, she got dressed and put on her trainers and she made it as far as the top step before she stopped herself. If Rob spotted her he'd guess she didn't trust him and what with that and the fact she hadn't yet trusted him with her money it could damage their relationship. Yes, but finding them at it would be worse. She had clutched her knees, sitting on the terrace getting colder and colder, before she finally made her way back to bed.

She felt like shit. When the sun came up, she made coffee and a tray of toast and carried it down. She made sure she was stealthy on the stairs, holding her breath for fear of what she might find. Rob was already awake and sitting up on the sofa. He complained of having a stiff neck. Did it mean he had stayed put all night? Part of her could not help thinking it could all be an act to throw her off the trail. *Stop looking for trouble. It will drive you crazy.*

'That toast smells wonderful,' Rob said as he kissed her. 'You're an angel.'

Sabrina appeared to be guilt free also. She did not want to leave her room and so they installed Maddy in there with breakfast and some toys.

Later on, they cleared up from the barbecue and then Rob had a nap in the shade. He looked so peaceful and innocent snoozing in the hammock. While he was sleeping, Ellie dug his shirt out of the laundry basket and she took a deep inhale. Could she smell Sabrina's perfume? Was there any trace at all of a lemony scent? Had he been with her? Or was she being stupid and torturing herself for nothing?

That afternoon, Ellie mooched around her poor rose bushes. They looked even worse than the day before, their leaves were curled and brown and most of the petals had dropped off. It was heart breaking. Adam replied to her message and a little while later he called by. His face said it all as he stooped to examine the damage.

'Sorry I couldn't come sooner. I knew it was serious when you sent me the photo, oh goodness look at the poor things, what on earth has happened.'

Adam was almost as upset as she was.

'I was hoping you'd be able to tell me.'

They fingered the leaves and the stems and examined the plants carefully, with Adam um-ing and ah-ing now and again, until he finally straightened up and looked her in the eye.

'What do you think?' she asked. 'Is it a disease? Can we save them?'

Adam slowly shook his head. 'I've never seen anything like it. And you said it happened suddenly?'

'Overnight. One day they were fine and the next.' She put her hand over her mouth to stop herself gulping air. 'It's bad, isn't it?'

'The only thing we can do is to cut them right back, down to about six inches of stem from the root and then hope for the best. Next spring they might regrow… but it's not a given. I'm so sorry. They were beautiful.'

'But why did it happen, I don't understand, did I do something wrong?'

'This isn't a disease as far as I can see and for them to die so fast, well, there's only one thing I can think of which would act so rapidly and that's weed killer.'

'Weed-?' Her mind struggled to compute it. 'What do you mean?'

'Someone sprayed your rose bushes with weed killer and that's why they've died because the product did its job.'

How could weed killer have been sprayed in her garden?

'You mean deliberately or an accident?'

Adam frowned. 'Your guess is as good as mine but look around and you can see none of your other plants have been affected. Weed killer acts on contact with green leaves. If you ask me, someone targeted these roses deliberately, I just don't see any other way this could have happened. You're a long way from any communal areas and anyway, the local council don't spray like that anymore.'

Sabotage? But that was crazy. Why would anyone target her roses?

She spent the rest of the day weeding the flower beds in the main garden, her mind a whirl of questions. When she told Rob what Adam had said he didn't buy it. He thought it was bad luck or the flowers had died because they got a sickness, but Ellie was much more inclined to believe Adam.

Chapter Twenty-one

Sabrina knew she had been reckless. Driven by an insane jealousy and fuelled by alcohol she had done something stupid.

After she had sabotaged the window, she had not meant to cut her own foot. She'd thought she would have plenty of time before it fell and then she realised Maddy might be in the kitchen when it happened and she had panicked because she'd not considered that possibility. And that's when it came down. Right when she had been standing beside it like an idiot.

What had made her do it? It was seeing Ellie and Rob getting intimate. It freaked her out the way he was all over his wife because from the way he behaved anyone would think he really had fallen for her. Or was Rob just a great actor?

Would she be able to hold it together? Be able to stick to the plan? Sabrina knew she had no choice. There was no other way to get what she wanted.

Ellie was there when the builder, Chandler, came to replace the window unit with a white pvc one. She had already decided she would be bringing down meals twice a day. This was partly spurred by guilt about the faulty pane and it was also a desire to get to know Sabrina better and to dig a little.

Sabrina spent the day on the sofa. She was able to hobble around the apartment though she wasn't very responsive to questions. Ellie supposed it was the pain, although she couldn't help wondering if Sabrina was avoiding talking.

The next day, determined to find out more, she invited Sabrina up to the terrace for coffee. Sabrina was wearing jogging trousers and a baggy top like she did when she first moved in. *See,* Ellie told herself, *she's not making herself super-attractive for Rob, you were wrong. Nothing happened.*

Maddy had brought paper and crayons and she installed herself in a corner and was soon engrossed.

'You've been very quiet the last couple of days,' Ellie said. 'I've been waiting for you to be ready to chat about Saturday night.'

Sabrina raised an eyebrow. 'I'm okay. My foot is a lot better.'

'I'm glad it is but I'm talking about what happened with the window pane.'

'What do you mean?'

Was Sabrina being deliberately dense?

'You got that nasty note, and then the damn thing breaks, don't you think it could be your ex?'

The idea hadn't escaped Ellie that the maniac might also be responsible for destroying her roses, however bizarre it might seem.

Sabrina put her hand to her throat. 'Yes,' she said in a small voice. 'Only I didn't want to think about it.'

'Ignoring it won't make it go away. He could be dangerous. Where did you say you lived before?'

'He isn't dangerous, he's obsessed.'

'Wasn't there anyone who helped you, I mean, a social worker or a doctor? Someone we could get in touch with?'

'I've cut ties. This is a new life for me, Ellie, I thought you understood. The only way for this to work is for me to lie low.'

'Right.'

'You didn't say anything to Rob did you?'

Ellie shook her head. No, but she should have done. Rob was waiting to get news back from Chandlers on the window frame. It made it more confusing to know what to do for the best. Had it been faulty?

'What if it was your ex-husband? What if he tries something else?' She glanced towards Maddy. 'What if he goes after your daughter?' she whispered. 'We've got to tell the police.'

'No! I told you, my ex is a senior officer and he's got connections. He'll find out and it will push him over the edge.' Sabrina was wringing her hands. 'Please. It will blow over, I know it will.'

Sabrina sounded so desperate Ellie started to feel sorry for her again. She made her tone as soothing as she could. 'It's okay. We can work something out together.'

'He won't touch Maddy,' Sabrina said. 'It's me he wants to punish.'

But wouldn't a great way to do that be snatching their child? The thought made Ellie go cold. 'How about I get cameras installed outside? And some security lighting?'

'Oh gosh, I don't want to put you out.'

'Don't be ridiculous, you've got to have protection, besides, Rob and I were talking about it not long ago.'

'Would you be able to get it done without Rob getting suspicious?'

'Yes, I think so.'

'Oh please promise me you'll keep it quiet about the note. It's humiliating. Being hounded is bad enough but I feel like an idiot for staying with him and for falling for him in the first place. You can't imagine how it sucked all my confidence away. You're such a good friend.' Sabrina wiped at her eyes. 'You see there's nothing I can do except wait him out and I know he'll get fed up with harassing me in the end. Who knows,' she spread her hands, 'perhaps he didn't have anything to do with the window, we don't know for sure, do we.'

Ellie did not feel reassured. In fact, she felt pretty certain the husband was part of the picture. Sabrina must be under an enormous strain and not thinking straight. The poor, poor woman. She must do whatever she could to help her.

Chapter Twenty-two

'You look a bit ruffled my dear,' Kath said, as she greeted Ellie at the door.

'It's been a hectic few days.'

'I bet it has. I heard about your poor roses and about the glass accident.'

Another confirmation the Lewes gossip tree was alive and kicking.

'Why don't you make yourself comfortable in the lounge and I'll bring through some tea.'

They sat in chairs close to the window and Ellie sank back and sighed.

'They're all dead, every single one of them.'

Kath shook her head. 'I'm so sorry and I can guess how dreadful you feel, if anything happened to mine I'd be cut up though you know there are plenty of infections they can get and some of them are unrecoverable.'

'Adam said they died so fast he didn't think it could be a disease.'

'He told me. Which makes it what?' Kath prodded at the tea pot. 'Done on purpose?'

Ellie shrugged. 'I know it sounds unbelievable. Rob thinks it could be spray drifting from someone's field.'

'What a load of rubbish. I've never heard of such a thing and there are no fields anywhere near.'

'I know and I recognise that look on your face. You're worried.'

'I suppose I am. The thing is, it reminds me too much of things which happened around here before.'

Ellie put down her cup. 'What sort of things?'

'I don't know why Rob didn't mention it to you himself, but after Hayley died, Rob was the target of a few unpleasant incidents. Nothing too dreadful mind you, and it was all put down to Hayley's young brother, Christian. Eggs were thrown at Rob's windows and weed killer was doused on his garden. It was just kid's stuff. Christian was only six at the time.'

'Right.' So weed killer had been used against Rob before. How strange. And odd how he hadn't told her.

'Although that was ages ago,' Kath said. 'I don't see how there could be any connection.'

They sat for a while sipping their tea.

'What happened to Christian?'

'He went away to boarding school and no one has heard of him since.'

'Do you think he might have anything to do with it?'

'Your roses?' Kath scoffed. 'I'm sure Christian has moved on and has got much better things to do. I can put out a few feelers if you like, but I think it will be a waste of time.'

'Thank you. I suppose Rob didn't want to worry me.' She sighed. 'I don't think I'm cut out for married life.'

Kath snorted. 'Ah, so you and Rob are coming out of the honeymoon phase, it happens to everyone you know. Sooner or later real-life challenges kick in.'

She raised an eyebrow. 'Are you sure you shouldn't have been an agony aunt?'

'It's interesting you say that because people have suggested I add a problems page to the blog.'

Kath poured out more tea for Ellie and for herself. 'But seriously, if there's something bothering you I'm sure you and Rob can work it out.'

Ellie wrinkled her nose. 'It's much simpler being single.'

'Of course, though much less fun.'

Kath busied herself with the sugar and the milk jug and offering Ellie biscuits.

'You've met Sabrina, haven't you,' Ellie said. 'What do you think of her?'

'Now that feels like a loaded question.' Kath gave Ellie a keen look. 'For what it's worth, I think she seems like a nice woman and her little girl is lovely, though I got the impression she's had a hard time.'

'Hmm, that's what she's hinted at.'

'Has she now. Are you telling me something is making you wonder about her?'

'I don't know, I just wish there weren't so many attractive women passing Rob's way.'

'Ah so that's it – the Rob Mitchell effect.' Kath laughed. 'Remember there've always been women doing their best to catch his eye, though you're the one who succeeded. Have faith in that.'

She was trying to.

'I can't break confidences,' Kath said, 'but Sabrina and I have had a couple of little chats and from what she told me she's got a lot to deal with at the moment, so I doubt you've much to worry about from her.'

Ellie sighed. If only it was so easy. And she stuffed a biscuit in her mouth.

Chapter Twenty-three

'There's a problem downstairs with the shower,' Rob said. 'I'd better check it out.'

Ellie's back stiffened. It was the end of the day and they were supposed to be having a relaxing evening, with a few glasses of wine, not running up and down after their tenant. She scrutinised her husband as he shrugged and gave her an apologetic smile.

'There are bound to be teething problems with the apartment,' he said. 'I'm sure it's nothing.'

Sure. Except it was the second nothing in as many days. Sabrina had Rob going down to see her whenever she flicked her little finger in his direction. Why? And why was Sabrina contacting Rob directly? Why hadn't she messaged Ellie instead? She couldn't shake a niggling feeling of unease.

The last time had been a problem with the light in the kitchen and it wasn't as if Rob was some kind of do-it-yourself mastermind. He didn't know one end of a screwdriver from another.

Rob didn't object either and he seemed to spend a huge amount of time down there on each visit. His excuse was they needed to keep Sabrina happy so she didn't make trouble about the glass pane.

'I'll come too,' Ellie said.

He looked surprised. 'Huh? I thought you were going to have a bath.'

She was. Except now she didn't feel like it.

'Don't worry,' Rob said. 'I can manage.'

Yes, I'm sure you can, she thought, and straight after she told herself off. *Come on, Ellie, nothing will happen downstairs. Sabrina is suffering from the stress of her ex and Rob just wants to be helpful and don't forget Maddy is around.*

Except Maddy was the sort of child to be so absorbed in playing, the house could fall down around her and she wouldn't notice.

Rob kissed her. 'Why don't you lie back in the bubbles and I'll come and see you when I'm finished?'

Why was he smiling so much? Why was he so happy he was visiting Sabrina? Ellie felt sick.

'I've looked up a few numbers for local tradespeople. Next time there's a problem downstairs, I'd prefer it if we call someone in.'

He was halfway to the door and he stopped and stared at her. 'Is that really necessary? We need to keep her sweet to avoid any problems.'

'Sure we do. Why wouldn't hiring a professional do exactly that?'

'I suppose so.' He frowned. 'Is there something else on your mind?'

'Not really.' *Except I don't like the way she keeps texting you.*

'Okay, well I'll be back in a jiffy.'

Sabrina was enjoying being able to summon Rob whenever she wanted. Every time she did it made her giggle. The lightbulb not working, the shower dripping, a problem with the tap – it was easy to invent reasons for her landlord to come downstairs. The first time, Sabrina had been in a low-cut blouse so as not to leave anything to his imagination. The second time, she wore a thin top with no bra underneath and he had hardly been able to keep his eyes off her.

The erotic tension between them was zipping up the charts. He hadn't touched her yet but she knew he wanted to. Rob Mitchell was the sort of man who was used to having the women he wanted when he wanted and marrying Ellie must feel like being strangled. Which led to the question, why had he done it? Sabrina wanted to know. Then she would be able to work out her best strategy.

This time, she was in her silk robe, loosely tied at the middle, with sexy lingerie showing in all the right places.

'Thanks for coming down,' Sabrina said.

Rob ran his hand through his hair and stared at her cleavage and then her legs. 'No problem, though my wife isn't liking it much.'

'Isn't she? Why not?'

'Where's Maddy?'

'In her bedroom, why do you want to know?'

'Because.'

Because then you'd know if you can slide your hand up the inside of my thigh? Push me against the wall and do it standing up?

She led him into the bathroom and closed the door behind them. 'It's the tap.'

'I thought you said it was the shower. What's the problem?'

'It doesn't work.'

He turned it on and off. 'There's hot and there's cold. I don't see anything wrong.'

'My daughter can't hear us in here.'

Rob put his hands on her shoulders. 'Sabrina, you're a very attractive woman. But we can't.'

Sabrina pouted. Ah, so he was going to carry on playing the charade of being the doting husband. How boring. She would have to see about that.

Chapter Twenty-four

A while later, the calls from Sabrina tailed off. It happened straight after Ellie phoned a plumber in response to one of the requests for help. Over the next few days Ellie started to relax. She was just getting back into a positive frame of mind when Rob received a bombshell text message.

'Ishtar's husband has deteriorated. He's being admitted to the hospice.' Rob ran a hand through his curls. 'That's sooner than expected.'

Ellie was taking an apple pie out of the oven. It smelled wonderful. She set it on the side and turned to her husband. Oh no, not more bad news. 'Goodness that's dreadful.'

'I'm going over there to help out.'

Her chest gave a little spasm of fear. It suddenly became vital Rob stayed with *her* and did not run to Ishtar. *Stop it,* she told herself. *Don't lose the plot*.

'Won't the nurses be supporting them? I mean this has been in the planning for a while now hasn't it?'

Rob was giving her a strange look. 'She's struggling, darling. Ishtar doesn't have any family to turn to. I can't let her handle it alone.'

'B-but she's so capable. Are you sure you won't be intruding? I know she's your boss but is it really necessary?'

'She's not just a colleague, she's a friend and this is the last stretch of the journey for Zachary. I can't abandon them.'

Ellie wanted Rob to put his arms around her and she hoped he would pull her close and tell her how special she was. Why, oh why was she so concerned about the attention Rob was giving Ishtar. She remembered the way he'd been fawning over Ishtar at the barbecue and how Rebecca had joined in. Or was it bothering her simply because it came right after her feelings being stirred up over Sabrina?

His keys clinked as he swept them up from the counter.

'I'm not sure how long I'll need to stay. I'll go straight to work afterwards and I'll let you know how they're doing.'

'Okay. Give them my love.'

When the front door slammed, she stood in the middle of the kitchen with her fists clenched. *He's supporting a friend in need. You can't be bloody jealous of that.*

Ellie did not go to the hospice. Instead, she sat in her loft room tying herself into mental knots. She should have gone with him. She should have been more supportive. She could have taken Ishtar some food, maybe some of the pie. Then again, comforting people wasn't her thing, especially since she hardly knew Zachary nor his wife. Rob was the one who'd known them for ages, not her.

She stared at her computer screen, trying to get words on the page. Damn it, why hadn't she handled it better. Zachary was dying.

It was no use, she wouldn't be able to get any work done. Was Ishtar crying on Rob's shoulder? Why was Rob so attentive? It felt like more than being a supportive friend. Or was she letting her imagination get the better of her?

The loft room was quiet and Ellie closed her eyes and tried to push away her insecurities. In a couple of hours it would be time for her regular trip and she would never manage it wracked with emotion. Why not take a walk to clear her mind because this was turning out to be a hellish day and she needed all her strength for her twice a week visit.

At the top of the South Downs the sun was bright. It was glorious up here, with the sweet-smelling gorse and the birdsong. The footpath meandered around the back of the golf course and then gave out to a magnificent view. It felt like you could see over the whole of Sussex. Ellie kept up a brisk pace.

There was a reason she stayed single into middle age. She was a woman who wrote about romance, not someone who let herself experience it. She had been in love once and she would never allow herself to fall for someone again. At least, that was what she decided, until she met Rob.

Now she had a wonderful husband all her insecurities were coming back to life, just like they had before. Was she going to go crazy again? Was she going to end up alone like before? Losing everything? She walked furiously, angry with herself for being so afraid.

A couple of hours later and she was back home. It was time to get ready because her whole life revolved around her visits. No one could understand how she dreaded and loved them at the same time nor why it was so hard to keep her feelings in check.

First, she got out the special products. She kept the hypoallergenic shampoo and moisturisers hidden at the back of the bathroom cupboard.

Taking a shower, she changed into a dress she had washed the day before in a special detergent. She could not risk wearing any perfumed products nor have any clinging to her, for instance, from Rob's aftershave or from her vanilla cream. Then she combed every strand of hair off her face and pinned it into a tight bun on the back of her head.

It would take an hour to get there. She pulled out of the drive knowing that by the time Rob got home, she would be back and have changed her clothes and her styling and would be looking just as her husband expected her to.

Chapter Twenty-five

'Mr Mitchell, good afternoon. There are seven people in the waiting area,' the secretary said. 'I've sent the details through to your agenda.'

Rob always liked the sound of his secretary's voice and especially the way she strung out his title *Mister*. Surgeons were never called by the title *Doctor* at the hospital because they had earned their place as Fellows of the Royal College of Surgeons. It was an accolade Rob was proud of. He was well above mere doctors.

Rob gave her a charming smile.

Patients had been stacking up while he was at the hospice. As the two senior consultants in the cardiac unit, he and Ishtar were rarely off at the same time. Although Ishtar was the boss, Rob had been stepping up during Zachary's illness and he felt it suited him just fine. After all, if Ishtar hadn't managed to wheedle her way in, the top job would have been his.

Rob gave the secretary a nod, enjoying how she gazed at him as if he were a god. The way her eyes shone when she looked at him and her red lips parted in adoration, had been prime reasons why he had chosen her for the post.

'Thank you. I'll buzz when I'm ready.'

'Yes, Mr Mitchell.'

He gave her another smile and was rewarded by her audible sigh. *Charming, charismatic, talented – he had it all.*

He had stayed as long as he could with Zachary and Ishtar. Zachary was too weak to speak and Ishtar was at his bedside, holding on to her husband's hand for dear life. Goodness, he thought with revulsion, how low people allowed themselves to sink in the name of devotion.

Rob checked his grooming in the mirror and then pulled up the files for his first patient. Today he was doing check-ups on people who had already received a heart bypass and speaking to those who would be having one soon.

A veteran at Brighton General Hospital, Rob had a good reputation for having a caring attitude towards his patients. He saw a lot of elderly people and he made sure he took time to answer their questions and provide a quality service. He was sure it was one of the reasons he was popular with the nurses, so he went out of his way to make certain they knew about the gratitude he received. Every time he got a thank you card, he showed it to the secretary, knowing she would be singing his praises to their colleagues all day long.

Recently, Rob had begun using a new heart bypass procedure. It was being experimented with in a number of cardiac units. The technique involved robotic arms which were inserted into the chest cavity. The surgeon manipulated the arms from the outside, with the aid of a computer screen which showed what was happening inside the patient. He needed to be extremely coordinated to carry out the operation successfully.

This new procedure wasn't suitable for all patients because there were increased risks. In contrast to a traditional bypass carried out by a surgeon's own hands, the advantage of the assisted surgery was it had a faster recovery time because it was less invasive and the chest cavity did not need to be cut open. However, there were potential problems compared to an operation carried out by human beings, as Rob had recently found out.

One of his previous patients had developed complications on the operating table. Rob had made a decision to continue with the robotic arms, rather than opening up the patient and finishing the procedure himself. It had been a close call and unfortunately the patient suffered some brain damage. The family were suing the hospital for negligence and an investigation was underway to determine if Rob had made an error of judgement.

It hung over him like a black cloud. He hated the idea of a slur on his reputation and he dare not tell Ellie. Why not? Because he fed off her awe. He loved talking about his life-giving work. It made him feel more than special, almost godlike and the thought of other people believing he made mistakes twisted him up inside.

Ishtar had put a stop to the assisted operations, and they had argued about it. Rob had been forced to swallow his pride and bow to her seniority, which he had hated doing.

Scanning his agenda, he spotted the name of someone who was a potential candidate for the new procedure. Why not talk to the patient about it anyway? After all, he was the one in charge at the moment. The thought of it made his morning go with a swing.

Halfway through the day, Rob received a personal call from Chandler and Sons, the builders.

'Sorry it's taken me a while to get back to you,' Chandler said. 'I've been hellishly busy. Like you asked, I had a good look at the frame we picked up from your place.'

It had been Chandler's son who had installed the pvc replacement for Sabrina's window and he had taken the old wooden frame away with him.

'And?'

'Well,' Chandler huffed out a breath, 'When we did your place up I inspected those old windows myself and they were good and sound and that's why I said they didn't need to be replaced. There's no way that pane would have fallen out on its own.'

'Then how did it happen?'

'I'd say someone did it deliberately.'

Rob paced his office. 'What do you mean?'

'I found marks along the top where someone used a blade or a chisel to attack the seal. That's why the whole thing dropped out.'

'Are you certain?'

'No doubt in my mind, I'm afraid. Are you going to get the police involved?'

And have another slur on his name, with rumours circulating? Just when the investigation was happening? No way.

'I'll deal with it myself.'

'You're the boss. What do you want me to do with the old frame?'

Rob's face was grim. 'I'll pick it up.' And then he'd get rid of it.

His mind flicked to what he knew about Sabrina's ex-husband and her divorce. Was her ex behind this? Bloody hell, Sabrina was supposed to have been a diversion. How could she have turned into a problem?

Chapter Twenty-six

When the next visit came around Ellie felt excited. Each time she waited until it was mid-day before she allowed herself to get ready. Taking out her basket of hypoallergenic products she carried them to the bathroom. Under a slow shower, she tried to relax though it was difficult with her shoulders tensed into knots. Would today's visit be a good one? She hoped so.

Changing into a freshly laundered dress, she did her hair, pulling it back off her face.

She got in the car and headed out. Her visits to Jacob were the high points of her week and it was also true that unfortunately, they also often turned out to be the lowest points. Why? Because Jacob was deteriorating and seeing him get worse and worse and not being able to do anything about it was torture.

An hour later, Ellie pulled into the visitor's car park of Clemence House. As she walked through the main doors the manager greeted her. An old friend to her now, Daniel was in charge of the nurses and carers in the facility.

'H-hello, Ellie. Shall I buzz Fiona for you?'

Daniel had a slight stammer and he always seemed to blush when he saw her. About her age, he was a kind and considerate man, extremely good at his job and excellent at dealing with desperate parents like her. It was Daniel who held Ellie together when Jacob had first been admitted to Clemence

House and he had supported her when she had her breakdown.

In the time Jacob had been here, Ellie had learned to rely on Daniel and when she married Rob it was Daniel who had been the hardest person to tell. Probably because in different circumstances and without Jacob's life hanging in the balance she always imagined there could be a little spark between them.

'Yes please and it's nice to see you.'

'You too, Ellie. How are you doing?'

'Fine thanks.'

Daniel had witnessed her at her worst – when she had spent three weeks under the care of mental health services. Ellie had been desperate. So exhausted. So alone. And she had tried to take her own life. It had been a long haul to get back on her feet and meanwhile, Jacob had been looked after by Daniel's staff.

'Is Jacob in the communal area?' she asked.

Daniel shook his head. 'He's in his room and I'll let Fiona explain why. I'll ask her to meet you there.'

Ellie's heart sank. Fiona was Jacob's main carer and if Jacob was in his room this likely meant he was not doing well today. Had he attacked another of the residents and they had confined him for his own and others' safety? It was happening more and more frequently due to the changes in Jacob's brain. It was terrible how the disease was stripping everything away from him. Ellie felt herself crumbling inside and Daniel took her arm.

'Please don't worry. We've adjusted his medication to try to help. Fiona will explain and if you've any questions afterwards please come and find me for a chat.'

She bit her lip and nodded, pushing back the tears.

Fiona was wonderful too. She had been Jacob's key worker for the last two years ever since he came to live at Clemence

House. Fiona was kind, experienced and steady and she had built a strong bond with Jacob.

When Ellie got to Jacob's room, she took a deep breath and walked in. Her five-year-old was lying on the bed. His head was enclosed in a protective helmet because he suffered horrific seizures which resulted in him bashing his head against the floor and causing himself injury. Jacob's wheelchair sat to the side and Ellie pushed it out of the way to draw up her chair. She took his hand.

Five years ago, Jacob had been born without any warning signs. There had been no problems with his development other than him being slow to walk and slow to speak. Then at two years old Jacob began to have difficulties with balance. He fell a lot. At first it happened when he was running and Ellie put it down to clumsiness, then it progressed to when he was walking and that's when she got worried.

Jacob started seeing doctors as his mobility diminished rather than built like with the other kids. Then he developed difficulties with talking. Jacob was diagnosed with metachromatic leukodystrophy. A rare, inherited disease, leukodystrophy slowly stripped Jacob of his abilities.

When the seizures started, it was the beginning of her slide into mental and physical exhaustion. Jacob needed constant supervision. His speech difficulties became worse and he developed problems with swallowing. Ellie had given up her writing to care for him twenty-four hours a day until it got to the point where she never dared leave him alone for a second in case he had a seizure or choked on his own saliva. She was in a constant state of hypervigilance. Though she had carers to be with Jacob overnight, Ellie hardly slept. He also needed frequent therapy to try to alleviate his symptoms.

Metachromatic leukodystrophy was a disorder of the brain and nervous system. She had become an expert on the horrors of the disease. It caused a breakdown of the fatty covering protecting the nerves, known as the myelin sheath.

Without this protection, Jacob's brain could not function properly and nor could his nerves communicate between his brain and body. The only hope for him was the miracle of finding a compatible bone marrow donor.

A specialist had explained to Ellie that a bone marrow transplant would be a means of slowing Jacob's decline. In the long term, if Jacob could be stabilised, he might be a candidate for experimental gene therapy.

She kissed Jacob's forehead. It was damp and her son's eyelids fluttered open although he didn't seem to recognise her and instead stared into space, somewhere over her left shoulder. The drugs did that to him – he was often spaced out. It was the best way for the doctors to control his seizures and his behavioural outbursts. Ellie had noticed how it wasn't just Jacob's speech that had faded, his memory was going too. Soon there would be nothing left of her dear child.

'Hello my darling.'

Jacob did not answer.

It had been a terrible decision to send her son to Clemence House. The doctors had convinced Ellie it was the best for him and for her because they said she had reached the end of the road and could no longer care for him at home. Jacob's needs had become too severe. Clemence House had staff on duty twenty-four hours a day with emergency equipment at hand. They had a therapy pool and a specialised physiotherapy suite – which Jacob needed every day. After looking after Jacob and struggling on her own for so long, Ellie had been on her knees, and her child was getting worse, not better. She still remembered the day the ambulance had taken him away. The torment of it still had the power to reduce her to a sobbing, wretched mess because having to let him go had broken her heart. The night after he left was when she took the overdose.

There came a light tap at the door and Fiona walked in. Fiona was absolutely dedicated to her work, and one thing Ellie really valued was how none of the care workers gave her less than the truth. There were other children here who were just as ill as Jacob, with different illnesses, and the staff never lied to the parents. They never tried to make it better than it was. Ellie appreciated that.

'Hi Fiona. How has Jacob been?'

'Doctor Venn is trying another adjustment to his medication regime. She'd like to get better control of his seizures.'

It was a constant battle – tweaking this or that medication in Jacob's cocktail. Doctor Venn was an expert and she was the one who suggested they put Jacob forward for a bone marrow transplant. She was also the one, in conjunction with the care staff and Ellie's own doctor, who had limited Ellie's visits to once a week at first. They didn't want Ellie to get overloaded, which, as they so rightly said, did no good for Ellie and did no good for her son either. Ellie had had to argue her case to increase her visits to twice a week and she had high hopes of making it three times soon. She had learned to be stronger since the dark days.

When she met Rob, she had just spent twelve months clawing her way back from being a physical and mental wreck. When he came to the art gallery talk and swept her off her feet, Rob gave her renewed hope. But she could not bring herself to tell Rob about Jacob. Metachromatic leukodystrophy was an inherited disease and likely one gene had come from Ellie and the other from Jacob's father. Both parents had to be carriers for a child to develop a disease of this sort. Of course, the chances of Rob being a carrier too were remote but she could not face the emotional pain of having another child. It felt like a betrayal of her son. Jacob needed her and she wanted to give him everything she had – she would give him her life energy if she could. If Rob had not been so set on having a baby, she would have told him about Jacob long ago.

Of course, she realised she was in an impossible situation. Back then, one date had passed without her telling Rob, and then another. She drank in the hope and it made her better, stronger. Before she knew it, weeks had gone by. She found out Rob wanted a baby not long before he proposed to her. Why, oh why, had she agreed without telling him? How much longer could she hide Jacob's existence? One day Rob would find out, and then what? It would be a disaster. So far, Rob was too wrapped up in himself to imagine her double life. Perhaps he always would be. She hated herself for being such a coward yet she instinctively knew Rob would never accept her son.

Ellie nodded. 'Has he been outside this week?'

'Yes, we took our usual walk down to the village.'

It was amazing how the local residents accepted the children being wheeled through their streets. Ellie appreciated that too. Before meeting Rob, she had been searching for a property here.

'And Jacob has been sitting in the garden,' Fiona said. 'He's not missed any physio sessions and his weight hasn't dropped.'

'That's good.'

'It is and his feeding has been going particularly well.'

Ellie couldn't help asking the question, even though she knew it was futile because Doctor Venn would have phoned if there had been any news. 'Have there been any updates on the transplant?'

Fiona smoothed the sheets on the bed. 'Not so far.'

Ellie had been told the chances of finding a bone marrow donor for Jacob were slim. Family members were always the most likely candidates but there was no one on her side to ask and she herself had been incompatible. If only she could have been the one to save him, but no, fate had cruelly not allowed it. That had been the blow which sent her spiralling into the abyss and led her to swallow too many pills and end up having her stomach pumped.

Jacob's father was dead and she had no contact with his side of the family. Which meant she was reduced to pinning her hopes on the kindness of a stranger and the miracle of a one in a million chance of a match on the bone marrow register.

Her son was trying to sit up and Fiona helped him while Ellie readjusted the pillows. When Jacob looked at her, Ellie felt as if the sun shone.

'Is it you again?' Jacob asked.

He had dark curls like his father, and the same dark eyes. His voice was whispery and he seemed younger than five years and so very, very fragile. Every time she saw him, the sorrow was so deep she felt it in her soul.

'I've brought something for you.' Delving into her bag, she took out chocolate. Fiona would melt it and mix in milk to make it thinner and Jacob would lick it off a spoon.

Ellie spent the next hour with her son. He had some chocolate, then she took him into the garden and they sat beside a little water fountain where the water trickled and bubbled. Daniel asked her to stay one hour only because otherwise Jacob became exhausted.

When it was time to go, Ellie did not want to leave. Her constant fear was that one day Jacob would be gone – he would choke in the night, or have a seizure the doctors could not control, or pass into a coma and never wake.

Daniel had the door of his office open and he came out and waited patiently as Ellie wheeled her son to the entrance.

'It's all right for you to go, Ellie,' Daniel said. 'You know I'd contact you immediately if there are any changes.'

Clenching her hands, she dug her nails into her palms. 'I know, it's just…'

She had seen other parents go through the same agony. The same torture of abandoning their own child. And Jacob had seemed more distant recently as if he really was slipping away.

'Bye bye, Mummy,' Jacob whispered.

She held him close, careful not to clutch too tight for fear she would damage him.

'See you soon my darling. Mummy loves you.'

Daniel waved goodbye and took hold of Jacob's chair as Ellie stumbled to the parking area. Once inside the car, she locked the doors. Daniel was slowly taking Jacob back to his room and she could see her son's head disappearing from view. He was so brave her heart ached.

You must be strong for him.

When Jacob was gone she let herself break, sobbing so hard her chest hurt. He was her life and her everything. She was paying her share of the bills at home and she and Rob had bought the house between them but she was not giving Rob open access to her money because it was in trust for Jacob. It wasn't just her money she was keeping for her son, it was her energy and her love. She could not bring herself to share it with another child. She was living a lie with her husband but she was in so deep now there was no way out.

Chapter Twenty-seven

'I have an idea about how to make it up to Sabrina for the glass incident,' Rob said.

Ellie was sitting at the breakfast table, buttering her toast and Rob was at the stove frying bacon. The aroma of it filled the kitchen.

'Are you sure there's something to make up?'

'She's not mentioned anything about our liability except I'm still worried about it and it doesn't mean she hasn't considered it.'

Ellie frowned. She couldn't help noticing how happy Sabrina seemed these days. Almost excited. Not at all like a woman who was being hounded by her ex.

'You remember how disappointed she was when we told her about the no pet rule?' Rob said, as he joined her and slapped several rashers of bacon onto his plate. 'How about we relax it?'

'That's not a bad idea.'

'I spoke to Sabrina and she told me Maddy has always wanted a rabbit.'

Her knife slipped from her fingers and clattered to the floor.

'No.'

'No what?'

Jacob had always dreamed of having a rabbit. A white one. 'I mean what about a hamster or something smaller.'

'I don't see why we can't give Maddy what she wants and with a rabbit can say it has to be kept in the garden. I was thinking about constructing a run for it.'

Ellie stared across the table. 'Don't you think that's going a bit far?'

'Not really and anyway I'd like to do it for Maddy.'

There was no reasonable way for her to object without it coming over as strange.

'What do you say?' he asked, his mouth full.

She shrugged. 'Okay.'

After breakfast, Rob went out to buy materials, whistling as he went.

Ellie made herself do some deep breathing. She could cope. It was only an animal, she kept telling herself, but please please don't let it be a white one.

Once she had calmed down she started to wonder why Rob was so keen to go over and above. Was he doing it for Maddy or for Sabrina? Ellie's imagination kicked in again. Was something happening between them? Were they doing it behind her back?

By the time Rob returned from his shopping trip, Ellie was upstairs. Through the open window she could hear Rob's happy whistling as he measured out the materials. Then came the noise of the electric saw followed by the hammering of nails. What the hell was he doing down there? Why wasn't it quick and simple? And what the hell had possessed him to do the job himself because he was far from handyman of the year. With each *bang* of the hammer, she felt her nerves jarring.

There was no point trying to do any writing. Her editor had sent two urgent emails about a missed deadline which she had ignored. How could she concentrate? From the garden below Rob yelped, and he and Sabrina laughed. Ellie bunched her fists.

If you don't like them being together, go down there, silly.

When she went into the garden Maddy was kneeling beside Rob, handing him wooden stakes one by one which he hammered into the ground to pin down the tunnel of wire netting. The little girl had a concentrated look on her face and her hair was falling in her eyes. She was fair and Jacob was dark but her expression suddenly transported Ellie back to when Jacob got his diagnosis. Her son had been lying on a hospital bed and his hair had been falling in his eyes. He had not understood the words the doctor had said. His innocence had made it even more devastating. It had been more than Ellie could bear.

Ellie swayed and grabbed on to the back of a garden chair.

'I keep asking and he won't tell me. What's he making?' Maddy asked.

'Just something to look nice,' Rob said.

'But what is it?'

'Don't ask so many questions,' Sabrina said. 'Can't Rob and Ellie decide what they do in their own garden.'

'It isn't in *their* garden, it's in *ours*,' Maddy said.

Rob laughed and so did Sabrina and Ellie squeezed her eyes shut. The image of Jacob faded.

'Are children always so inquisitive?' Rob asked.

Sabrina nodded. 'Always. Oh, what's wrong Ellie?'

'I think I'm getting a bit of a headache.'

Rob squinted up at her, shading his eyes from the sun. 'We can manage here, why don't you relax and save yourself for this afternoon?'

He winked at her because that was the other part of his surprise. He was organising a party for Maddy. Rob had been so proud of his idea and Ellie had wanted to pour cold water on it and not been able to because he had already sent out the text messages inviting their friends. And why shouldn't Maddy have a celebration?

At the little gathering Sabrina was going to present her daughter with the animal. Sabrina had already been to the pet shop and Rob would be going into town to pick the animal up and bring it back in secret.

Ellie rubbed her forehead. 'I think I'll take some work and read it through on the terrace.' *Though not a word on the page is going to make sense to me.* She tried hard not to look at Maddy as she walked away.

Chapter Twenty-eight

Later in the day, Sabrina brushed her daughter's hair. It was another gorgeous sunny afternoon and perfect for the surprise party. When Rob told her his idea she had been pleased. In fact, she had spent the rest of the morning preparing herself with a long soak and face mask, and painting her nails to look extra pretty. She had carefully chosen an outfit which fitted with a little girl's party and yet was seductive. Ellie and Rob were going out of their way to be nice to her and deep down she knew the rabbit had been Rob's idea, though he didn't say so. Good.

Perhaps they felt guilty about the glass accident. So they should, though it wasn't in Sabrina's plan to hold a grudge. Instead, she would do the opposite and make sure she looked after Ellie, who was trying to get rid of a headache. She made lemonade and then a summer pudding and brought both to her new friend, together with an ice pack.

'You're an angel,' Ellie murmured, pressing the ice pack to her temple.

'Just relax,' Sabrina said. 'You looked after me when I was unwell and now it's my turn.'

It was amazing how Ellie drank it in. So naïve and trusting. *Like putty in my hands.*

'Why are you brushing my hair in the middle of the day, Mummy? And why are you wearing that dress?' Maddy asked.

'Wait and see.'

Her daughter had picked up on the excitement even though everyone did their best to keep it a secret. Lian was coming with her two children and so was Rebecca.

Sabrina inspected herself in the mirror. The dress fell to just over the knee and she'd chosen it to show off her curves. She squirted on some more citrusy perfume, tossing her hair. Wasn't everything turning out well and now it was time to enjoy the afternoon with her new friends.

A while later once everyone had arrived, the rabbit was unveiled. White and fluffy, it came to the netting when Rob pushed in a carrot. Maddy screamed.

'Is it mine!'

'Yes it is,' Sabrina said. 'Now all you need to do is think of a name.' She noticed Ellie clutching at her throat. Was the woman ill?

They gathered around and the children oh-ed and ah-ed.

'I'm going to call her Cleopatra,' Maddy proclaimed.

Rob passed over the carrot. 'Great name. Hold it nice and steady so she can chew on it.'

Sabrina smiled at him. He definitely likes children, she thought, whilst Ellie positively dislikes them even though she tries to hide it. Look at her skulking in the corner trying to keep as far away from them as possible. And why has she gone such a funny colour?

Going over to Ellie, she took her friend's arm.

'Are you still feeling ill? You look a bit pale.'

'I'm fine.'

'It's so kind of you to do this. I don't know what to say.' Sabrina squeezed Ellie's arm.

'You're welcome and I think it's about time to cut the cake, isn't it?'

'Are you sure you're all right?'

Though Ellie nodded, Sabrina knew she was lying.

'Well, I made a special one smothered in pink icing. Shall I get it?'

When Sabrina carried it out, she smiled radiantly and proudly held it high. The cake had two long ears and a rabbit face and she knew it would be a show stopper.

'That looks wonderful,' Lian said. 'And how clever. I'll have to get some ideas from you because it will be Samuel's eighth birthday soon and cakes really aren't my thing.'

'They are mine and I'd love to make one for you. What theme would he like? A sport? Or has he got a favourite hobby? Let me know and I can come up with a design.'

'You're very generous, Sabrina, which reminds me, when are you free to come to see the craft space at school? I'd really appreciate your input.'

'Anytime you want.'

'Is tomorrow too soon?'

'Perfect,' Sabrina said. How easy it was to slip in with Ellie's friends.

She had given the cake an orange flavour. Everyone had complimented her on its appearance and now they did the same for the taste.

'This is sublime,' Rebecca said. 'I hope there's enough for second helpings.'

Whilst she chatted to the other guests, Sabrina kept her eye on Rob. Ellie had disappeared inside the house whereas Rob seemed enamoured by Sabrina's daughter and her excitement about the rabbit. He would definitely make a great father. She waited to get him on his own and, later on, when she saw her moment she seized it.

'Fabulous cake,' he said as Sabrina brought him another slice.

'It was such a lovely idea of yours to fix up a run for Cleopatra. Thank you.'

She gazed up at Rob with big eyes and Rob put his finger in the icing and licked it off. 'Glad she liked it.'

Smiling, she tossed her hair and wiped a finger in his cake herself and then slowly licked it off. 'Ellie's so lucky to have you.'

Rob glanced around, checking if anyone was watching or listening.

Slow and steady, she told herself. *One step at a time. Her plan was underway but she was far from the home stretch yet.*

As she leaned closer to him, he didn't move away. She felt the tension between them as her chest brushed his arm. Then she sensed a change in his breathing. Making a pass at him in the open made her tingle with excitement. She was about to press herself against his leg when Rob's phone buzzed and then it was too late because his damn wife was coming across the lawn.

When Ellie came outside and spotted Sabrina and Rob far too close and personal, a wave of light-headedness passed over her. She hurried over. It looked like their chat was turning much too intimate and the way Sabrina's face was tilted towards Rob made Ellie want to run as fast as she could. How long had they been together like that?

Rob took a step away. He was staring at his phone.

'Is it the hospital?' Ellie asked breathlessly. 'Is there an emergency? Are they calling you in?'

'No, it's Ishtar,' Rob said. 'Her husband has passed away.'

'Oh goodness that's dreadful,' Ellie said.

'I'm going over there.'

'What? Do you have to go now?'

'Yes. Ishtar is asking for help. What do you want me to do, abandon her?'

Ellie had just been throwing up her lunch in the toilet. She had forced herself back into the garden and all she wanted was for everyone to leave so she could curl up in the dark until she felt better.

'I mean, she's a doctor, why can't she handle it herself?'

'Ishtar isn't a *doctor* she's a *surgeon*, and what is wrong with you? Zachary has died. Wouldn't it be nicer if you offered some support instead of creating problems?'

'I'm not creating problems, you are, and what do you expect me to do with our guests?'

'How about you look after them? Or is that too much to ask?'

Sabrina was wide-eyed as if she was enjoying the drama. Ellie ignored her and followed Rob back to the house.

'What were you talking to Sabrina about?'

'Nothing.'

'It didn't look like nothing.'

'What?'

Ellie bit her lip. 'I don't know. You seem to be spending a lot of time with her these days.'

Rob frowned. 'Isn't that an exaggeration? She's clocked a couple of DIY issues downstairs and I checked them out. Nothing more. Now we've got the list of tradespeople you sorted for her so what's the problem?'

'And then there's the rabbit.'

'You said you thought it was a good idea.'

I know I did but that was before I saw what it looked like. 'Maybe I changed my mind. You two seemed to having a pretty cosy chat.'

'I don't know what you're getting at.'

'Don't you?'

'Listen, I'm not sure how long I'll need to stay at the hospice.' Rob sounded annoyed. 'I'll let you know.'

'Okay. Give Ishtar my love.'

When the front door slammed, she paced the kitchen. Well, she'd really messed that up hadn't she. Rob was going to think she was behaving like a bitch. He was being nice to

Maddy and he was supporting Ishtar. Ellie took a glass from the cupboard, poured herself a huge glass of wine and slugged half of it down. She had to get a grip or she risked losing everything.

Chapter Twenty-nine

Rob hurried away. As far as he was concerned Ishtar was a priority since she held the power to break him over the malpractice case. My god, she could ruin everything he had worked for, simply by speaking against him, which left him with no choice but to fully and convincingly play the part of a devoted friend.

At the hospice, Ishtar was sitting by Zachary's side. The room was quiet and the blinds had been drawn.

Rob and Ishtar had worked together for almost ten years and he knew her better than most people did. Ishtar put up a strong façade yet her devotion to Zachary had shown her vulnerable side. Rob sat with her, then the nurses coaxed her away from the body and Rob helped with the formalities and afterwards he drove Ishtar home.

He had to admit a tiny part of him felt sad for her. He could see her heart had been broken as she walked into an empty house. For months, her life had revolved around juggling work and caring for her husband. She had fed him, washed him, and taken him to the bathroom. All the paraphernalia for his sickness was stuffed into their living room.

Though she was a strong woman, Rob felt Ishtar was cracking with Zachary gone and he knew she was isolated from her family because they had long ago shunned her for marrying outside their religion. It made him the ideal person for her to rely on.

At the same time, he could not afford to neglect Ellie too much and Ellie always seemed so uncomfortable around Ishtar. For sure, Ishtar was stunning and he supposed it might make a woman like Ellie feel insecure. He did his best to silence his wife's self-doubts though sometimes it seemed an impossible task. Goodness, wasn't it difficult to balance his own priorities.

A while later, Rob left Ishtar alone and by the time he got home it was close to midnight and Ellie was asleep. Quietly, he got ready for bed, studying the outline of his wife's face. When was she finally going to trust him with her money? And what about his fallback position and the descendant he so badly wanted? Though he was a patient man, it was very trying not having all his needs met.

Rob turned away, glad he didn't have to fuck her tonight. *This is going to be worth it. It's just a matter of time. You've stuck it for a year so keep going a bit longer.*

When was she going to give way? With his casino debts sky-high, he really could do with getting his hands on Ellie's money soon.

Chapter Thirty

Ellie put the finishing touches on her potato salad. She had asked Lian and Rebecca for lunch. The only awkward thing was they had both suggested Sabrina be invited to join in. Ellie had tried making excuses but had finally given way under Rebecca's strong persuasion. Now she regretted it.

Rebecca was the first to arrive.

'Hi,' Ellie said, kissing her sister-in-law. 'Great you could come.'

'Thanks for the invite and I'm glad Sabrina's coming too. I think it's wise. Litigation avoidance and all that.'

Ellie sighed. Were they going to be paying the price forever?

'I guess Rob's at work?' Rebecca said.

'Yeah. He's covering for Ishtar again.'

Rebecca had brought goodies. She began unpacking, putting baguettes on the kitchen counter and then pulling out several bottles. 'Isn't it dreadful. I feel sorry for her. Zachary had been hanging on for so long.'

'Rob is pretty cut up. Wine or fruit juice?'

'I've got something much better have a look at this, I mixed us some punch.' Rebecca jiggled one of the bottles. 'I bet he is. Rob and Ishtar have got each other's backs and they need to have with a job like theirs. They have so much responsibility but if anything goes wrong it's them on the block.' Rebecca ran a finger across the front of her own neck.

Ellie was getting a bowl out of the cupboard and she paused. 'I'm not sure what you mean. Has there been a problem at the hospital?'

'Oh it's nothing.'

That sounded like a lie. Ellie frowned. She didn't want to get between brother and sister, but it seemed pretty obvious Rebecca was holding back. Was Rob in trouble?

'How's Sabrina doing?' Rebecca said quickly.

Well, that was a deft change of subject. Rebecca was definitely hiding something.

'She's better. Listen, if there's something Rob's not telling me I'd appreciate if you'd fill me in after all I am his wife and...'

Rebecca ignored her, opening a bottle and pouring it into the bowl. The set of Rebecca's mouth was obstinate, warning Ellie not to push. Then Lian arrived and she had to let it drop.

Sabrina was so jittery getting herself ready, her earrings kept slipping through her fingers and landing in the sink. *It's only a lunch date,* she told herself. *Sure, except it's vital to get this right.*

She had a whole stash of jewellery which she used to put on when she worked at The Grosvenor Casino and she picked out a gold necklace of three twisted strands. It was one of her favourites because she'd been wearing it the first night she met Rob. It would be fun to wear it in front of Ellie without Ellie even realising what it meant.

For the lunch date she even had childcare because Lian's husband was taking his own children to the park and Lian had suggested he bring Maddy with them.

Sabrina had a major wobbly moment being separated from her daughter and at the last minute, she almost called it off and it was Maddy herself who made the decision by telling her mother she *wanted* to go and play with the other children.

The way she said it turned the screws on Sabrina's guilt about keeping her isolated.

Watching her little girl being driven away, she tried not to hyperventilate. Carrying a huge chocolate mousse up to the terrace, she knocked at Ellie's kitchen, the dessert trembling in its bowl.

'Hey let me take that,' Ellie said. 'Wow it looks fantastic.'

'Nice dress,' Rebecca said.

'Thanks. It's something I grabbed out of the wardrobe.' A lie. She had spent hours deciding how to present herself.

Lian kissed her on the cheek. 'Hmm you smell great too. Love your perfume.'

They were being nice and all three of them stood around her being concerned. They must have witnessed how she had been slightly hysterical when Maddy left.

'Don't look so worried,' Lian said. 'Your little one is in safe hands and she couldn't have been happier running off with her new playmates.'

'I know, the thing is with her father being so…' Sabrina gulped, '…difficult, it was always safer to keep her close by.'

Rebecca made sympathetic noises. 'Sounds like you had a rough time.'

'It was horrible.' Sabrina shook her head. 'Oh listen to me moaning on about my own troubles. I don't want to put a damper on the party vibe.'

'You're not,' Ellie said. 'Come and sit with us and have a glass of something.'

Rebecca pulled out chairs and patted the one next to hers. 'You don't have to be worried about creating a good impression with us. We're not those kinds of friends.'

'Oh gosh it's ages since I've had real friends.'

That got her more sympathy. Sabrina wriggled to get comfortable and Ellie passed her a drink.

'Don't ask me what's in it,' Ellie said. 'It's Rebecca's secret recipe and it's perfect as long as you're not driving anywhere.'

Sabrina clutched at the table, as her imagination conjured up a whiff of eau de cologne. A familiar mix of musk and sandalwood overpowered her senses. 'Wh-what? What do you mean?'

'Huh?' Ellie looked puzzled. 'Nothing. I'm saying it's got a kick.'

Sabrina placed her hand over her chest. 'What has?'

'The punch.'

'Take it easy,' Lian said. 'Everything's fine.'

Sabrina inhaled and exhaled slowly until the scent dissipated. Ellie wasn't deliberately making a jibe about drinking and driving. *It doesn't mean she knows.*

Lian was frowning and Sabrina forced herself to take a couple more deep breaths and she hoped they would assume she was still messed up about saying goodbye to her daughter. She took a sip. 'Gosh. It sure has.'

'So, er how's it going with the new book?' Rebecca asked Ellie.

'Slowly. It's been so difficult with Zachary passing away. I haven't been able to concentrate and Rob's been a bit odd lately.'

Rebecca took a swig from her glass. 'Maybe it's because of the pregnancy thing.'

'Maybe, or perhaps because of Zachary.'

'Sorry if I'm being too nosey,' Sabrina said. 'What is it you're saying about pregnancy? Are you expecting a baby?'

'We're trying for one,' Ellie said. 'And Rob is impatient.'

Well, that was interesting and no wonder it was taking time at Ellie's age. She must be sure to put a stop to it. 'Oh.'

'Maybe Rob's mood is a bit to do with poor Ishtar,' Rebecca said. 'They've always been close and he's bound to be worried about her though Rob always gets the blues this time of year – sorry Ellie, I guess you've not been with my brother long enough to realise.'

Ellie raised her eyebrows. 'Are you going to tell me why? He didn't mention anything.'

'He wouldn't.' Rebecca shrugged. 'Earlier this week it was the anniversary of the death of his first wife and even though it happened over twenty years ago he always gets the blues. It tends to hang around for a while. You need to know he's so much better this year than he usually is and I'm pretty convinced it must be because of you.'

Rebecca's comment hit Ellie like a slap in the face. Her hand flew to her mouth. She couldn't believe she had forgotten about Hayley's anniversary. 'I should have realised. How stupid of me.'

'Listen if Rob didn't mention it, then it's not important. I put a bouquet by Hayley's headstone and there was already one other so I think he placed flowers there too. It's what he usually does.' Rebecca tossed a handful of snacks into her mouth. 'Don't worry about it, even Rob and I don't talk it over anymore, and listen, I'm starving, why don't we get started on the food?'

When Ellie didn't respond Rebecca went to the kitchen and brought through two loaded plates. 'This side are stuffed with tuna and the other is houmous and avocado. Help yourselves.'

Ellie felt dumbstruck. How thoughtless she had been. She must make it up to Rob and be sure to jot down the date so she never forgot again.

She went to help Rebecca. They brought through the rest of the food and Ellie heated up Lian's gorgeous looking pasta dish. Soon there was the wonderful aroma of melted cheese and everybody loaded their plates.

'Yum this is mouth-watering,' Rebecca said. 'I love your lunch dates.'

'Me too,' Lian said.

'I wanted to tell you your brother has been so supportive,' Sabrina said. 'Being nice to Maddy and being kind to me. He's even offered to put in outside cameras and lighting.'

Ellie stopped herself from saying the security had been her idea, not Rob's.

Rebecca smiled indulgently. 'Rob's like that. He's a great guy.'

Sabrina nodded. 'He definitely is.'

Ellie passed over the potato salad. 'Here, would you like some?'

'He's even fixed up a couple of squeaky hinges downstairs, and a dripping tap.'

Rebecca laughed and Ellie tried not to cringe. Sabrina was definitely layering on the praises and Rebecca was lapping it up.

The lunch went really well and it was amazing how Sabrina fitted in with her friends. Ellie couldn't help thinking it seemed as if she had been part of their circle for ages. They chatted and they ate, and later on, Sabrina told them how she had been to the school and she loved it and had already put down Maddy's name to start next term.

'I'm sure you're going to be lucky,' Lian said. 'It will be fun having Maddy at my school and of course I'm biased, but my boys are there and they really like it. Wow, I am so full I don't think I can eat another mouthful.'

The talk went on for ages and there was a lot of laughter. When it was time for dessert Sabrina's chocolate mousse was a big hit.

'Oh this is sublime.' Rebecca held up a spoonful and inhaled. 'Hmm, you've got to give me the recipe.'

'It's really easy to make.'

'Uh huh,' Rebecca said, as she smothered hers in cream and vanilla sauce. 'I bet it isn't.'

'My puddings are always a disaster,' Lian said. 'Luckily no one at home notices and they wolf them down anyway.'

'This has got to be the best chocolate mousse I've ever tasted,' Ellie said, and she meant it. 'Sabrina, you've got to promise to make this again because I don't think I can live without it.'

They all laughed and Sabrina looked radiant. A blob dribbled from Ellie's spoon onto the floor and she giggled. 'Oh dear can someone give me a serviette please?'

Lian passed one, Rebecca was helping herself to another serving. Sabrina smiled at Ellie, put a hand to her neck and fingered a gold necklace. Ellie's eyes dropped to the flashy twisted strands around Sabrina's neck. It was then she recalled the Celtic shamrock she had seen in the book box on moving in day. A cold tingle raced up her spine because it suddenly came back to her where she had seen the exact same Celtic necklace before. It had been hanging around the neck of Hayley.

Chapter Thirty-one

On his way to work Rob stopped by Ishtar's house. He was calling by every morning and evening and being careful not to let his wife know. He definitely didn't want Ellie finding out about the negligence case.

That morning he received another email from the casino. They had suspended his account until he paid off his debts. It had been lucky for him Hayley's fortune had been massive and together with his generous surgeon's salary, it had been easy to make frequent trips to London and splurge whatever he wanted. When he married Ellie, he continued his habit, disguising his weekends at the casino as medical conferences. Rob told himself it wasn't an addiction, it was a fun pastime and he loved every minute of it but it was over time for a new injection of funds. Which is where Ellie was supposed to come in. He hadn't expected it to take so long to access her money.

The casino were still being polite although soon they wouldn't be. His gambling had caught up with him.

Ishtar had not yet drawn the curtains in the lounge. There was a stale smell. Three days since her husband passed and she sat in the gloom. Rob found the front door on the latch because she wasn't bothering to lock it.

'I brought some food,' he said. 'Did you forget to close the front door again? It was open when I arrived.'

'It must have slipped my mind.'

'You should do it straight after I leave then you won't forget.' Rob hesitated. 'Unless... have you had other visitors?'

He needed to know because it was so much better for him if she remained isolated.

Ishtar looked bleak. 'The ward sister wanted to call by and I managed to put her off. I can't face people. Of course, no one in my family even knows and if they did, they wouldn't care. Actually, most likely they'd be happy because they always hated how I married Zach.'

'And what about his family? Any word from them?'

'Zach's brother contacted me and he's flying over for the funeral. He told me his parents aren't well enough for the flight.'

Rob went to the kitchen where he put the bread and yoghurts away and washed fruit at the sink. 'It's stuffy in here. Shall we open a window?'

'No I don't want to. Not yet.'

He wondered if she had slept, and if so, had she stayed where she was on the sofa? Every time he visited she was sitting in the same place, in the same clothes. Her hair was greasy and lank. Had she eaten anything since the night before when he had made toast for her and waited until it was gone?

Bringing grapes and peaches back to the lounge, Rob perched on a chair opposite and took her hands.

'I know this is hard.'

'Zach was everything to me. I gave up my family to be with him without a second thought and now I'm left with nothing.'

'Not nothing. You've got me.'

She had diminished. She was smaller and greyer. Bowed down. This was not the woman who battled for patients, who was capable of spending eight hours in the operating theatre with the stamina of an ox. Ishtar had endurance performing surgery which he struggled to match. This was the person everyone admired and the woman who was invited to every top conference on heart surgery on the planet.

Rob helped himself to some grapes. Where was the sliver of hope that would pull her through this? She had no family, no children, and Zachary's family lived too far away. Would her commitment to her work rekindle her will to carry on? He hoped not.

'I think I've found a second patient who's suitable for the robotic procedures. I had a preliminary consultation with him and he's interested.'

Rob waited for a response. Ishtar had put a stop on any more procedures until they knew the outcome of the medical negligence claim. She felt it was too risky.

'I'll leave it to you to decide,' she said, slumping back on the sofa.

He could hardly believe his luck. It was a pleasing response and at last she wasn't acting the part of the big boss. He smiled to himself.

Lying down, Ishtar pulled a blanket over her legs. 'I'm so tired and yet I don't want to go to sleep because I keep seeing his face.'

'That must be horrible, I'm so sorry.'

'I can't find peace. Not without him.'

'You will, give it time.'

Pulling the blanket up further, he stroked the side of her face, keeping his distaste from showing. 'Try to get some rest and I'll check back later.'

'I'm being too much trouble. You don't have to keep calling, I'll be fine.'

'Nonsense, and listen, have you got a spare key? That way I can lock up on my way out.'

'Sure. Take Zach's. They're in the entrance.'

Before he left, Rob pushed the bowl of fruit a little closer. In the hallway he spotted the set of keys on a side table. Pocketing a dead man's key gave him a slight shiver but he wasn't worried because they would be very useful for what needed to be done.

Chapter Thirty-two

When Rob got home Ellie was waiting for him, sitting at the bar in the kitchen.

'Rob!'

She flew to embrace him, wrapping her arms around his neck.

'Hey babes. Has something happened?'

For a moment, he felt hopeful. At bloody last he was going to be a father and Ellie could sign her savings into a trust fund for said baby. It would be the icing on the cake because with an heir, Ellie was bound to be generous with the child, even if she wasn't ready to share with him. Then he could get control. After a quick hug, he rubbed his hands together and gave her an expectant look.

'Have you got good news?'

He knew Ellie understood what he meant and he scrutinised her expression. When she shook her head his rage came quick and fast. He bit back a retort. A couple of days earlier he had received the test results on his own ability to father children and Doctor Greenwood said the difficulties were not on Rob's side. How best to handle the fertility without alienating her? Rob went to pour himself a drink.

'I'm sorry I've been a bit distant. Work and stuff, you know, it's been high pressure. And Zachary.'

'I want you to be able to talk to me about anything.'

Rob nodded and got ice-cubes from the freezer.

'I had the girls over for lunch. Rebecca told me she put flowers on Hayley's headstone and you did too.' Ellie came to stand by his side and he could see she was upset.

'Why did she tell you that? I don't want you to think it's because I'm still in love with her because I'm not. I let Hayley go a long time ago. You're the only one who matters.'

'Oh darling.'

'To be honest I sometimes have difficulty remembering how Hayley really was, though that makes me sad.'

Ellie put her hand to his face. 'I'm so sorry.'

'Be sorry for Hayley not for me.'

'Er, you kept some pictures of her, didn't you?'

'A few.'

'Hmm.' She turned away to push a stool tidily back under the bar. 'Where are they?'

'In the garage I think.'

'That's where we put the junk. Why are they plonked out there?'

'I dunno. I guess I didn't want you to find them by accident.'

'That's silly Rob, so what if I had?'

'Oh I don't know.' He ran his hand through his hair. 'Yes it was stupid to hide them if I think about it now.'

'I want you to know I understand she was important to you and I want you to commemorate her passing without keeping it a secret from me.'

He pressed his lips together. This was starting to get annoying.

Ellie tipped her head on one side and gave him a quizzical look. 'What is it?'

'Oh nothing, it's just I got an invitation to present at a big surgeons' conference in Berlin. Well, actually Ishtar was invited and seeing as she's not in any shape to go she needs to cancel and I was thinking about stepping in. It's really short notice and I won't go if you don't want me to, though it would only mean a few days away...'

'Of course you should go.'

It was typical of Ellie not to object. She never did when he told her he needed to go away for a conference and he had been to several since they got married, or at least, that's what Ellie believed. In fact, this was his first actual conference date because Ishtar had been the one who got all the invites, not him. It was another reason he resented Ishtar's success so much.

He swirled his glass and the ice cubes tinkled. 'Are you sure?'

'Go and enjoy it and have a break from the stress.'

He imagined standing on the podium and his name coming up on the screen as he gave his presentation to an audience of worldwide experts. Ishtar did so many international presentations and she had never once asked him to be a keynote speaker in her place. Everyone regarded her as the expert. Now it was his turn.

Ellie poured a lot of praise on him for the conference and Rob lapped it up. *An inspiring surgeon, handsome and way ahead of his field.* He had a few more drinks to celebrate and spent the rest of the evening imagining the admiration he would receive in Berlin.

Chapter Thirty-three

As soon as Rob left for work the following day, Ellie went to the garage.

It had been hard holding back on her search yet she knew it would be safer once he was gone. She didn't want him asking questions. First of all she needed to find out if she was right about the Celtic necklace. Or was her mind playing tricks?

The back of the garage was a storage area for items from Rob's old house. Ellie searched the boxes. She found his old school reports and sports trophies, medical books, a few souvenirs from past holidays – until she came to the photograph albums. Perching on an old stool, she leafed through them – Rebecca and Rob when they were children, family shots of Rob and his sister with their parents wearing clothes that were the fashion at the time, Rob at medical school and then at graduation. He was just as handsome with lovely curly hair and a generous smile. He and his sister had looked quite alike when they were small.

Ellie took the next album. The cover had faded and she turned the pages carefully. At the beginning there were photographs of school classes. Rob had told her he and Hayley started school one year apart and Rebecca and Hayley had been in the same year.

She examined the faces. Her husband she could spot and Rebecca too, but without Rob's help she couldn't pick Hayley out. Then she turned the pages and came to a shot of Rob and a girl playing with a hose pipe. The girl was about ten years old and she wasn't Rebecca. Was it Hayley? Ellie peered at the child's face. She was laughing and so was Rob and they were both getting very wet. The girl had brown hair and long lanky legs and Rob was wearing swimming shorts.

The next photographs were pictures taken from Rob's first wedding and yes, she could see now the girl with the hosepipe was definitely Hayley. The young woman on Rob's arm looked quite ordinary and a little lost in her wedding dress.

Now that she examined Hayley's pictures, Ellie was surprised how plain Hayley was. In fact, there was nothing remarkable about the young woman and it gave her a funny feeling because it was the point she and Hayley had in common. Why on earth would a man like Rob have chosen *them*? *Love moves in mysterious ways*, she told herself.

Hayley and Rob were young when they married – twenty, Rob had told her. After a few more pages, she came to the ones she remembered Rob showing her of Hayley on honeymoon. One in particular stood out because in this one Hayley looked quite captivating, and not at all like the girl in the other shots. Hayley was sitting at a table, resting her chin in her hand as she gazed into the distance, with a happy dreamy look on her face. She wore an open neck shirt and a necklace was in plain view.

Ellie's breath caught in her throat. It was a silver Celtic shamrock. She had not been mistaken – Hayley had a Celtic necklace, intricate and with the same design as the one she had seen when Sabrina moved in.

She sat for a long time with tingles playing up and down her arms. Was it a crazy coincidence? Or was Sabrina somehow connected to Rob's childhood sweetheart? How could that be? She stared at the picture, a cold shiver running up her back because this was not good. No, no, no, my god. What the hell was going on?

Chapter Thirty-four

After passing by to see Ishtar, Rob went to the hospital. He had a full day of appointments, most with patients who had undergone surgery and he was carrying out their follow up consultations. The morning went with a swing because it really was fantastic to be the one in charge at last.

Towards the end of the morning, he found himself face to face with the owner of a garage in Lewes. Rob knew him from many years of taking his car to Morris Road Garage for servicing. The man had had a triple heart bypass by Rob's hand and he had recently returned to work.

'My wife and I are taking up hiking and my son is bombarding me with tips on being much more healthy, you know eating right and stuff,' the man said. 'The bypass has been a real wake-up call.'

'Lots of people say that,' Rob said. 'I'm glad you're feeling positive.'

'Sure,' the man said, as he buttoned his shirt. 'I aim to live to see my grandkids grow up and before I forget, I told that lovely wife of yours she should think about trading in her vehicle. With the mileage she's packing on she could do with a newer model and one came into the showroom yesterday. It's only six months old and a real bargain.'

Rob looked up sharply from his notes. 'What mileage do you mean?'

'She's put twenty thousand on the clock in the last six months, that's why the servicing was brought forward. Didn't she tell you?'

'Oh yes, of course she did, it slipped my mind.'

'Like I said, Mrs Mitchell told me she was interested in getting a new car and you're not going to get much nicer than the one which came in yesterday.'

'I'll let Ellie know, thanks.'

'You do that doc. You saved my life, the least I can do is offer a small favour in return.'

Once the man left, Rob rubbed his hands over his face. Goddam it, he was supposed to be in control of the woman, what was going on? Ellie hadn't mentioned anything about her car and what the hell had she been doing to amass thousands of miles?

As far as Rob knew, the furthest she went was Brighton to go shopping. His wife infrequently went to London to see her publisher, and when she did, she took the train. Didn't she spend her time in her loft room or going to yoga or walking on the Downs? That's what he had believed.

He balled his fists and felt his chest go tight. It was a feeling that made him want to lash out. Rob was a man who had a temper. Which was why he kept it tightly under control although now he felt it churning inside. What the hell was his wife playing at? Was she keeping secrets?

Later that day, he passed by the office of one of his friends. Maybe it was about time to get some advice and, of course, spread rumours about Ishtar being depressed. He knocked on Doctor Sajid Bakir's door.

'Hi Rob, I meant to come and see you for news. How's Ishtar doing?' Sajid asked.

'Badly.'

'Hmm.' Sajid nodded his head. 'That's to be expected.'

'Yeah except she's really taking it hard. All the fight's been knocked out of her and I've got to tell you I've never seen her so low.'

'My wife tried calling and Ishtar didn't answer. It's difficult because we don't want to intrude if she needs to be private. Grief is a terrible thing.'

'To be honest I'm worried about her.'

'There's really nothing we can do except be available when she needs us.'

'I know but the way she's talking, it's as if she's given up, you know, on life.'

Sajid shook his head. 'They were terribly devoted to each other and I can imagine the grief will pull her down but I'm sure it's not more than that.'

'Hmm, as long as she's not sinking into some sort of depression. I've heard bereavement can do that.'

'I don't think that's Ishtar's style.' Sajid patted Rob on the shoulder. 'She'll pull out of it, don't worry. Has there been any news on the negligence case?'

Rob was pacing the room. 'Nothing so far. Ishtar hasn't yet given her professional opinion and I guess they're going to have to wait for that now.'

'Don't worry about that either, it'll all blow over.'

Rob doubted it. He knew he'd made a mistake during the operation and he also knew Ishtar was the only one who would be able to interpret his decisions and pinpoint the error he had made.

'There was something else I wanted to talk to you about.'

Sajid tilted his head.

'Well… this is going to sound weird… and it's a bit delicate… I just found out Ellie has been putting thousands of miles on her car and I've no idea where she's going or why.'

'Did you ask her about it?'

Rob ran his hands through his hair. 'Should I? I mean, why hasn't she told me.'

'You can only find out by talking to her.'

'Saj, you are so damnably reasonable.' Rob started pacing again as his chest tightened. 'I just don't understand why she would hide this from me.'

'Ah so you suspect something you don't want to hear about?'

'Maybe, I don't know. I mean if I ask her isn't that like saying I don't trust her?'

Sajid shrugged. 'Do you?'

Rob wagged his finger at his colleague. 'Don't ask me stuff like that. I'm trying to build a relationship not destroy it. You're the one with the long marriage. I need help.'

'What else am I supposed to say? I know you couldn't wait to marry Ellie but if you've got doubts, you need to check it out. You could always employ someone to watch her, you know.'

'Snoop on my wife! You've got to be joking.'

'Well it's either that, ask her, or keep quiet and let it eat you up.'

'I am not hiring a spy.'

'I think they're called private detectives and it's the best way of finding out if Ellie is up to anything.'

He shook his head. 'Ellie isn't *up to* anything.'

'Then why are you so upset? Isn't it because there's something she isn't telling you and now you're imagining all the worst things it could be.'

That was exactly the problem. As far as he had been concerned, Ellie was an open book – a lonely woman who earned a fortune, ripe for the picking. He thought he had her in the palm of his hand. He only wanted two things from her – money and an heir. Was that too much to expect after all the bloody effort he had put into bolstering her – fucking her, telling her how great she was, being all over her every hour of the bloody day? My god, the woman owed him and if his plans had gone awry… if he'd been wasting his time… Rob felt his fury rising.

'When my patient told me about the mileage I thought I'd heard him wrong. And then I had to cover up so I didn't look like a complete idiot.'

'Calm down. Listen, Ellie is a great person, you know my wife and I were so pleased for you, but how well do you actually know her? I mean, you got together very quickly. What do you know of her life before she met you?'

'The basics. In London, she had a close circle of writer friends, all of whom wished her well. I met them at the wedding and you spoke to a couple of them there too didn't you?'

'Hmm, what about her family? They weren't at the ceremony were they?'

'Her parents died and she's an only child. We're not teenagers and we didn't need to dig into the past. Love is love, and I mean, I'm a good example, I didn't tell Ellie much about the horrible episode of losing Hayley. Like me, I kind of assumed she'd had past relationships which didn't go as expected. We were two people who thought they'd missed out and then we got a second chance.'

'But you're not a mystery like Ellie. You're tied to someone from your past because you have your sister. And do you actually see any of Ellie's friends from London? Do they keep in touch?'

No, he hadn't seen any of them since Ellie moved to Lewes and Ellie didn't mention them. It hadn't seemed important. Until now. He had known from the start she was the one for him. From the moment he met her in the rain he knew he would ask her to marry him. That had been the plan. Seduce her. Ellie had been picked out for having a string of bestsellers to her name and a savings fund to prove it. The only drawback had been her face.

Rob stared at his friend. 'What are you getting at?'

Sajid crossed his arms. 'I'm not getting at anything though I've got to ask a serious question and it's one you probably don't want to hear - how well do you know your wife?'

Rob wanted to say he knew her very well except it wasn't strictly true. In terms of hard information he knew about her money and her loneliness. Carrying out his plan to ensure he had money to fund his habits had meant he had seduced and he had proposed and they had bought a brand new house. Being engrossed in each other and their new plans had taken up all his time and attention.

'No ex-husbands, no serious relationships,' Rob shrugged. 'What is there to know?'

'The thing is, with women you can never tell.'

He had believed it was only a matter of time before he got his hands on her money. As for supplying a baby, the way he'd been going at it, he'd expected it to happen by now and that would be his golden ticket to her bank balance.

Sajid was right and it made Rob want to clench his fists. His wife was not the open book he had imagined.

Chapter Thirty-five

Sabrina finished the phone call and she frowned. She had been speaking to one of her old friends at the casino, Angelique. She'd asked Angelique to check the records on Rob Mitchell which had been a big favour to ask and it had taken some time for Angelique to have the opportunity to access the files but she'd done it. The findings had not been good.

Sabrina knew Rob was a gambler. It was the reason she attended a crash croupier training and groomed herself for employment at The Grosvenor Club, which was the casino he frequented.

It had been in Sabrina's favour she had worked in the past as a receptionist at a high-class hotel. Before she had Maddy, she had been used to being polished and dealing with demanding customers. Landing a job at the casino had been child's play and so had meeting Rob because he was the type of man who enjoyed women. The only sacrifice Sabrina had to make, and it was a huge one, was leaving her daughter asleep at home with a babysitter.

She jotted Angelique's information in her notebook. On average, Rob spent fifty to one hundred thousand on his casino weekends, which wasn't news to Sabrina. What was more disturbing was on his last splurge, Rob's account had been frozen due to an unpaid debt of thirty thousand.

Did it make sense of why Rob had proposed to Ellie? Had his inherited funds been running low and he had needed a top up? Ellie likely had considerable savings.

Sabrina had not imagined the man could be so devious. She laughed to herself. Two could play that game. Soon Rob would find out what she was capable of.

Chapter Thirty-six

There was a strange tension in the house which Ellie could not explain. The next day Rob dropped several heavy hints about them pooling their resources, saying his investment dividends were late being paid again and it would make things so much easier with cash flow if their finances were joint and transparent.

Ellie had tried again to make herself tell him about Jacob, but once more, she failed to break through her own barriers. Instead of explaining the reason she could not share, she transferred several thousand to their joint account. Rob hadn't said much but she knew it was starting to annoy him how she was keeping her affairs separate.

She was glad when he finally set off for the Berlin conference. Standing in the drive, Ellie waved until the car was out of sight and when she turned to go back into the house, she spotted Sabrina watching from her window. Sabrina waved. It gave Ellie an uneasy feeling.

How the hell could she dig about the Celtic necklace? She had been putting off a confrontation. How likely was it there could be an innocent explanation? Very unlikely, she thought.

But she could not use her energies on it today, because it was a Friday. She would go for a walk on the Downs and then get ready for her visit to Clemence House. Nothing came before her son.

When she arrived, Daniel greeted her.

'Hi, it's nice to see you.'

'You too, Daniel.'

'Jacob is in his room and I should warn you he's had a rough few days. I might need to shorten your visit a little, just so he doesn't get too tired.'

She nodded, knowing that for Daniel to say this, it must be bad. As soon as she entered Jacob's room, she could see he had deteriorated. She didn't need doctors to tell her because she could see it with her own eyes.

Jacob did not respond at all and she sat by his bedside crying. Daniel was kind, and so was Fiona and there was nothing any of them could do.

Once she had left her son's side, Ellie went to find Daniel again.

'He's in a sudden decline, isn't he?' she said.

Daniel shut the door of his office. 'His illness is very aggressive at the moment. If you like, I can arrange for you to talk with Doctor Venn. Jacob is also suffering from the side effects of his medication.'

What was the point? Ellie thought. Doctor Venn could not save Jacob either, all she could do was ease his suffering.

'Has nothing at all come through about the transplant?'

Daniel shook his head. 'I'm sorry, not so far.'

When Ellie got home, she sat through the night sending out more of the Anthony Nolan bone marrow donor information. Then she targeted companies in France, asking them to promote donations programmes with their employees. She had already devoted months to the same task and had focused on France too because that's where Jacob's father was from. According to Doctor Venn, one reason they had not found a match might be because the matching was highly dependent on ethnicity. What was Jacob's father's background,

Doctor Venn asked? All Ellie knew was his family was from France.

Enlisting the help of companies was an uphill struggle, like wading against a never-ending current of apathy. The companies never moved fast because they needed time to organise, and her son did not have time.

Ellie dreaded seeing another child Jacob's age, like Maddy or Lian's two boys or Rebecca's son. How would she hold it together?

Chapter Thirty-seven

The next day when the doorbell rang, Ellie felt like hiding. Through the spyhole she saw Sabrina and thankfully with no child in tow. Reluctantly she opened the door.

'Hi, I know Rob is away and you said you had a thing for chocolate, so I decided to make us a treat,' Sabrina said. 'Ta da.'

She was holding out the gooiest chocolate cake imaginable. A delicious chocolaty scent wafted towards Ellie. It was so powerful it made her mouth water.

'Oh my, you shouldn't have.'

'Yes I should because you deserve it and Rebecca has taken Maddy to the playground so I've got time to myself for once, hey is something wrong?'

'It's nothing. I had some bad news recently, um, about a friend.'

'Sorry to hear that. Is there anything I can do?'

'Bringing cake is a big help. Come in and let's give it the attention it deserves.'

Ellie stomach rumbled as she got out plates. She could not remember the last time she'd eaten. Had it been before she went to Clemence House? She really must do better. She could not allow herself to slip downhill. With her hair unbrushed and wearing crumpled clothes, she must look a sight.

'Have you been hard at work?' Sabrina asked.

Ah, so Sabrina presumed all writers were eccentric and barricaded themselves in to devote themselves to their manuscripts? And with Rob away Ellie had done the same? People thought all sorts of weird things about authors.

'Sort of.' She dragged her hair out of her face and tied it back.

Sabrina pulled out a chair. 'I feel as if I'm finally finding my feet.'

'Right.' She cut slices of Sabrina's cake and they settled at the kitchen table.

'Helping Lian has reminded me how I used to enjoy going out to work though it seems so long ago. Lian is lovely isn't she, and she's boosted my confidence.'

'She's a breath of fresh air.' Ellie spooned cake into her mouth. 'Wow, this is delicious.'

'Desserts are the best comfort food, aren't they?' Sabrina toyed with her spoon. 'You know, Lian mentioned that while Rob's away you're having a surprise girl's night? I wondered if you'd like me to make a pudding, I mean only if you don't have other plans and I'm not trying to elbow my way in.'

'Oh right, yes. Tomorrow night.' Though the way she was feeling, Ellie now regretted inviting over Rebecca and Lian.

She had not included Sabrina which was now a bit awkward, although she wasn't obliged to. It was her dinner party. The three of them had been holding dates for ages, although she was well aware of a message on her phone from Rebecca, asking if Sabrina was coming. She had stalled answering that one because she had not challenged Sabrina about the Celtic necklace.

'I could make a cake if you like?'

Shit. 'The thing is, I didn't know if you'd be interested what with Maddy and everything to take care of.'

When Ellie reddened, Sabrina laughed. 'You're right about me having no babysitter and you saw me getting hysterical when I came for lunch, didn't you?'

Ellie kept silent.

'Well, Lian said her husband would be willing to look after Maddy with their two.'

Damn. She hadn't expected Sabrina to be free for an evening.

'Lian even offered for her husband to come and babysit downstairs if it would make me feel better to have Maddy close, which I've got to admit it would. Lian is so lovely, isn't she?'

'Yes she is and well…'

Sabrina was giving her a puppy dog face.

Just resist. You don't have to invite her if you don't want to. Say no.

'…I suppose if you're free and if you'd like to...'

'Oh thank you so much.'

Ellie slumped back, defeated by her own politeness. She was so preoccupied with Jacob it was hard to think straight.

'Are you asking me just because of my cakes?'

'Of course not.'

'I'm only joking, oh goodness this is really exciting. I haven't been invited to dinner for years!'

'Hey don't talk it up too much. It's only a cosy night in.'

Sabrina clapped her hands. 'I can't wait. I *love* the idea.'

Maybe it was because she had been starving herself, but the sugar had whooshed straight to Ellie's head and was making her feel a bit sick. But it gave her a sudden idea.

'Wow, my tummy is full. Shall we go and sit in the lounge? I need to flop.'

She had left Hayley's photo album lying on the coffee table. As they settled themselves, Ellie flipped it open and found Rob and Hayley's wedding picture.

'What's this? Is it Rob's previous wife?'

'Uh huh.'

Now Sabrina was perching on the edge of the sofa and turning the pages. 'Rob looks the same,' she said.

Reaching over, Ellie turned to the picture of Hayley – the one with the necklace. She watched Sabrina like a hawk and Sabrina didn't give any reaction to the necklace though she was staring straight at it. Should she ask outright? It would mean letting on she had been nosey and spotted it in the box, but what the hell.

'Poor Hayley, Kath told me what happened,' Sabrina said. 'Actually I've been meaning to speak to you about Hayley.'

'Have you?' Ellie gripped the edge of the sofa. Was this it? Was Sabrina going to confess to being Hayley's long lost relative?

'Yes I have because Kath Nettle told me a disturbing story about the young woman's death.'

Ellie sat bolt upright. 'There was nothing disturbing about Hayley's accident.'

'That's just the thing, Kath told me there was and she said specifically the police thought Hayley died in mysterious circumstances.'

'The poor girl fell and the newspapers did the usual with the story and sensationalised it. That's all.'

'Did Hayley slip, nobody knows do they? Please don't take it the wrong way, I'm only saying this to you because you're a friend and… well it's also because I was blinded to the shortcomings of my husband and friends tried to warn me again and again and I ignored them and I even thought they were being malicious or jealous…when actually they were trying to protect me.'

'I don't know what you're getting at.'

'The thing is, however hard it is to face the possibility, what if Rob *was* involved in Hayley's death? Haven't you ever considered it?'

'That's ridiculous.' It came out indignant. Yet a little voice inside said – *but it had seemed strange hadn't it* – the way Rob swore Hayley had been alive when he left her, not to mention the strange choice of a honeymoon in the middle of nowhere hiking in hazardous terrain. And what about the vast wealth Rob inherited? All because Hayley died. *Shut up Ellie, he's your husband and you love him.*

Sabrina was toying with the corner of the album. 'I know you don't want to hear it though I'm not a good friend if I don't voice my doubts, am I?'

'Why are you so interested in her?'

Ellie could feel her heart beating hard. She half expected Sabrina to say she was Hayley's long-lost sister, except that was stupid, besides, Hayley only had a brother.

Sabrina pursed her lips. 'The story seems so strange, and frankly, suspicious.'

'No it doesn't. Kath has been filling your head with nonsense. You know she writes the Lewes blog, right? She just likes a good story.'

'I don't see it that way.'

'Listen.' Ellie took a deep breath. 'The day I helped with your boxes I noticed you had a necklace the same as Hayley's.' She tapped the page. 'Exactly like this one. What's going on, Sabrina?'

Sabrina leaned forward, scrutinising the photograph. 'It's very pretty but you're mistaken. I don't have anything like it.'

'Don't deny it. I saw it with my own eyes. It was a silver Celtic shamrock. A twin of the one Hayley is wearing.'

'You've got it wrong. It's not my sort of jewellery at all.'

She's lying. 'It was there! In your book box.'

Sabrina shook her head in bewilderment. 'In my book box? No way.'

'For goodness sake. I didn't imagine it.'

'If you don't believe me then let's go and have a look. I haven't had chance to unpack those ones yet.'

'Right. Come on then and I'll show you.'

She followed Sabrina down to the apartment and they found the two cartons exactly where Ellie had put them against the wall of the lounge.

'I haven't touched a thing. Take a look for yourself.' Sabrina stood with her arms crossed.

Ellie knelt down. She couldn't remember which box it had been in, but when she opened up the flap of the closest one there was no necklace on top. She took out the first layer of books and stacked them to the side.

'Take them all out if you want, just to make sure. I don't mind.'

Ellie did. There was nothing except novels and definitely no necklace. *Right, well it must be in the other one then.* She turned to the second carton. Now her hands were trembling as she piled the books on the floor. But when she got to the bottom, she was staring at brown cardboard. There was no silver chain in sight.

'See? I told you. I haven't got a necklace like the one in the picture. What's got into you?'

'It was here. I know it was.' She started picking up each book and shaking it.

What the hell was going on? She had seen it. She had held it up. She knew she had but she had no proof of that. Could the little girl have something to do with it? Had she taken her mother's chain? No, this didn't make any sense. Ellie peered into the empty carton again and felt suddenly light-headed. Shit. She shouldn't have binged on the cake.

When Ellie groaned and pitched sideways, Sabrina rushed to prop her up and then ran to the kitchen. She came back with a glass of water. It looked like Ellie was on the verge of fainting and it took a couple of seconds for her to come to her senses.

'Oh goodness, what happened? Did I pass out?'

'Just sit quietly until you feel better, please don't tell me you've been working too hard. I thought you looked dreadfully pale today.'

'The necklace,' Ellie said. 'What happened to the necklace?'

'There was no necklace. I promise you.'

'I've not been well the last couple of days.' Ellie levered herself up. 'I don't feel too good.'

'I think you need a rest.' Sabrina waited patiently. Would Ellie continue with her questioning about the shamrock? She doubted it. The woman looked a complete mess. It was like she had hardly slept.

'What you were saying about Hayley, that it wasn't an accident,' Ellie said 'You shouldn't repeat it, especially with it being the time of Hayley's anniversary.'

Sabrina opened her mouth to say something, then thought better of it. If Ellie wanted to deny suspicions about Hayley's death that was her right and who was Sabrina to tell her otherwise? After all, many women brushed aside warnings from their friends. She knew from experience how strong the loyalty could be between husband and wife – even if it did turn out to be based on lies.

'Sure,' Sabrina smiled. 'And you do believe me about the necklace, don't you?'

'Maybe I'm confused, I don't know. I can't think straight.'

'Don't worry about it and I didn't talk to you about Hayley to spoil things between us.'

'There's nothing to the story. Rob is a good man.'

'I only said it to help you.'

Ellie rubbed her hands over her face. 'Please don't get upset,' she said.

'I can't help it because you probably think I'm being mean. I don't want us to not be friends.'

'Calm down, it's okay. Listen, I appreciate your offer of making a dessert and right now I think I need a nap. And tomorrow night let's not talk any more about Hayley.'

Taking a tissue and blowing her nose, Sabrina nodded.

Chapter Thirty-eight

Ishtar was even weaker than when Rob last saw her. How the mighty fall, he thought.

'How are you doing?' he asked.

'Okay I guess and maybe a tiny bit better. I haven't been able to eat but I was thinking of taking a shower later.'

Ah, so her energy was dribbling back and her morale wouldn't be far behind.

'That's good to hear. I'm heading off to the Berlin conference soon.'

Ishtar nodded, though he wasn't sure she had any recollection of them speaking about it. She started talking dreamily about some absurd memory of hers, when she and her husband had been running in the rain and she slipped and Zachary had taken her hand.

'And Zach never let go,' Ishtar said.

My god, what did she think life was, a romantic movie?

The more Rob thought about it, the more she was a problem. Other experts examining the malpractice case would probably put the blame on the robotic inserts but Ishtar knew Rob's surgical habits too well. She would understand he should have made a decision to stop. Brain damage may well have been prevented and, at least, lessened.

He could lose his licence to practice. Lose his job and his income. *And his reputation.* Was this an opportunity not to be missed? An all-time low which Ishtar could never recover from? Rob fingered Zachary's keys, safe in his pocket. His plane left for Berlin in a couple of hours, which would be sufficient to ensure an alibi.

Ishtar was lost in her memories when she heard the key turn in the lock. For a moment, she expected it to be Zach, then she remembered it would never again be him. She remained motionless hoping whoever it was would go away. It must be Rob because he was the only one who had a key.

He didn't announce himself, instead going straight to the kitchen. Ishtar heard the sound of the kettle boiling and she sighed and closed her eyes.

A while later, when she opened them, there was a bowl of fruit and two cups on the coffee table in front of her. One was empty and the other was full. Had she fallen asleep? Had Rob sat with her for a while and then left? How much time had passed?

With the lounge gloomy from the drawn curtains, the house was quiet. She propped herself on one elbow and took a sip from her cup. It was lukewarm, so he can't have been gone long. She drank half of it and then tucked herself back into her blanket. She preferred being alone. That way, she didn't need to apologise for being in such emotional pain, nor have to make an effort for visitors.

It wasn't long before her eyelids began to droop again though, this time, it was a strange, heavy feeling and it took a few moments for her to register it wasn't normal.

Sitting up, Ishtar's head spun. Her vision was off and it was difficult to breathe. Something was wrong. She searched for her mobile phone and couldn't find it because it wasn't on the table where she left it, nor on the sofa.

'Are you looking for this?'

She turned. In the half light, someone was standing behind the sofa. Her vision was now so blurry she couldn't make the figure out properly. Was it a man or a woman?

'Wh-what's going on?'

There was no reply and Ishtar realised too late the danger she was in.

'I added sedative to your drink. That way, when I push the tablets down your throat, you won't be able to resist.'

As she tried to stand she was grabbed and her head forced back. She kicked out, banging her legs against the coffee table.

'Let's not delay too much, or you know as well as I do, you'll lose your swallowing reflex.'

Ishtar stared upwards as a gloved finger forced more and more crushed pills down her throat. She tried to spit them out but could not manage it. Her eyes bulged and she fought with all her strength but there was nothing she could do to resist. It was too late, the drugs from the coffee were taking hold and in her final moments of consciousness, she knew with terror that her assailant was sending her to her death.

Chapter Thirty-nine

It was Saturday afternoon and Ellie had spent most of the day in bed. All she could think about was Jacob. Then she dragged herself up and hastily prepared as nice a dinner as she could manage. A while later, she led her friends through to the lounge. Or rather she greeted her two friends and a third person whom she could no longer completely trust.

'I've got to warn you I've not been feeling good today,' Ellie said. 'Though I didn't want to cancel. I just hope it's up to your expectations.'

'Whatever it is it smells great,' Rebecca said. 'I just appreciate the invite.'

'Don't be silly, what expectations,' Lian said. 'I'm here to relax and no pressure on the hostess, and what do you mean you've not been well? What's going on?'

She wafted her hand. *I'm going mad dreaming of necklaces which don't exist. My son is dying and no one can save him*. 'Stress.'

Lian frowned.

'Nothing serious,' Ellie lied.

'Is it because you can't bear being separated from my brother?' Rebecca laughed. 'I don't blame you, come on let's crack open the wine and kick back and I'm so glad you're here too, Sabrina. Where's your daughter?'

Lian put her arm around Sabrina's shoulders. 'My husband is at Sabrina's place supervising Maddy and our two kids. They'll be fine.'

Rebecca took a bottle of red wine. She rummaged in a drawer for a corkscrew. 'Great idea.'

'Gosh, this is my first night out for ages,' Sabrina said.

'Then you'd better enjoy it.' Rebecca popped the cork. 'Where's your glass?'

It wasn't long before the evening was in full swing. As they moved to second glasses of wine and finger snacks, Ellie relaxed. Perhaps this was going to be an easy night after all and it would be good to take her mind off searching desperately for bone marrow donors.

Her sister-in-law had brought onion bhajis and samosas. When Ellie heated them up, spicy aromas wafted across the room.

'Hmm, wonderful.'

'Not made by me, you'll be glad to hear, given my poor track record with Indian food. I know a woman who's started a party company and I got them from her.'

'They're delicious – you'll have to give me her number,' Ellie said. 'I tried making some once and it was so fiddly I gave up.'

Lian laughed. 'Was this when you were in London?'

'Uh huh. Seems like a lifetime ago now.'

'I bet it was different to sleepy Lewes. My brother was so worried you'd be bored down here.'

'Well I'm not. I love my new house and my loft room and the South Downs are heavenly.'

'Tell you what, I've some news I've been dying to tell you.' Rebecca sounded excited. 'My husband is taking me to the Caribbean for my birthday. Let me show you pictures of the hotel.'

It looked fabulous and very expensive. They oohed and aahed over the turquoise water, the tropical beach, the perfect pool and the in-pool cocktail bar. Then Lian talked about her husband's online music lessons which were becoming really popular. Lian was helping to set up his website. Ellie busied herself keeping the supply of alcohol and snacks flowing and she noticed Sabrina was a bit quiet. It was Rebecca who tried to draw her into the conversation.

'I remember when you first moved down to Lewes, Ellie, and you told me how it seemed such a quaint town with its quirky high street,' Rebecca said. 'How about you, Sabrina? Are you finding your way around?'

'Oh yes and I'm taking it slowly,' Sabrina said.

'People are friendly here, I think it's because it's not as hectic as big cities,' Lian said. 'They've got more time for people.'

Sabrina helped herself to another bhaji. 'I didn't have a positive image of the south before I came but you're right, people are nice and actually, a friend of mine was wondering about moving down this way too. She has a disabled son and she's interested in a specialised care facility. She's got her eye on one, though I guess it's a bit of a way from Lewes, in Kent I think. Have any of you heard of it, it's called Clemence House?'

Ellie stopped breathing. She blinked. She had been about to take a sip and her hand froze halfway to her mouth. When she looked across to Sabrina, Sabrina was looking directly back at her so she put down her wine and the glass clonked against the table. It was near impossible to keep the shock from her face. *Please don't let Sabrina notice. Please don't let anyone notice.*

Lian took some olives. 'I don't know the name. Is it a hospital?'

'I think so, or sort of, it's for children with extensive needs.' Sabrina smiled at Ellie. 'My friend said it's got a national reputation.'

Ellie hadn't managed to breathe or move. *Act normal.* She took a shaky in-breath and licked her lips. Then reached to take a samosa and pushed it around her plate. Oh goodness, how could that name have come up. No, no, no, it wasn't possible.

'What's wrong with her son?' Lian asked.

'He has an inherited illness though I've forgotten the name. Unfortunately it's pretty serious and she's looking for the best care she can find.'

'How terrible,' Lian said.

'Sounds dreadful.' Rebecca took a swig from her glass. 'Every mother's nightmare.'

Indeed. A disabled son. An inherited disease. How could it be possible? If she stood up, Ellie wondered if she could make it out of the room without falling over. She doubted it because her legs had turned to jelly.

'I'm starving,' Rebecca said. 'Shall we move to the table?'

They all looked at her and she nodded, not trusting her own voice. There was movement and noise as her friends took up their glasses and moved chairs. Ellie felt faint.

'You okay?' Lian asked.

'Uh huh. Just a bit tired.'

Lian swept up Ellie's glass. 'Let me help you with the food.'

'Thanks,' she said, and she tottered to the kitchen. It can't be true, she kept thinking, it's simply impossible for a friend of Sabrina's to be in the same situation as me. First the Celtic necklace and now Clemence House.

On automatic pilot, she got the food out of the oven and onto the table. She served her friends. She found mineral water and ice cubes and got another bottle of red and one of white for Rebecca to open. It was like an out of body experience. Her hands did the work while her mind was whirring and struggling.

What could she say that wouldn't sound completely crazy? No one else had seen the necklace and Sabrina denied it existed. And no one knew about her son and Clemence House.

Sabrina seemed to be acting totally normally, chatting to Rebecca, and only Lian seemed to sense something was not right. Did it mean Sabrina knew about Jacob? Ellie could not accept that to be true. Or was it a one in a million chance Sabrina's friend had researched Clemence House, after all like Sabrina said, it had a national reputation.

Ellie felt drained. She picked at the contents of her plate. It all tasted like cardboard and she couldn't wait for the evening to end.

They were halfway through the main course, when something else very strange happened. Sabrina suddenly clutched at the edge of the table. Ellie startled. For a moment, she thought Sabrina was choking.

Rebecca must have thought the same because she slapped Sabrina on the back. 'Oh, did something go down the wrong way.'

Sabrina seemed agitated, then she had a coughing fit.

'Here, have a drink.' Lian poured water.

Shaking her head, Sabrina jumped to her feet. 'Someone… at the window,' she said, her voice hoarse. She was pointing behind Ellie's head.

'What are you on about,' Rebecca asked.

Ellie swivelled in her seat, as her mind flew to the threatening note and the broken pane.

Rebecca went to the window and peered into the dark. 'There's nothing there. Are you sure you saw something?'

'Not something! Someone!'

'The new security lighting didn't come on,' Rebecca said. 'It would have done if there was an intruder, wouldn't it?'

'Yes, it should have been triggered,' Ellie said.

'Oh gosh, what about Maddy,' Sabrina whispered, and she clutched at Ellie's arm.

Oh god, Ellie thought, is it Sabrina's mad husband. 'Should we phone the police?'

Rebecca gave her a strange look. 'Huh? What for?'

Sabrina was shaking her head. 'No, no. I don't know. Maybe I'm overreacting. Perhaps I was mistaken.'

'Jesus.' Rebecca rolled her eyes. 'Make your mind up. Did you see someone or not?'

'Something has spooked Sabrina,' Lian said gently, 'and she needs to know Maddy is safe. Why don't I call my husband and check everything is all right, then he and I can check around the house.'

The voice of Lian's husband came through on speakerphone.

'Hi hun, is everything okay?' Lian asked.

'Sure. Why?'

'No… disturbances? We thought we saw someone peering in the window but we're not sure.'

'That's odd. You want me to call the police?'

Sabrina was violently shaking her head.

'Well,' Lian said. 'Only Sabrina saw it so we're not sure…'

'I'm just being silly,' Sabrina said, flapping her hands, 'and I'm sorry to disturb you but can I have a quick word with my daughter.'

When Maddy came on the line the little girl sounded cross. 'I'm fine, Mummy. Why are you phoning?'

'No reason,' Sabrina said. 'I love you.'

Lian hung up. 'Let's all take a few deep breaths and calm down. I'm going to take a walk around the house with my husband, anyone else want to come?'

Rebecca grabbed her jacket. 'Yeah, me.'

'But what if there is someone?' Ellie said. 'It might not be safe.'

She wanted to tell them about the note and the ex-husband. What if the bloody maniac was out there? But Sabrina was biting her lip and shaking her head. Oh bloody hell. She didn't want to be the keeper of Sabrina's secrets anymore. Although she still felt a ridiculous loyalty to her promise.

'What about the security cameras,' Ellie said. 'Rather than you going outside, can we check the footage first?'

'I guess,' Lian said.

Ellie stared at Sabrina, willing Sabrina to tell the others the truth. But Sabrina kept shaking her head.

'I think the footage is a much better idea,' Ellie said.

Rebecca sighed and peeled off her jacket. 'I'm for giving it a go and that way, we don't let the dinner spoil.'

'The videos are stored on the cloud and I've got a password and that's all I know.'

'If you can lend me your laptop, I'll try to access them,' Lian said.

'I'm so sorry.' Sabrina seemed close to tears. 'I don't know what got into me. There was something pale and I thought it was the side of a face although now when I think about it I'm really not sure.'

'Maybe it was a reflection?' Lian suggested.

'Oh gosh, now I've gone and ruined our evening.'

Lian patted Sabrina's arm. 'No you haven't.'

Sabrina was too disturbed to eat more and Ellie didn't feel at all like it either. Rebecca was the only one who went back to her plate and tucked in while Lian got to work on Ellie's laptop. By the time she accessed the footage, the ambience was well and truly dead.

'There are four cameras in all and as far as I can see they show the three of us arriving and then nothing. Have a look for yourselves.'

They watched Lian and Rebecca coming to Ellie's door, and Sabrina leaving her apartment and then appearing at Ellie's door. All the rest was a dark, grainy blur.

'Nothing,' Lian said.

'It was stupid of me,' Sabrina said. 'Now I've spoiled everything.'

It was a huge relief to see nothing had been caught on camera and be reassured Sabrina's ex wasn't lurking outside. Ellie plumped into a chair. 'Let's have the dessert and then call it a night.'

'I feel such an idiot,' Sabrina said.

Rebecca poured herself more wine. 'Why on earth did you get spooked like that?'

When Sabrina didn't answer, Ellie pulled Rebecca away. 'Rebecca, can you help me with the pudding please?'

In the kitchen, Ellie hissed in Rebecca's ear. 'Sabrina has got a violent ex. I didn't want to tell you before but he might have been the cause of the broken window.'

'Shit. Does Rob know?'

'No.'

'What! Why not?'

'Because I promised not to tell. There've been a couple of odd things recently.'

Rebecca narrowed her eyes. 'Like what?'

Clemence House. The necklace. But would Rebecca believe her about the shamrock? Ellie wasn't sure.

'The window. And Sabrina acting all jittery.'

'My god, yes. Poor Maddy having to put up with her mother embarrassing her in front of her friends. You know as well as I do there was no one outside, Sabrina was imagining it. If there had been anyone there, even her ex, it would have been caught on camera.'

'I suppose.'

'I'm going to ask her about it.'

'Okay.'

For the next twenty minutes, Ellie managed to steer the conversation towards lighter topics like a yoga weekend which she and Lian were hoping to attend. Lian talked about the craft area at school and Sabrina's great ideas for it.

'You lot are so creative,' Rebecca said.

Sabrina had fallen quiet again since the incident.

'It's a lovely dessert,' Lian said. 'Such a heavenly mix of strawberries and creamy sponge.'

'Thank you,' Sabrina said.

Rebecca turned to face Sabrina. 'Listen, you know you can trust us, so please can you tell me what the hell is going on?'

'You won't believe it if I do.'

'Try me.'

Sabrina gave a strange laugh. 'What the hell, you already think I'm crazy, don't you?'

Lian tutted. 'No, we don't.'

'It's my ex-husband. When we managed to escape I knew he'd come after us. He was a monster.'

Lian stared. 'Oh my god.'

'What do you mean, come after you?' Rebecca said.

'He's a control freak. He couldn't stand me having any life and he didn't like me leaving the house. He used to yell at me and tell me how worthless I was until, in the end, I started to believe it. He took away my self-confidence and after Maddy was born I had post-natal depression and his yelling made it so much worse.'

Rebecca pushed back her hair. 'Jesus. The son-of-a-'

'And you think he might have found you here?' Lian asked. 'If that's true we need to contact the police.'

'No! Like I said, I overreacted earlier. It was nothing. Probably just a trick of the light and me being on edge all the time.'

'I'm not so sure,' Lian said. 'Isn't it better to go on the cautious side, just in case? Shouldn't we at least let the police know we're worried? What do you think, Ellie?'

Ellie didn't know what to say. Was Sabrina going to tell them about the threatening note? And if Sabrina didn't, would it be wrong of Ellie to spill the details? Were her concerns about the necklace and Clemence House sufficient to give her the right to break the confidences of a vulnerable woman?

'Please,' Sabrina said. 'Please don't make trouble for me.'

Ellie hesitated.

'Oh goodness, we're trying to help you,' Rebecca said.

There was an awkward silence and then Sabrina started crying.

'I think you're very brave to escape him,' Lian said. 'Women our age are supposed to have it all – brilliant careers, kids, fantastic husbands,' she shrugged. 'And sometimes life throws curve balls and we find ourselves in situations we can't handle. One thing is for sure – you're not alone Sabrina. We're here to support you.'

They murmured their agreement and gathered around to console her.

Chapter Forty

The day after the dinner party, Ellie felt as if her head had been run over by a lawn mower. Her guests had eventually gone home, with Lian offering to stay at Sabrina's and Sabrina turning her down.

When Sabrina came hammering at her door late morning, Ellie downed her coffee in one scalding go. What had happened now? She dreaded to think what it might be.

Sabrina tripped over the doormat and practically landed in Ellie's arms.

'Cleopatra is gone.'

Ellie's mind could not compute this. 'Who?'

'Maddy's rabbit is missing. She's not in her hutch.'

And this was important because…?

'Oh gosh I've got a splitting headache after last night.' She had slept really badly, dreaming of Jacob and Hayley and trying to decide if the Clemence House coincidence was innocent or contrived. 'Are you sure she's not hiding under the hay or…'

'Of course I am and Maddy is in pieces. I didn't want to tell her Cleopatra might have been *taken*.'

'Wait a minute, please don't tell me you're thinking the rabbit has been stolen by your ex? That's really not likely.'

'I know and I don't believe that's what's happened, but I can't get my brain to work properly. And thank you so much for not talking about the note last night. It was humiliating enough without them knowing the whole embarrassing story.'

'Right. Except I wasn't comfortable keeping it back. You've got to tell people yourself.'

'When I feel stronger, I promise I will. But please help. Maddy is distraught.'

'Well, maybe she left the hutch open and Cleopatra escaped?'

'No way.'

'Or she dug her way out.'

'She can't have done. The hutch has a wooden floor.'

'I don't know.' Ellie flapped her arms in exasperation. 'Have you searched the garden?'

Which was how, an hour later, Ellie found herself crawling around the lawn. She scanned the bottom of the hedges, she peered under bushes, she searched everywhere a fluffy animal could hide. She could hear the child calling Cleopatra's name and it was the only thing which kept her at it because little Maddy sounded heartbroken.

'This is ridiculous,' she muttered to herself. No one had taken the damn rabbit. It had got out or been let out, most likely by Sabrina's five-year-old. They should get a new one in fact, she would suggest it, just as soon as she found the right moment and then they could end this. Or better still, could they get one which looked the same as the old one and then pretend they had found Cleopatra?

Ellie was congratulating herself on a wonderful plan, when she heard Rob's car on the drive. She breathed a sigh of relief as he pulled into the parking area the other side of the hedge. He would help calm Sabrina down. The evening before, Lian and Rebecca had done a stellar job doing the same.

She was on her hands and knees right by the hedge when the boot of the car clicked open. Then came the plonk as luggage landed on gravel. Rob's footsteps crunched as he came around the car. Wouldn't it be funny if he knew she was on the other side of the hedge with her face in the grass? It would be hilarious if it were not so tragic for poor Maddy.

Instead of going towards the front door, Rob seemed to be going away from it. Ellie peered cautiously under the bushes and caught sight of Rob's shoes and the hem of his trousers. He was over by the ornamental bushes opposite the front door and he was scrabbling with his foot under the honeysuckle. What was he doing? Did he have something disgusting on his shoe? Rob bent quickly, doing something in the earth with his hand and then he straightened, pushing at the ground with his foot. After that, he retrieved his luggage and went inside the house.

Ellie wasn't sure why she did it but she scrambled to her feet and scooted over the other side of the lawn, so she was right next to Sabrina when Rob appeared on the kitchen terrace.

'Hello,' he called down. 'What are you up to?'

'Hi darling, did you have a good conference?'

'It was fantastic and it looks as if I've missed something?'

'Cleopatra has gone,' Maddy wailed.

Rob came down the steps and he hugged Ellie and then rolled up his sleeves. 'Then we'd better find her hadn't we? How did she get out?'

They were about to explain, when they heard another car draw up outside and then came voices and someone rang on Ellie's door.

'Are we expecting anyone?' Rob asked.

'No,' she said. 'I'll be back in a minute.'

Rob followed her up to their kitchen and as they went through the house, they heard banging on the front door.

'Whoever it is, they're insistent,' she said. She peered through the peephole. Outside were a man and a woman both smartly dressed.

'Good morning,' the woman said as Ellie opened the door. 'I'm Detective Inspector Hunter, and you are?'

'I'm Ellie Mitchell. How can we help you?'

'I'm here to speak to you and your husband, Doctor Robert Mitchell.'

Ellie turned to Rob.

'My name is not Doctor Mitchell it's *Mister* Mitchell.' He titled his chin. 'I'm a cardiac surgeon and a Fellow of the Royal College of Surgeons. As such, my correct title is Mister.'

'Yes of course. I'd like you to come with me to the police station,' Detective Inspector Hunter said, her tone icy.

'Have I done something wrong?' Rob asked with a laugh.

'We need you to assist us with our enquiries.'

'What's this about please?' Ellie said.

DI Hunter stared at her. 'It's in connection with the recent death of Ishtar Khan.'

Chapter Forty-one

Ellie sat with Rob in the back of the police car. She had never before been spoken to by the police, let alone been asked to go with them. The pavements sped by and pedestrians peered in when the car slowed at the lights. With her stomach winding itself into a knot, she turned her face away. Ishtar was dead? How? And why on earth did the police want to ask them questions? Relax, this is only routine, she told herself, but her palms were practically running with anxious sweat.

They arrived at a drab building and parked around the back and she and Rob followed DI Hunter inside.

'If you don't mind I prefer to speak to you separately,' DI Hunter explained, though the way she said it left little room for refusal.

As they were led in different directions, Ellie's anxiety spiked.

'Are we under arrest! What's going on?'

'There's nothing to worry about,' Rob said. 'They already told us this is an informal interview which means we don't even need to be here, do we inspector?' DI Hunter gave a curt nod in response. 'Although since we're law-abiding citizens, why shouldn't we help the police if they ask us to?'

DI Hunter's attitude towards them was brusque and officious. No, that wasn't quite right – actually the detective didn't have a negative attitude towards *them,* she had it towards Rob. Why? Against all logic, Ellie started to feel frightened.

She was led to a chilly interview room and left on her own. Her bare arms were quickly covered in goosebumps. Sitting at the grey plastic table, she tried to stay calm. This was unnerving. If it was all routine, why was DI Hunter so stern? And how could Ishtar be dead? It didn't make any sense. And so soon after Zachary's death.

She had to sit for over an hour on her own. When DI Hunter came in, she was accompanied by someone else in plain clothes.

'That took longer than expected, I'm sorry,' DI Hunter said. 'Let's get started shall we? This is my colleague Detective Sergeant Delaney.'

Ellie wanted to ask what had taken so long, was DI Hunter referring to her interview with Rob? Or had other events happened to drag the inspector away? The questions stayed locked in her throat.

Delaney was carrying two mugs. 'We thought you might need warming up,' he said. 'It's a bit cold in here.'

'Thanks,' Ellie mumbled. 'Do you mind telling me what this is about?'

Chairs scraped as they two of them sat down and Delaney pushed a mug over to her and kept one for himself.

Hunter had penetrating dark eyes and chestnut hair pulled into a ponytail. With no trace of makeup and a navy trouser suit and pale pink shirt, she had an efficient air about her. Ellie got the feeling DI Hunter was very good at her job.

'As you know I wanted to talk to your husband first about events surrounding the death of Doctor Ishtar Khan, sorry not doctor, your husband has been very clear that her correct surgeon's title was Ms Ishtar Khan. He's very picky about that isn't he. Ms Khan was found dead in her own home yesterday evening. A couple of colleagues had called by her house to offer their condolences for Mr Khan's passing and they raised the alarm.'

Both officers were intent on Ellie's reactions, which made her shift awkwardly, even though she had nothing to feel guilty about.

'What happened? Ishtar seemed in good health, I mean, she'd recently lost her husband and it was a terrible blow but still I don't see how…'

'When did you last see Ishtar Khan?'

'A couple of weeks ago at our barbecue. We invited a bunch of friends over and Ishtar called by. She didn't stay long because she needed to get back to her husband. He was ill, actually he was dying, and then Zachary passed away a few days later.'

'How well did you know her?'

'Not very. Ishtar and my husband work together, as I'm sure you know. I first met her a few weeks before our wedding, just over a year ago.'

'Hmm,' Hunter nodded her head. 'From what your husband told us, he and Ms Khan have known each other a long time. Were you aware that since Mr Khan's death, your husband was regularly visiting Ms Khan at home?'

She tried to stifle her surprise. Rob had told her he had dropped by to see Ishtar *once*, the morning after Zachary died. He hadn't mentioned any other visits. Why not? To stall before answering, she lifted her mug and took a sip of lukewarm liquid. Whether it was tea or coffee she couldn't tell and neither did she care.

She nodded. 'Uh huh.'

'You're saying your husband informed you of his visits?'

'Of course he did.'

She hoped they couldn't see her blushing. She really was a terrible liar. It wasn't so much she was covering for Rob, but rather she was covering for herself because he *should* have told her. She didn't want DI Hunter to think they had a dishonest relationship, or worse, that there was something wrong in their marriage, and now she thought about it, it made sense Rob had been going to Ishtar's regularly. Why shouldn't he?

DI Hunter tapped a pen on her notepad. 'Can you tell me when your husband last went to Ms Khan's house?'

Oh shit. 'I don't know, I guess it was a few days ago before he went away on his conference.'

'Morning or evening?'

'I'm not certain.'

'Right. Can you be more precise about the day and the time?'

Ellie shook her head. 'Not really, look, is this important? My husband doesn't have to let me know every time he decides to see a bereaved friend. I don't keep tabs on him.'

DI Hunter smiled. 'Of course not.'

'Why are you asking these questions?'

'The thing is, Mrs Mitchell, we need to investigate the circumstances of Ms Khan's death. We're awaiting the outcome of the post-mortem examination, but it seems she overdosed on sleeping tablets.'

Ellie's hand flew to her mouth. 'Oh my god that's not possible.'

'Why not?'

'Because… because Ishtar was so…' She searched for the right word, '…vibrant.'

'Are you saying you find taking her own life to be out of character?'

'Like I said, I didn't know her well but she was a strong woman, everyone will tell you that.'

'Yes, they already have,' Hunter said. 'which is why we're trying to understand what might have been going through the doctor's mind to cause her to take her own life. If you've any information to pass to me, I'd be grateful.'

Ellie knew what it was like to plunge to the depths and not be able to get out because she'd been there herself. But Ishtar? It just didn't seem right.

'I don't understand – how on earth might I have information? Do you mean about her emotional state?'

The inspector said nothing and the only sound breaking the silence was DS Delaney slurping from his mug.

'You tell me,' the inspector finally said. 'Are you aware Mrs Mitchell, that your husband was under investigation at the hospital for malpractice? As we understand it, Ms Khan's conclusions about the case were going to be very important in deciding the outcome.'

She went hot all over and this time she could not cover up her ignorance – it must be written all over her face. 'I don't know anything about that.'

'I see.'

'Wait a minute, if you're insinuating my husband might have had anything to do with Ishtar's death, you're badly mistaken. Rob cared for her. He was visiting her to support her in her time of need. There's nothing sinister about that.'

'Of course not. And did your husband have keys to Ms Khan's house?'

It was a focused question and one of a few the inspector had slipped in. Ellie's anxiety notched up and her instinct was no longer honesty – rather it was to protect Rob. She stopped herself from biting her lip. Was this a trick? What was the right answer?

'I don't know.'

'Think carefully, are you aware of your husband having a key?'

'He's never mentioned it, and so what if he has? That's not a crime is it?'

'Keys belonging to Mr Khan were not in the house nor in the cars owned by the couple. An elderly neighbour has been visiting every few days and she noticed straight away they were missing from their usual place. It's possible if someone was involved in Ms Khan's death, this person had the keys and were able to let themselves in and out.'

Feeling her heart beating fast, she started to feel faint.

'What I mean is, it would have been perfectly possible for someone to give the doctor those pills, for instance by force, and then let themselves out and lock the door behind them.'

The inspector stared at Ellie, dark eyes unblinking.

'Ishtar Khan had some small marks on her body. It could indicate there had been a struggle.'

A struggle? Was the inspector talking about murder? Ellie opened her mouth to say there was no way in hell it could have anything to do with Rob. Instead, she heard a buzzing in her ears. DS Delaney scraped back his chair and then the sergeant's hands were on Ellie's shoulders, as she passed out.

Chapter Forty-two

When Ellie came to, she was slumped forward. DI Hunter was holding the back of Ellie's head so it was between her knees.

'Breathe nice and calmly,' DS Delaney said. 'A slow breath in… and now a slow breath out. That's it.'

Staring at the linoleum floor, she could see the shine on Delaney's shoes. She felt a complete idiot, yet the shock had been total. Did the inspector think Rob had supplied the pills? Or worse, had administered them himself? How ridiculous. Rob would never do something like that. Ever!

'I can sit up now.'

'Are you sure?' DI Hunter asked. 'It can take a few minutes for a spell of dizziness to pass.'

Ellie removed the inspector's hand. 'I said I'm okay now. I don't know what happened.' She smoothed her hair and took a few more deep breaths. 'I'd like to go to the bathroom.'

'I'll show you where it is, and if you feel better perhaps we can quickly finish afterwards?'

Her heart sank because she had been hoping to get away. Maybe she should have pretended to be more ill and then she might have been able to avoid Hunter's interrogation, because that was what it was beginning to feel like, not a casual voluntary interview.

In the ladies restroom, she splashed water on her face and stared at herself in the mirror. *There's no need to panic. Rob is innocent and if Hunter is good at her job she'll realise it and go after who might really be responsible.* Or maybe Ishtar had done it herself, however unlikely that seemed.

Back in the interview room, she sat down.

'Do you feel able to continue?' DI Hunter asked. 'Otherwise we can do this at your house if you prefer?'

'Let's get it over with, please.'

The inspector glanced at her notebook. 'Your husband mentioned you didn't like Ms Khan very much. Can you explain that to me?'

It came like a slap in the face and she almost flinched. Why the hell had he told Hunter that? Here she was standing up for him while he'd been...

She stared at her cold cup of tea and managed a half-hearted shrug. 'Like I said, we weren't best friends. Ishtar was Rob's buddy not mine.'

'Buddy or colleague? Or was there more to their relationship than that?'

The bloody nerve of the woman.

'Let me put it more bluntly, did you dislike Ms Khan because you suspected she and your husband were having an affair?'

'How dare you! No I did not! Ishtar was a highly respected surgeon. I guess I felt I wasn't good enough for her since I'm just a romance writer. Like a lot of Rob's friends she probably looked down on me because I didn't meet her high standards.'

'Though perhaps your husband did meet Ms Khan's standards?'

'Stop it! You can't make those sorts of insinuations. They were friends, nothing more and nothing less and this interview is over. I'm going home.'

She and Rob took a taxi and Ellie sat fuming in the back. She was furious at him for betraying her. There she had been lying for him and all he could do was drop her in it. *Come on*

Ellie, you're being ridiculous, there was no harm in him telling the inspector the truth. But that wasn't how it felt.

Why hadn't he stood up for her? Now Hunter wondered about Rob and Ishtar having an affair which was the very thing Ellie had been worried about.

When they got out of the car, Rob tried to put his arm around her shoulders and she shrugged it off.

'Are you all right?'

'Fine,' she snapped.

She stalked into the kitchen, took a mug from a cupboard and banged it down onto the counter, then turned her back as she went to the tap and gushed water into the kettle. When he came up behind her, she whirled to face him.

'Why did you tell that vile detective I didn't like Ishtar?'

'Is that what you're mad about?' Rob ran his hand through his hair. 'I dunno. Because it's true.'

'So what if it is! And why didn't you tell me you were visiting Ishtar every damn day. Why did you lie to me?'

'It wasn't a lie, I simply didn't mention it.'

'Same thing.'

'Because I knew you'd get upset.'

'Yeah? Well I'm upset now!'

He said nothing, which made her even more angry.

'Hunter told me Ishtar killed herself. Aren't you going to ask me how it went with them bombarding me with questions?'

'I will if you give me a chance,' he said. 'I was thinking it was all routine stuff, the same as she asked me.'

'So you think Ishtar took her own life?'

'Poor woman, I knew she was going through hell but I never imagined it would affect her so deeply.'

After her breakdown, Ellie joined a support group and she had met others who had attempted to end it all. None of them were like Ishtar. She stabbed an accusing finger at Rob's chest.

'Me neither – grief wouldn't have derailed her like that. She wasn't that sort of person.'

For a moment, she imagined Rob's expression flickered and he no longer looked at her kindly. She suddenly felt the need to be careful. Ellie withdrew her finger.

Rob walked over to the coffee machine, sliding a cup underneath.

'Detective Hunter told me Ishtar took an overdose,' Ellie said. 'The pill container was found by her side.'

She didn't know why but she would have liked to be able to see his face because something about Rob's behaviour was making her uneasy. The coffee machine made its noise, and few moments later, he slid a little cup of espresso onto the counter.

'The bereavement must have been too much for her,' he said.

'You think?'

'It's the only explanation I can come up with.' He came to her and touched her arm. 'Hey, you're shaking.'

'I know, because the stress got to me. It was horrible them searching for foul play and it was pretty obvious Hunter believes Ishtar may have been murdered.'

Rob shook his head. 'I didn't get that impression.'

Didn't he? When Hunter's agenda had been perfectly clear to Ellie?

'The police are suspicious because some keys are missing,' she said, scrutinising his face.

'Which hardly sounds like cast iron evidence of anything weird to me.'

She started making herself a herbal tea. 'What a hellish morning. And I had a dinner party here last night with the girls and Sabrina was freaking out so I didn't get much sleep either.'

'They took my fingerprints,' Rob said. 'Or rather, I gave them voluntarily since they're going to be all over Ishtar's place anyway.'

'Are they?'

There was a silence as he stirred his coffee and took a few sips. It was remarkable how calm he was whereas she was a bag of nerves.

'And Cleopatra went missing and we were searching all over the garden for her.'

'Sounds like you had a busy few days,' he said with a smile. 'I did too at the conference.'

She didn't miss his hook fishing for compliments. This was the moment she would usually ask about Berlin and sit and listen in awe as he talked about his achievements. Ellie didn't take the bait.

'You can tell me about it later,' she said. 'Right now I need a long soak in the bath, oh, and Hunter told me about the malpractice case…' She made sure to keep her tone light and she knew she had been right to because she saw Rob stiffen.

'There's nothing to it.' He dismissed it with a wave of his hand.

'What's it about then?'

'You wouldn't understand it darling, but basically I used some hi-tech to assist me in a heart bypass. Do you remember I told you about that new technique where robotic probes are inserted into the chest and I can manipulate them externally via monitors? It's a big advance in my field. Anyway, an operation didn't go as well as I hoped and the patient's family complained.'

'What will happen?'

'They'll investigate and they won't find me at fault because I couldn't have done anything differently.'

She knew Rob habits and his nuances because she'd been learning them. Which was why she knew his response was too glib and too smooth. He was lying.

Ellie took a hot bath and let the questions swirl around her head. Nothing made sense. Ishtar was a vibrant woman who had fought for Zachary right to the end. Suicide seemed out of the question. Rob had talked about the malpractice case but he had missed out crucial information because he had not told her how Ishtar would have been the one with the vital input. Ellie only knew this because Hunter had told her.

That night when she snuggled in Rob's arms the warmth she usually felt had disappeared and instead there was a cold feeling in the pit of her stomach. What if her perfect husband was not so perfect after all?

Chapter Forty-three

Sabrina sipped her coffee. At the girl's dinner evening, when she dropped Clemence House into the conversation, the look on Ellie's face had been priceless. How she hated Ellie for what she had done in the past, and here Ellie was, living a lie with Rob, carrying on as if nothing had happened.

Soon after Jacob's birth, Sabrina discovered Ellie had a son. *Now I've got power over you, Ellie Mitchell.*

Wasn't it time to sow a few seeds of doubt amongst Ellie's nice friends?

It was a glorious afternoon and Kath had arranged chairs in the shade. Maddy went straight to the pond, taking a slice of her mother's cake with her. They chatted about the weather and Kath told Sabrina about her latest blog article which had been an interview with the gardener at Southover Grange.

'He's so knowledgeable and would you believe that man has worked there for over forty years,' Kath said.

'Did it get a good response?'

'Oh yes, lots of people around here are keen gardeners.'

'I bet, and did Adam like it?'

'Actually, Adam came with me and videoed the whole thing.'

'Him and his green fingers,' Sabrina said.

Kath took a drink. 'Look at your daughter, she's coming out of herself, isn't she?'

'She's been playing with some other children and I've managed to let her go a bit. I guess I'll have to get used to it for when she starts school in the autumn.'

'That's so good to hear and what about you? No more nasty messages from your ex-husband, I hope.'

Sabrina shook her head. 'Thankfully not and I'm starting to feel more positive, perhaps it's because I've realised my own troubles aren't so bad compared to other people's.'

Kath nodded sagely. 'Sympathy for others often makes us realise we're not as badly off as we thought we were.'

'Yes.' Sabrina put two sugars into her cup and left a decent pause. 'Except I wasn't expecting to hear Ellie had such a dreadful history, the poor woman.'

The shock on Kath's face said it all.

'I'm sorry, you've taken me by surprise. Ellie is a friend of mine.'

'I didn't realise, gosh I apologise. I didn't intend to be tactless, but I'm guessing she hasn't mentioned her past to you then?'

Kath was frowning. 'Ellie and I get on very well indeed, though I don't think I'm aware… I mean she doesn't talk about her previous life much.'

'I can't break confidences.' Sabrina smoothed her skirt. 'But her secret took the breath right out of me and to think she tells everyone she isn't a mother.'

'Oh dear.' Kath's hand came to rest on her chest. 'I don't know what to say…'

She firmly shook her head. 'I shouldn't have mentioned it, it was wrong of me, please forget it.'

'Well yes. I think that's probably best.'

Passing Kath another slice of cake, Sabrina tried not to smile. The old woman was flustered and far too decent to try to delve more into the juicy information. Yet a gossip like Kath, would she really be able to keep this to herself?

Chapter Forty-four

Things did not go back to normal between Ellie and her husband, how could they? She found it hard to forgive him for dumping her in it with the detective. She went for regular walks to try to keep her emotions in check because she needed to keep balanced for Jacob. When she got back from her walk that morning, Ellie knew she must talk to someone or she would explode. She decided to head over to Kath's.

'Lovely to see you,' Kath said. 'Come through, come through.'

'Sorry I didn't phone ahead. I just called by on the off-chance and I hope I'm not disturbing you.'

'Nonsense, of course not, you know you're welcome any time.'

She followed Kath to their usual seats in the lounge.

'How about a cup of tea.'

'I'd love one.'

'Then you wait here and I'll be back in a jiffy.'

The tray was soon arranged on the table and Kath was busying herself prodding at the tea bag.

'Maybe it's my imagination but you seem a little unsettled today,' Ellie said.

'Do I? Well yes, to be honest, I'm glad to see you.'

'You're being mysterious.'

'Oh goodness, and very rude I'm being too, because there was probably a reason you came to see me. You first, my dear.'

'But if there's something you want to tell me....'

'No, I insist. You first.'

Ellie sat back and she sighed. 'I've had a hellish couple of days. I don't know if you're aware but one of Rob's colleagues took her own life and Rob and I were questioned by the police.'

Kath nodded, confirming most of Lewes knew the morbid news.

'It's even worse because I'm sure they're viewing Rob as a suspect.'

Kath gasped. 'The poor man. Not again. Are you sure?'

'Yes and it was horrible. They grilled us like criminals and then we had a big row about it afterwards.'

Kath stirred her cup, with a little frown on her face. 'That doesn't sound very nice and no wonder you needed a chat.'

Slumping, Ellie took a biscuit. 'I *knew* you'd understand and it's all been going around and around my head and driving me mad, and Rob has been acting very strangely lately. I don't know what's going on with him.'

'Ah, I see, and have you managed to patch it up after the argument?'

'He doesn't want to talk about it.'

'Then he's an idiot. Couples have to communicate or it leads to all sorts of misunderstandings, I've seen it so many times, and er, how's it going with Sabrina?'

She caught the casual way Kath had dropped it in on a light note and it made her instantly curious.

'It's funny you should say that.'

'Is it? I just wondered if you two are still getting on.'

Ellie wagged her finger. 'Don't hold back on me, you know I've been wondering about her. She's been acting very strangely and I didn't tell you before but the bizarre thing is that when I helped her to move in, I spotted a necklace.'

'And?'

'Not just any necklace. It was a Celtic shamrock like the one Hayley had. You might not remember it but it's clear in one of Hayley's photographs. And when I challenged Sabrina about it she denied it existed. Then we checked in the box I'd seen it in, which hadn't been unpacked, and it wasn't there anymore.'

'You're saying Sabrina has the same necklace as Hayley?'

'Yes.'

'And it disappeared?'

'Right.'

She watched as Kath straightened her sleeves

'That doesn't make any sense.'

'And she has an abusive ex-husband who has been threatening her. Which makes it difficult to be hard on her.'

'I see. Well, it's a bit awkward but I'm glad you called by because I had a visit from Sabrina myself and I found it pretty disturbing.'

'Disturbing? In what way?'

'Though I like Sabrina I couldn't help thinking she was trying to make trouble and disguising it as concern for you.'

A frisson of fear raced up Ellie's back. 'Go on.'

'She hinted she knew secrets about your past...'

Ellie's eyes widened.

'....and about you being....'

Now Ellie couldn't breathe.

'...a mother.'

She squeezed her lids shut.

'Whether it's true or not, I really don't care, and your life is your affair. The only reason I'm telling you is so you can protect yourself.'

A wave of anxiety flooded over her. Ellie thought of Clemence House. Could Sabrina know about Jacob? It sounded very much as if she did. Thank goodness Kath was so understanding, she really was a good friend. Then Ellie heard the *creak* of a floorboard in the hallway. Her eyes sprang open, just in time to see Kath hurry across the room. For a woman her age, Kath was surprisingly quick.

'Adam, if you're out there, you'd better show yourself,' Kath said, flinging the door open.

Adam slunk into the room with his hands in his pockets. Damn it. How long had he been listening?

Ellie didn't know whether to hit Adam, shout at him, tell them both a lie, or tell them the truth about her son. She must be smart. Sabrina could not use Jacob against her if he was no longer a secret, could she? The big question was, could she trust Kath? Could she trust Adam? But what about the part of her son's story which shamed her the most? The part about Jacob's father? Ellie had to make a quick decision or risk ruining her own life forever.

Chapter Forty-five

Sabrina organised a meeting with Lian. When she arrived at the school, Lian was waiting in the room which the school wanted to transform into a craft area. Good luck to them. At the moment, it looked more like a dumping ground for old equipment and broken desks.

'Hi,' Sabrina said. 'Gosh is this the space? It's much bigger than I thought it would be and it's got plenty of light. I think we can make something of it.'

'You're an angel for being positive. I was worried you'd say there was no hope and I know it's going to be a lot of work. I've got to warn you the budget is pretty tight too,' Lian said.

'Don't worry, you said there are desks and stools we can bring in and I'm sure I can come up with ideas for décor which aren't going to cost much.'

Lian sat on a desk. 'Thanks so much for offering your time. I've got loads on at the moment what with the end of term and the school play. It's wonderful when parents get involved and help out.'

'No problem and before we get started, I brought some refreshments.'

'That is so lovely of you! I am completely starving and I didn't have chance to pop out and get something.'

Sabrina brandished two stuffed baguettes. 'Chicken or veggie burger, your choice,' she said with a smile.

Lian shrieked and hugged her.

They sat and ate, Lian chatting about her day and her class, while Maddy occupied herself with a drawing.

'I've been wanting to make sure you were all right,' Lian said. 'You worried us at Ellie's house.'

'You mean freaking out about a non-existent intruder? I've been cringing about it ever since, it was so brainless of me.

'No it wasn't. We all understood you've been under tremendous strain.'

Lian's expression was so sympathetic, and in another life Sabrina might have felt bad piling on the lies, except that sort of thinking went out the window a long time ago. Needs must.

'Actually it made a huge difference having your support. I've been lacking friends and having you believe me made it, well, more bearable. It reminds me what I went through with my ex wasn't right and you've all been so nice, especially you and Ellie.'

Lian munched on her sandwich. 'Yeah, Ellie is a wonderful person. You're lucky to have moved into her place.'

'I know, and they're such a great couple, except…' Sabrina bit her lip.

'Except what?'

'Thing is, Ellie and I are forming quite a bond and I don't mind telling you I'm worried about her.'

'I don't understand what you're getting at.'

'Ellie. She's under strain, you know, to do with Ishtar's suicide and Rob and Ellie being questioned.'

'Yeah, I know although it's not serious. The police will work it out in the end.'

'I've heard Ellie and Rob arguing loads and last night they were going at it yelling at each other and Ellie screaming at Rob and I don't want to repeat what she was accusing him of, the poor man. I was really glad Maddy was asleep so she didn't get to hear it.'

'Oh no. Ellie? Are you sure?'

Sabrina nodded.

'Well, I suppose we all have our off days,' Lian said.

'I get the impression it's more than that. Hmm, so do you think it's possible?'

'Sorry, you've lost me.'

'Do you think Rob was… you know… having an affair with Ishtar? That's what Ellie accuses him of when she has her screaming fits.'

Lian almost choked. 'Are you mad? He's crazy in love with Ellie and she is with him.'

'She's been tearful and moody. She was sobbing in my lounge yesterday telling me how much Rob has let her down. I did my best to console her because she was in a real state. If you ask me that woman is on the edge. Looked to me as if she was about to crack.'

'No way,' Lian said, 'and Rob and Ishtar no way either. I can't explain what you overheard but whatever's going on it will pass, you can bet on it. It's just a lovers' tiff. We all have them.'

Even so, Lian had a concerned look on her face and Sabrina could see she'd given her plenty to think about.

'I only hope you're right,' Sabrina said. 'For Ellie's sake.'

Chapter Forty-six

When Detective Inspector Hunter turned up again, a feeling of dread swept from Ellie's head to her toes. She froze on the doorstep. It was raining and the forecast was for a downpour the whole week. Drops plopped from the porch onto Hunter's shoulders, soaking into her jacket. Ellie definitely did not want to invite her in.

'May I come in for a moment?' Hunter asked.

Oh no. Ellie reluctantly stepped aside. She was glad Rob already left for work so he wouldn't be subjected to Hunter's unpleasant suspicions. They stood awkwardly in the kitchen, or rather, Ellie stood awkwardly while the inspector dripped and took up space.

'We've found your husband's fingerprints at Ms Khan's house, as expected. Of course, the place is full of the couple's prints and aside from these, there are traces of another person who we've not yet been able to identify. If we're to eliminate you from our enquiries, I'd like you to come down to the station so we can take your prints.'

'I already told you I've never been to Ishtar's house.'

Hunter nodded. 'Yes, you told me that before.'

'So then why are you asking?'

'As I said, it's a process of elimination at this stage.'

Ellie wanted to object on principle, except that felt childish. Since she had nothing to hide, wouldn't it be best to comply?

She gave a sigh. 'Okay.'

'That's wonderful. Would you like to follow me or can I give you a lift?'

'I hope this is going to be the end of it and you can leave us both alone.'

Hunter gave a smile completely devoid of humour. 'The process won't take long, Mrs Mitchell, thank you for cooperating.'

Several hours later, when Lian called by to see Ellie, Ellie was still disturbed by Hunter's request.

'Sabrina told me about you and Rob being questioned by police and if you don't mind me saying, you look like shit.' Lian squelched into the house. 'Sorry for the mess. I shouldn't have walked up because it's awash. The ground is so dry, the rain is running straight off and they're forecasting heavy rainfall for the rest of the week with the river predicted to rise.'

Ellie wasn't listening. She led the way to the lounge.

'I'm so pleased to see you. The police called by earlier.' The words were tumbling out and Ellie felt like she couldn't breathe. 'We didn't get to talk much since the dinner but Ishtar took her own life and the police are investigating. A couple of days ago an inspector dragged us to the station and she was very unpleasant and I thought she suspected Rob was involved except now I'm pretty certain she suspects *me*.'

Her voice cracked.

Lian pulled her close. 'You must have got it wrong.'

'I haven't. Hunter's targeting me. Hunter was here earlier asking for my fingerprints. She told me a suspect's prints have been found at Ishtar's house.'

'And?'

'Don't you get it? If she wants a sample from me, it must be because she thinks they might *be mine.*'

Lian made a sound of disbelief. 'There's got to be a reasonable explanation.' She motioned for them to sit side by side. 'Tell me exactly what this detective person said.'

'She said she needed my prints to eliminate me from her enquiries.'

'There you see? It's nothing.'

'It was a trick! She misled me into giving her what she wants.'

'How? You can't have left your fingerprints at Ishtar's if you've never been there, can you?'

'Are you sure?'

'You're sounding irrational and, you know, a bit paranoid.'

'Lian, that's what Hunter *said* only it's not how she *acted*. She treated me like a criminal and she already knows I didn't like Ishtar. Hunter knows I suspect Rob and Ishtar of having an affair.'

'That's ridiculous.'

'It isn't! I *did* think it!'

'Calm down and take it from me this is all going to come to nothing. You're innocent and this detective is soon going to realise it.'

Ellie furiously shook her head. 'Killing your husband's illicit lover – it's a motive for murder isn't it, and I wished her dead loads of times even when poor Zachary was dying.' Ellie buried her face in her hands.

'We all wish things and it means nothing,' Lian said. 'Hunter can't possibly think you're involved – it's preposterous.'

'But is it? Do you really know me? There are terrible things about me I haven't told you or anyone.'

About Jacob. And Jacob's father and how he died.

'What? You're not talking sense.'

'I am talking sense, I am, I am – because I thought I knew Rob and now I'm not sure. I think he's hiding something. Hunter told me there's a malpractice case against him at the hospital and Ishtar was going to give evidence.'

Ellie's phone rang and she grabbed at it. One glance at the screen and she jumped to her feet, her eyes wide. It was Daniel from Clemence House. She pressed it to her ear.

'Please don't panic Ellie. I need to tell you Jacob is having a crisis and Doctor Venn has asked me to contact you,' Daniel said.

'I'm coming.' Ellie's mind went blank and she clutched at the back of the sofa.

Lian was alarmed. 'What's happened!'

'I've got to go!' She screamed it at her friend's face.

'Go where, Ellie? This is crazy, you're not in a fit state to go anywhere.'

Pushing Lian out of the way, she swiped up her handbag and then her keys from the table in the hallway. She stuffed her feet into trainers and didn't bother to do them up.

'I don't think you should drive,' Lian said. 'Let me take you. I can drive your car.'

She marched out of the door with Lian running after her.

'Where are you going? You haven't even got a jacket on.'

Ellie didn't stop and she didn't speak. It was too late to explain, not after all the lies. All this time she'd pretended she wasn't a mother. That she never had a child.

Jacob needed her. He was in crisis. God, he might be dying. It was what she dreaded. What kept her awake at night. What gave her nightmares. She yanked open the car, her own jagged breathing filling the space as she fumbled with the ignition.

Her darling boy. She imagined him in his little safety helmet, thrashing in bed, or being taken by air lift to hospital in a desperate attempt to save his life. Was he struggling to breathe and the doctors battling to clear his airways? Or having a stream of never-ending convulsions they couldn't get under control?

She ignored Lian's gesticulations, promising herself she'd sort it out later. She had been so stupid. She should have told Lian long ago. She left her friend standing in the middle of the drive, staring after the car.

Rain poured down the windscreen, until she remembered to turn on the wipers. Her brain wasn't functioning properly. Jacob, she had to get to her son. She wouldn't allow herself to crumble. She had learned to be strong and she must get there as fast as she could. She put her foot down hard on the accelerator.

With no rain for weeks the road was slippery, which was why several minutes later, accelerating along a country road, the car skidded. She fought to get control of the vehicle and as she careered towards the trees, she called her son's name. Then came the crunch of the impact and everything went black.

Chapter Forty-seven

Ellie awoke in a clean white room. She lay in a hospital bed and a doctor bent over her, his glasses slipping down his nose. Then he shone a bright light into her eyes.

'Can you hear me? My name is Doctor Hemmington.'

His blue eyes kept going out of focus. When she tried to speak, Ellie's mouth was stuck and she couldn't get words out.

'Just blink if you understand what I'm saying.'

She did.

The doctor repeated the thing with the little light and then he helped her to take a drink.

'You came off the road and your car hit a tree and it's left you with a severe concussion,' Doctor Hemmington said. 'You have three cracked ribs and a lot of bruising to your torso which means you're going to feel pretty sore for several days.'

Gingerly, she moved her hand to her face. There was a horrible pain in her head and a ringing in her ears. The slightest movement caused such agony in her chest she wanted to cry out.

'Can you tell me your name?'

'Ellie Mitchell.'

'What do you recall of the accident?' the doctor said.

The more she tried, the more she couldn't remember. She had absolutely no recollection of driving or of a crash. A feeling of panic gripped her. Was there something wrong with her mind?

'I don't remember.'

'Do you recall getting in the car?' he asked.

'No.'

'Or the events before you drove?'

She remembered Rob going to Berlin for a conference. 'My husband is away in Germany. He left this morning and I waved him off.'

There was movement behind Hemmington and she shifted her gaze there.

'That was a few days ago,' Rob said.

Hemmington was writing on a clipboard. 'How many exactly.'

'Three,' Rob said.

'But it's a blank. That's the last thing I have memory of.'

As she started to cry, Doctor Hemmington gave her a kind look.

'It's quite common after a concussion to have memory blanks. Please don't be alarmed.'

Rob came to stand beside Hemmington and his face was full of concern.

'You remember your husband, and you recall events from a few days ago and that's a good start,' Hemmington said. 'With trauma to the brain it's usually more recent events which are affected.'

'Lian said you were rushing off and she tried to stop you,' Rob said. 'She said you were in a panic and it was because of a message you got but your phone was destroyed in the crash so we don't know who contacted you or where you were going.'

'I don't know. The more I try the more it won't come to me.'

The doctor cleared his throat. 'Think of it like this – the brain has suffered the equivalent of a severe bruising and it needs time to recover. In most cases memories return fully.'

'So there's no permanent damage?' Ellie asked.

'Not as far as we can tell. You need time and the best thing you can do is rest. Forcing yourself to remember won't achieve anything – if they're going to, the memories will come back on their own, though they might be a bit muddled at first because they don't always come back in the right order.'

Wiping at her eyes, she nodded. Thank goodness she didn't have some kind of lasting brain damage. Hemmington had a reassuring manner whereas Rob, on the other hand, was edgy and tense.

'How long have I been here?'

The doctor was back to writing on her chart. 'You've been unconscious for twenty-four hours and I'm going to keep you here for at least another twenty-four so we can monitor your progress.'

'Then can she come home?' Rob asked.

'We can talk about it tomorrow once we've assessed Mrs Mitchell's balance and coordination.'

'Thank you, doctor,' Ellie said.

After Hemmington left, Rob tried to pull her into an embrace only it was so painful she gasped.

'Sorry,' Rob said. 'I didn't realise.'

'And with you a surgeon,' she teased him. 'You should know better.'

'I'm not a trauma specialist, I'm a heart surgeon.'

His tone was huffy and she did her best to smooth his ego. 'Yes and I remember that too.'

Rob sat on the edge of her bed and she winced because she was worried he might jog her by mistake.

'And you really can't recall where you were going in such a rush?' he asked.

What a strange question, of course she didn't know otherwise she would have told Doctor Hemmington.

'I've no idea. Didn't I tell Lian?'

'She had no clue and it seemed like it was urgent.'

Rain was battering the window in a real downpour. 'Was it raining as hard as this? Is that why I crashed?'

'The police said there were no other vehicles involved and you skidded because of the weather. Apparently you were travelling pretty fast at the time.'

She could feel his insistence to know where she had been going and why. Ellie closed her eyes. If only she could remember just to please him but her brain was full of fog and the more she pushed the worse her headache got.

'I'm sorry I can't tell you,' she said.

'Can't tell me or won't?'

It wasn't a joke. The cruelty of Rob's tone went in like a knife making tears prickle the back of her eyes. Why was he being so unpleasant? The doctor had already explained she wasn't to blame, so why might he think she was deliberately not telling him?

Ellie kept her eyes closed and pretended to be drifting to sleep. Some minutes later, Rob kissed her lightly on the forehead, and as he did he whispered in her ear. The nasty way he spoke made her clench her stomach. Why on earth was the man she loved behaving so badly?

'Whatever it is you're not telling me – you know I'll find out.'

Chapter Forty-eight

Ellie had no explanation for Rob's behaviour. It made her sick with anxiety and her mind came up with all kinds of crazy explanations. Had they had an argument? Was there a dispute she couldn't remember? Did her husband have something to hide? Or did she?

The more Ellie turned it over, the more she dug herself into a hole and given she could not recall events before the crash, she had no way of solving it. Since he was working in the same hospital, Rob called by several times and each visit she felt her anxiety notching up. It became impossible to rest and she wished he would stop coming. Part of her wanted to tell the nurses except it seemed silly to, and she didn't want to make waves at Rob's workplace and neither did she want him to lapse into a bad mood. It seemed better to put up with his visits.

Her friends did not come, which made her sad and her only visitor was Doctor Sajid Bakir, one of Rob's colleagues. Ellie knew Sajid and his wife since the wedding.

'Rob told me about your accident,' Sajid said. 'Seems like you've got a nasty concussion.'

She pulled a rueful face. 'Unfortunately.'

'I can't stop long. My wife asked me to pass by and to give you her best wishes, and of course, mine as well.' He gave her a light kiss on the cheek.

'Thank you, being a surgeon's wife doesn't help you know, the nurses are all being odd with me.'

He laughed. 'Are they? They're just nervous because they don't want to make mistakes with Rob watching their every move, though I noticed your husband is in a great mood at the moment. I guess it's because his first keynote speech went so well. Did he tell you Berlin was a success? Apparently they loved him. Let's hope it's the first of many.'

What an odd thing for Sajid to say because Rob had given plenty of conference speeches. As her scalp prickled, a little instinct told her to dig around a bit more.

'The first of many?' she said. 'I see. And here was me thinking you and Rob were asked to conferences all the time.'

Sajid raised his eyebrows. 'As if. Rob's further up the pecking order than me but he still gets nada. Everyone wants to invite the big boss, not the underlings.'

And Ishtar had been the boss. 'Of course. Though you often get invited as participants, right? Even if you don't get the red-carpet treatment and do the big presentation?'

'Not even that. I'm sure my wife prefers it because she gets to keep me at home, but Rob and I, we haven't been to a conference in years.'

A day later Rob brought her home. He was full of care getting her into and out of the car and there were flowers and chocolates waiting on the kitchen table. He was so attentive, Ellie would have liked to think she imagined his nasty whispers. Yet she knew she had not.

The concussion had given her a balance problem which the doctor said would fade with time. She still had the ringing in her ears which meant she planned to spend her days lying down. The headache was the worst. It was constant and sometimes flared although it was manageable with the medication Doctor Hemmington had given her.

Rob helped her to the sofa and then went to prepare supper.

'Lian sends her love,' he called through to her. 'So does Rebecca. They wanted to visit at the hospital and I put them off and Lian wanted to be here when you came home except I told her you'd prefer to be quiet.'

She would have liked to make that decision herself. Why hadn't he discussed it with her because it would have been so nice to see them. She had been thinking of phoning Lian although without her mobile she didn't know Lian's number.

Rob had not got around to getting her a new phone yet either, which was why, at the hospital, she had to ask one of the nicest nurses to help her make a call and to promise to keep it private. She hoped Rob hadn't found out. She had wanted desperately to check on Jacob and when she spoke to Daniel she was horrified to hear Jacob had had a crisis and Daniel had phoned her. That must have been the call which led her to leave the house in a panic, although of course, Ellie had not told Rob this. Though Daniel reassured her the crisis had passed, she felt bereft not being able to see her son. How could she without her husband knowing? Daniel had been very clear that Jacob's condition was now stable but it wasn't enough to console her. At the thought of it, she pushed back the tears.

'I'd like to speak to Lian and Rebecca soon, could you jot down their numbers for me?'

'Sure though remember, you need to rest, not be pestered by visitors.'

Her friends would not be pestering her, they would be helping.

'And did you have time to call by the phone shop?'

'I've been really busy though I promise I'll do it tomorrow.' Underneath his smile his tone was testy. 'We've got the landline haven't we, so you're not completely cut off.'

It was in Rob's study which was at the end of the downstairs hallway and not the easiest place for her to get to. Still, she supposed she could manage for now.

To walk around the house, she had to hold on to the wall. She really hoped her equilibrium would sort itself out because clinging to the furniture was so limiting. In fact, it was worse than her headaches because it effectively kept her housebound.

'I'm not sure I can stand living my life with dizziness and brain fog,' she said.

'Of course you can and I'm going to make certain you are well and truly pampered until you feel better.' He blew her a kiss. 'I'm making your favourite, pasta carbonara, how's that for service?'

To help keep the peace, she made appreciative noises. Being pretty much a prisoner did not sit well with her. She could only hope the concussion would soon fade.

A while later, once they finished supper, Rob sat beside her on the sofa. She noticed how he hadn't yet jotted down her friends' telephone numbers only she didn't want to spoil his mood by asking again. Rob had a glass of wine, though Ellie did not because of her medication.

'That was delicious,' she said.

He took several sips from his glass. 'I forgot to mention we got the demand for payment for the second half of the landscaping work. Maybe you don't remember but you were the one who wanted the garden done exactly how *you* wanted. I've got to say I do so hate it when these people send out bills according to their own timetable to suit their tax planning, but it's a whopping tab and it needs to be settled as soon as possible.'

Frowning, she rubbed her forehead. 'I'm not sure I'm in a fit state to sort it out but I'll have a go tomorrow.'

'Don't worry, if you give me the information I can do the transfer.'

Actually, she would prefer it if he settled the bill for her and she would sort it out with him later, like they usually did. Whereas Rob meant he needed her banking details.

'Ellie?'

'Sorry, my head is really hurting. Like I said, I'll log on tomorrow.'

'Okay, if you're sure. Anything come back to you yet about the day of the accident?'

She was immediately tense – oh no, he wasn't going to go on about that again, was he?

'Nothing.'

'Are you being serious?'

'It's a complete and utter blank – sort of like walking into a fog and seeing nothing around you.'

He took another slug of wine and she could sense his annoyance yet what could she say?

Slipping a couple of pain control tablets into her mouth, she washed them down quickly. She looked forward to going to bed and blanking out, though she couldn't shake the feeling there was something vital she needed to remember and she could not for the life of her grasp it. Was it about Rob? Had he always been so quick to take offence? So quick to accuse her? She didn't think so but had something happened recently to change things? When she struggled to get hold of what was bothering her, all she got was an image of a white fluffy rabbit. What the hell did Cleopatra have to do with anything? She really hoped her memories would come back soon and in the right order because it was horrible to feel so out of control.

It was a while later, as they were getting ready for bed, there was a ring at the doorbell.

'What now?' Rob said, rolling his eyes. He quickly checked his mobile. 'No messages from work. I'll go and see who it is.'

She hoped it might be a late visit from Lian or Kath but it wasn't. It was bloody DI Hunter.

Chapter Forty-nine

'My wife is upstairs and she's unwell.'

Ellie listened to Rob protesting and then she heard the voice of Detective Inspector Hunter. Oh no, what the hell did Hunter want?

'If Mrs Mitchell is too ill to come down, I'll have to speak to her in her bedroom.'

Heavy footfalls came up the stairs. Ellie quickly grabbed a robe and covered herself. Hunter knocked.

'Come in.'

When the detective entered she was accompanied by a uniformed officer. Then Hunter opened her mouth and the words that came out froze Ellie to her core.

'Mrs Mitchell, you are under arrest…'

It washed over her like a tidal wave.

'Do you understand?' Hunter asked.

'Yes. No. I'm not sure.'

The inspector turned to Rob. 'What's wrong with Mrs Mitchell? She doesn't seem herself.'

'Ellie crashed her car and she's suffering from concussion. Her grasp on reality is slim and she's in no fit state to be questioned by you.'

'The Force Medical Examiner will be the judge of that,' Hunter said. 'Mrs Mitchell do you understand you are now under caution?'

Ellie nodded.

'No she does not,' Rob said, 'and there's no way in hell I'm letting you take her away. Besides, my wife can't remember a damn thing because her memory has been wiped.'

The inspector frowned. 'Mrs Mitchell please get dressed and you will accompany us to the station for questioning. Meanwhile, I have a search warrant.' She brandished a sheet of paper at Rob. 'It would be best to cooperate with my officers so we can get this over with quickly and efficiently, Doctor Mitchell.'

Rob bristled and Ellie felt sure Hunter had made a mistake with his name deliberately. She slumped.

Oh my god, they were going to search the house? And the police were taking her for questioning? The shock sucked the air out of her. Arrest her for what? She wanted to be sick. Her legs wobbled as she swung them over the edge of the bed.

'Rob, please can you help me get my things.'

Her voice was shaky and she stuck her chin out and made herself be brave. *This will be over soon. It's all some terrible mistake.* She kept repeating the mantra as she pulled on jogging trousers and a sweatshirt, as she made her way downstairs doing her best to blank out the sounds of thumping and slamming as a fleet of uniformed officers rummaged through their things. In the hallway, she fumbled with her shoes and Rob had to do them up for her.

'If you'll go with my sergeant, please,' DI Hunter said.

Ellie cast a desperate look at her husband, and then followed the officer to a waiting car.

At the station, she had to wait to be seen by the Force Medical Examiner. He proclaimed her fit to be questioned but not fit to be detained overnight. What seemed like ages afterwards, she was led to an interview room, though now Ellie called it by its proper name, an interrogation room. She had refused a solicitor, believing in her own innocence, though now she wondered if that had been wise.

Sitting at the grey table, she remembered being questioned here before and how Rob had told the inspector Ellie disliked Ishtar. She also recalled Hunter afterwards asking for her fingerprints.

Hunter and another officer arrived and they all sat down. Hunter said the date and the time and her rank and name out loud, and so did the second officer.

'If you would state you name for the recording please,' Hunter said.

'Ellie Mitchell.' She pushed her hair out of her eyes. 'Have you finished turning my home upside down?'

'I'm the one asking the questions. I've brought you here because we've cross checked your fingerprints with those found at Ms Khan's house.' Hunter paused. Her dark eyes coolly met Ellie's. 'They are a match.'

Her mouth almost dropped open. 'I've never been there, I swear it. How is that possible?'

The inspector's expression was unreadable. 'I was about to ask exactly the same question. Perhaps you can explain it to me?'

She rubbed her hands over her face as the ringing in her ears got louder. 'I'm telling you the truth. I've never set foot in Ishtar's house.'

'But you don't deny disliking the doctor?'

Clasping her hands in her lap, she tried to stay calm. 'She and I didn't get on though there was no animosity, it was just… we didn't click.'

'Hmm. You had no animosity towards Ms Khan even though you suspected her of having an affair with your husband?'

'I never said that.'

'It's true though, isn't it? You believed they were having an affair.'

'Okay maybe I did, except it was baseless. It was just my own stupid insecurities tripping me up.'

'Tripping you up enough for you to go to Ms Khan's house and force pills down her throat.'

'No!'

Hunter had a pile of papers and she pulled them closer, reading from the top sheet. 'At the initial post-mortem, tiny scratch marks were discovered on the inside of Ms Khan's throat. This triggered a special post-mortem examination which has now been completed. The marks were consistent with the deceased being forced to swallow something she did not wish to, for instance, pills.'

As Ellie fidgeted, both officers stared at her.

'We have also discovered a substance in the doctor's blood stream which causes a sedative effect. This leads me to believe that someone administered a sedative to the doctor, likely without her knowledge, and then once she was incapacitated, they proceeded to force her to swallow an overdose. Why did you do that, Mrs Mitchell?'

Ellie shook her head.

'Though some bruises were evident at the time she was discovered, more have since become visible on the victim's body. This is quite usual because hematomas sometimes take time to manifest.' Hunter cleared her throat. 'Bruising now shows on the doctor's wrists. These are consistent with the deceased being held down against her will. Is that because she struggled against you despite having been drugged?'

'No. It wasn't me.'

'It would be much better if you tell me the truth, you know that don't you? The court is always more lenient to those who confess. Why did you do it, Ellie?'

'I didn't do it,' she whispered.

'Then how is it we found your fingerprints in Ms Khan's home? Even though you claim you've never been there?'

'I don't know.'

'You don't know or you don't want to tell me?'

'I don't know.'

'Please speak a little louder for the recording.'

'I said I don't know.'

Taking her time, the inspector took another item from her pile. She pushed a paper across the table and spoke for the recording. 'I am showing Mrs Mitchell the suicide note found at the victim's address. Please look.'

Ellie squinted at it.

'I would like you to read it. This is the suicide note supposedly left by the victim. Have you seen it before?'

'No.'

'Take your time. Are you certain?'

'Of course.'

'Then why does it have your prints all over it? Please explain that to me.'

'I can't because I've never seen it before. I don't know how my prints got on it.'

A chill stole into her as she realised that if she had been involved she might not even remember. But that was crazy. And she was not a murderer, she was sure of it.

'Your responses are really not very credible, you realise that, don't you?'

'But it's the truth.'

'I see.' Hunter steepled her fingers. 'Have you ever supplied paper to Ms Khan?'

She shook her head.

'Please answer a clear yes or no for the record.'

'No I have not.'

'I see.'

Ellie was sweating and she couldn't think straight. She got the impression Hunter looked triumphant. As if she were closing in for the kill.

This time, Hunter pulled a plastic evidence bag from the stack and slammed it down on the table.

'I am showing Mrs Mitchell the item discovered at her house. Take a good look and tell me what this is.'

She bit her lip. It was a pad of plain paper. The paper itself was standard size and ordinary in every way, although the cover was not because it had a pretty flower motif. She had bought it at Camden Market in London. 'It's my paper pad.'

'Your pad, which my officers found on *your* desk in the loft room of *your* house.' Hunter slowly ran her finger along the top edge. 'You see this tear line where a sheet has been taken off? And this little bulge where it didn't come away smoothly? And you see the tear line on the doctor's suicide note?'

Hunter laid the two side by side. On one there was a bite missing. It was matched by a bit of paper left at the top of the pad.

'Of course, I will be seeking expert opinion but perhaps you can explain to me how it is this tear line seems to be a mechanical match to Ms Khan's suicide note? Even to the naked eye it's obvious. Because the only explanation I can see is that the suicide note was written on paper taken from your pad, and it has your prints all over it, because you planted it in Ms Khan's house after you killed her.'

Oh god. Ellie felt as if she were drowning. None of this was true yet it all sounded so plausible. And that's when she put her head in her hands and felt like giving up. *No,* a little voice whispered, *remember you're a fighter. You've learned to be strong.* She would have to dig deep if she was going to get out of this and discover the truth.

Chapter Fifty

The next day, Sabrina phoned Rob at work. 'I saw the police came round last night.'

'Yes, they ransacked the place and Hunter arrested Ellie and grilled her but she hasn't been charged. Yet. She wasn't well enough for them to keep her at the police station so they let her come home. She's pretty much at an all-time low ebb.'

Sabrina tried not to laugh. 'The clock is ticking for your wife.'

Rob tutted. 'I told you before, no fucking until it's in the bag, so don't get impatient. Hunter is closing the net on her. Things are moving in the right direction and I've got a good chance of Ellie coughing up access to her funds. With her so fragile, I know I can make it happen. If you ask me she's at a tipping point.'

Sabrina suppressed a sigh. Rob had promised her everything – him, a plush Lewes lifestyle, a new Dad for Maddy. Meanwhile, she would have to let Rob play his little game with his wife. What he didn't know, was what Sabrina wanted from Ellie was worth far more than her bank account – because nothing tasted sweeter than revenge.

Chapter Fifty-one

When Rob left for work, it was still raining and Ellie watched out of the window. The forecast was more heavy rain, though what did she care? Hunter was waiting to throw her in prison and she shivered at the memory of the inspector's accusations. And her evidence.

Ellie realised too late she had forgotten to remind Rob to leave Lian and Rebecca's numbers. Damn.

Creeping to the sofa, she wrapped herself in a blanket. She must get to the truth about Ishtar's death. Otherwise she was finished. And how exactly was she supposed to do that, housebound and practically disabled?

Her balance was still weird and Doctor Hemmington had told her it would go back to normal once it was ready to, which had been far from helpful. Flicking through the television channels, she caught sight of the day. It was a Wednesday. Friday was her usual day for visiting Jacob. Perhaps she should take a risk while Rob was at work and go in a taxi, before she ended up behind bars.

She knew she was in no state to see her son, physically or mentally and that made her wobbly too. What she should do was tell Lian the truth and ask her friend to drive her to Clemence House. Lian would understand and Ellie hoped she would be forgiven for all the lies.

She was lost in her own thoughts, when there was a tapping at the door. Goddam it. Ellie made her way there, swearing under her breath.

'I'm coming as fast as I can,' she yelled.

She was sweating and though she had done her best to rush she was sure whoever it was must be wondering what took so long. Luckily it hadn't sounded like Hunter's insistent thumping.

Adam stood on the doorstep holding a big bunch of roses. 'These are from Kath, from her garden. She wanted to come herself except she was worried about slipping in this nasty weather. Kath sends her love.'

'Thank you so much.'

Adam put his arm around her shoulders and gave a squeeze.

'It's all right, Ellie, please don't get upset.'

Taking off his coat and shoes, he smiled sympathetically while she dabbed at her eyes. She didn't have the energy to explain about Hunter, and she didn't want the news to worry Kath.

'The accident has knocked the stuffing out of me. Sorry for being silly.'

'You need to take care of yourself and get better and it should be me apologising for traipsing in mud. The river is massively swollen and there's water running along the high street, but hey, I can't stay long. I wanted to bring you the info.'

'Sorry Adam, I've no idea what you're talking about.' She touched her temple. 'The concussion has been messing with my head and not everything has come back to me yet.'

'Oh right, that's a bit tricky.'

She put the roses in a vase. 'I'll arrange these properly later. Let's sit down and you can fill me in.' They went through to the lounge together, Ellie holding onto Adam's arm.

At the sofa, he opened up his laptop. 'Okay, you asked me to follow up on Sabrina's references and get new copies. Here they are, do you want to take a look?'

'Why did I ask for these?'

'Not sure exactly.' He gave her a worried smile.

'Just tell me, it's okay.'

'Well… I think it was something to do with your, er, son.'

She blinked several times.

'Yeah, well I did say it was a bit tricky. You told me and Kath you have a son who is five years old and you asked us to keep it quiet. You were worried Sabrina had found out about him. I think you wanted to check she was who she said she was.'

Ellie knew she was blushing. It was made worse by not remembering what exactly she had told them.

Adam smiled again. 'Don't worry about it, Ellie.' He passed over the screen. 'Maybe these will put your mind at ease.'

He was being so nice it almost made her cry. Jacob was such a precious secret and here was Adam being so kind and accepting. She pushed the feelings aside and made herself concentrate on the computer.

Sabrina had three references. Two were from prestigious hotels, dated from before Maddy was born. It seemed Sabrina had worked with them as a receptionist. The third was much more recent. It was dated one year ago and came from The Grosvenor Club in London, which appeared to be a hotel and a casino.

'They all say great things about Sabrina Gibson and I called to request them myself so I can vouch they come from the people she said they came from. The first two were in the original file I gave to your husband and the more recent London one was listed on her application form.'

'Don't you think it's odd she worked at a casino?' Ellie said. 'And not as a receptionist but as a croupier?'

'I couldn't see her doing it myself, but there you go.'

'It would have meant being out the whole night. What about Maddy?'

'I guess she had a babysitter.'

'Maybe.'

It didn't make sense with Sabrina so nervous about leaving her daughter. Of course, it was possible Sabrina had a trusted child minder but what on earth would motivate her. It would have to be a vital reason otherwise Sabrina would never have wanted to leave Maddy. And as a croupier? Why that choice? Didn't you have to have a specific training to work on gambling tables? It was downright odd.

'I thought Sabrina had funds from her divorce?' she said.

'She had a healthy bank balance and I know that's true because she showed me the statements herself.'

'So Sabrina didn't need to have a job.'

'I suppose not, but sometimes people do strange things. You'll have to ask her the whys yourself, all I can vouch for is these references are genuine.'

'Coffee?' she asked.

'I'm on my way to the office sorry I can't stop longer.'

When he left, Ellie made herself think it through. Sabrina didn't need money. She hated leaving Maddy. So why would Sabrina take employment in a casino. Doing a search online, she found out you did need specific qualifications to work on gambling tables. It seemed so strange. Why would Sabrina go to all that trouble?

The only reason Ellie could think of was perhaps Sabrina wanted to meet a new partner. Had she been looking for romance? Yet why not go back to working as a receptionist? Still, probably there were plenty of wealthy men who liked gambling and maybe ones looking for romance too. If you worked as a croupier you would be right in the thick of it side by side with them. That must be it, lots of flirting opportunities.

A horrible thought suddenly occurred to her.

She went to Rob's study, negotiating her way along the hallway. A calendar sat on his desk and Ellie studied the dates. He had been to a medical conference every couple of months since they got married and it made her think of Doctor Sajid Bakir's odd comment at her bedside. It had been niggling her because Sajid would know about conferences and he would know about Rob's engagements, wouldn't he? So like Sajid said, did it mean her husband had not been to conferences at all. Perhaps Rob had been lying to her.

Logging on, she scanned the details of The Grosvenor Club. Then she checked her and Rob's joint bank account. There were no receipts showing from the casino or the adjoining hotel. She went further back for the last few dates Rob had been away. Nothing. But hey, that was strange too, because there were no bills from anywhere at all, not a single tab for a restaurant or hotel room or taxi. She had never looked properly before and, if she had, she would probably have assumed Rob put all his expenses through the hospital. Yes, but even if he was going to conferences he would have had to pay for *something*. Didn't doctors foot the bill like everyone else and then claim it back? Why was *nothing* showing?

He must have a separate account. One she didn't know about. *Yes, and that way, he can hide where he goes.*

No, no, this was crazy. Was she losing the plot? Her arms were prickling with goosebumps and she gave them a vigorous rub. What if Rob had been deceiving her? How could she find out?

Casinos must be more strict than most places about confidentiality, still, it was always worth trying a little trick. She picked up the phone and a few minutes later, she was speaking to customer service at The Grosvenor Club.

'I understand from reception you've lost an item of jewellery?' the young woman said.

This was the second person Ellie had spoken to at Grosvenor. 'Like I explained to your colleague, it's not mine, it's my husband's. He's mislaid one of his cufflinks and he only realised recently though it might have been missing a while. We've searched everywhere and the only place we haven't checked is with you. I'm wondering if it's possible he mislaid it when he was with you last month. He was so upset because they were a Christmas gift from his late mother.'

'If you can give me a name and dates and a description of the item, I can check for you.'

'Thank you so much.' She described one of Rob's sapphire cufflinks.

The young woman tapped at a keyboard. 'We log every item we find meticulously, whether it's in the hotel or the casino, let's me see, oh I'm sorry, there's nothing like that listed for the dates you've given me.'

'Oh dear, he's going to be very upset. I hope we haven't made a mistake with the dates…' She left a hopeful pause, and breathed a sigh of relief when the young woman filled the space.

'Hmm, let me check for you. What was the name again?'

'Rob Mitchell.'

'Yes the dates are correct, Mr Mitchell was in our hotel on those dates ma'am, but I'm sorry I don't see any cufflink listed as items found.'

'Thank you so much for checking.'

'My pleasure.'

She put down the receiver. The lying hound. The next question being, had Sabrina met Rob there? Had she spotted him and liked him and come after him to Lewes? It seemed absurd. Or did it? The more she thought about it, the more it made sense of all the little clues she kept picking up on.

Ellie took a bath and she spent a long time in the bubbles trying to decide if she wanted to save her relationship with Rob. She had fallen so completely in love with him, it was hard to let that dream go. More importantly, if she was going to end their marriage, she wanted to be the one to do it, not have herself kicked out by Sabrina.

Was he having an affair with Sabrina? And what about Ishtar's suicide note left on her paper? After all, she and Rob were the only ones with easy access to her study. Could this all be linked? She would have to find out.

Chapter Fifty-two

There was still no new mobile for her when Rob got home. He told her the most recent model wasn't in stock and he'd put in an order. She didn't bother telling him she had bought one herself online, and she should get the delivery the following day. Rob also told her he had engaged a lawyer to represent her.

'Why do I need one? I'm innocent.'

Rob took her hands. 'Hunter has your prints on the note. The lawyer said we'll have to wait to find out what other evidence they have linking you to Ishtar's death but he found out your prints were nowhere else at the house. Apparently they haven't yet located Zach's keys either.'

'But there can't be any other evidence against me, can there? And the thing is, how did my paper get to Ishtar's?'

Did you take it? The accusation stuck in her throat. She wanted to ask him again although she already had and he insisted he had never taken anything from her loft room.

'That's the big mystery. The lawyer said there's no need to be worried and he doesn't think it's enough for them to charge you.'

'My note pad never leaves my office.'

He was being remarkably calm. 'I know, darling. Relax and let me take care of everything. It's going to be okay.'

Like hell it was.

'Let me make supper,' Rob said. 'Oh yes, and I got a call from the landscapers today. I suppose you didn't have a chance to settle the bill?'

Ellie felt a sinking feeling.

'I guess I don't feel as well as I thought I did because it slipped my mind. Could you deal with it?'

'Sure I can, if you give me the details.'

Under Rob's expectant gaze, she fidgeted. 'I've got an ID file on my computer with my bank account information. The password is Jacob and then the number 17.'

Jacob's name and his birthday.

'Jacob?' Rob was staring at her. 'Is he an old boyfriend?'

'Of course not, why on earth do you say that? It's the name of one of my favourite characters.'

'I see,' he nodded. 'And I forgot to ask about your memories, have they come back yet?'

Her stomach clenched. Most of them had though she didn't want to let him know because Rob would likely return to his insistent questioning about where she had been going. At least it meant he didn't yet know about Jacob and Clemence House.

She shook her head, noticing the twitch of temper at the corner of Rob's mouth. Would he go straight to her account and transfer funds? She would soon find out.

'What do you fancy, pasta or curried fish, your choice?' he said.

He was smiling at her again and Ellie chose the fish and she sat through Rob's chatter and then through supper, waiting for her moment.

When her husband went into the bathroom that night, Ellie was in bed, her heart beating hard. This was her chance. She listened to him taking off his clothes and dumping them on the floor, then came the sound of running water. She waited for the *clunk* of the glass door closing.

As quickly as she could, she slid from under the covers. Through the open bathroom door, she could see his mobile on top of the clothes. If Rob spotted her, she would be in trouble. She trod quietly and while he had his back to her, water running down the panels, she took a few steps, crouching low and reaching out, ignoring the throb in her torso and swiping up his phone.

Back in the bedroom, she hugged the pain in her ribs, her knees and hands shaky. To unlock it, Rob used a finger pattern of joining up dots and she had seen him enter it many times. Pressing her lips together to stop them trembling, she traced her finger across the screen.

Bingo. Up flashed the home page. Scrolling through to messages, she scanned the list of names. One of them was a repeater – *Sab*. The harsh reality hit her like a drench of cold water. There was message after message from *Sab*. It could only be one person – Sabrina, and it looked like the exchanges between them dated from way back, from not long after Ellie and Rob got married.

She read the last few and groaned. Oh god, from the content, at least on Sabrina's side, it looked like they had been lovers for months. What a fool she had been. She had so wanted Sabrina to be the one who was deceitful and Rob to be innocent. But how could it be like that if two people were lovers? And the messages didn't leave much to the imagination.

She was so crushed and betrayed, when the shower cut off, it took a few moments for her to react. She jumped, realising Rob was already out of the shower, which meant he would notice his mobile wasn't there. A sudden surge of anger spurred her into action and when he walked into the bedroom, towelling his hair, she tossed his phone onto the bed.

Rob frowned.

'I was trying to get Rebecca's number, except I couldn't open it.'

As he picked it up, she pulled the duvet closer around her.

'You only have to ask,' he said.

I did. Several times, you bastard.

She really hoped she had put it back the same as it was and Sabrina's love messages didn't pop straight up.

'Here,' Rob was showing her his contact list, 'you can write it down if you want, only I don't have Lian's or Kath's.'

'Thanks.' She averted her eyes and Rob waited until she wrote the number and then he took his phone back into the bathroom.

She had been holding her breath and she let it go. Rob was a cheat and a liar and all she wanted to do was get as far away from him as possible.

Chapter Fifty-three

Sabrina smiled to herself. Today was going to be a special day and because of it she put on her favourite eau de cologne – the one that always reminded her of her ex-husband. It was why she could smell it when she had her panic attacks. She puffed on several squirts of musk and sandalwood. Well, today she would wear it in celebration.

Taking her cake making ingredients from the cupboard, she weighed them out. Sugar and butter first and she blended them in the bowl, remembering with bitterness how her heart had been ripped in two. It made her feel like spitting in the mixture. Now Ellie was going to pay.

She beat the mixture until it gleamed, then spooned in the flour, added vanilla flavouring and a touch of salt.

Once the cake came out of the oven, she left it to cool and got started on the topping. She was going to make a dark chocolate one, so any aftertaste would be masked. As she melted chocolate in a pan, the rich aroma filled the kitchen. Then she took a small container from her handbag, handling it carefully.

It was a little bottle of clear liquid. This would do the trick nicely. She held it up to the light, then added half to the melted chocolate and mixed it in. Lunch with Ellie was going to be such a treat.

Chapter Fifty-four

The next day, Ellie felt hollow inside. She went through the motions of their usual goodbye routine, hiding her rage and berating herself for it, yet not feeling physically strong enough to have a full frontal shouting match. The blazing row her pride screamed for would have to wait until her headaches were gone. Instead, she would leave quietly and screw Rob on the finances. Once she had finished with him he would have no idea what had hit him, and for that, it was best to be sneaky. She waited until he left before she packed.

Her bag was almost done when who should show up at her door? Sabrina. Woman on woman, she could handle that, couldn't she? She would have liked to feel better for the encounter but now was as good a moment as any. Time to tell Sabrina exactly what she thought of her.

'Oh gosh, Ellie, are you okay?'

'No.'

Sabrina was all smiles and sympathy, though this time, Ellie understood it was an act and a very good one too. As Sabrina came in, she was oblivious to Ellie's mood. She chatted about her daughter and apparently Maddy was playing at Kath's house. That made Ellie even angrier because Kath was *her* friend not Sabrina's.

She had brought a huge cake. 'Here you go. It's one you'll really like.'

Rage about the affair had been boiling inside her waiting to rampage out and she felt like smashing the cake into Sabrina's chest. 'I'm glad you popped by.' *Because I'm going to enjoy telling you what I think of you.*

'That's what friends are for,' Sabrina said, again missing the tone of Ellie's voice. 'Shall I bring through plates?'

Ellie snorted. 'I suppose you know where they are.' *Though now we both know you're far from a friend.*

Cutting two slices, Sabrina carried them to the lounge. Ellie followed, dismayed when a new dizzy spell caught her unawares and left her having to creep her way back to the sofa. Damn. How best to play this. Was she really in a fit state for an outright confrontation?

'It must be horrible and Rob tells me you can't remember the days before the crash?'

'No, they're a bit of a blank though my memories are perfectly fine from earlier.'

'That's good.'

'Sorry?'

'I mean it must be weird though at least there's not much missing.'

She waited for her vision to stop swimming. On automatic, she took a plate and wiped a finger in the icing. Delicious. Well, no point in wasting it. She took a couple of bites.

Sabrina launched into news about Lian's craft room as Ellie remembered how Sabrina had first sat here and given a sob-story of being alone, and then used Ellie's sympathy to wriggle in amongst her friends. It made her furious to have been manipulated.

Swallowing the cake, she sat back. 'Let's cut the crap. There's no point in continuing your little game because I know what's going on.'

'What do you mean?'

'You're after Rob. You came to Lewes for him.'

Sabrina's eyes widened. 'What?'

'Don't play innocent with me.'

'Ellie, if I've offended you in some way, please-'

'For goodness sake stop!' As Ellie slammed her hand onto the coffee table, a sudden rush of wooziness made her head spin. 'You've been seducing my husband.'

'How on earth can you say that!'

'Because it's true.' Breaking out into a sweat, she wiped at her top lip. 'You're a liar and a con artist.'

Sabrina laughed, which infuriated her.

'You came here for Rob! Now get out of my house before I throw you out.'

'Oh, I don't think you're in a fit state to make me leave if I don't want to.'

Sabrina's voice had changed to a slow drawl and she sounded confident and smug and it was around then Ellie realised something was not at all right. Why did she feel so strange? She wiped again at her top lip and found it slick with perspiration.

Sabrina made a *tutting* sound. 'Not feeling good?'

Doctor Hemmington had told her if she got any funny spells she should contact him straight away. She needed to call him. Trying to get off the sofa, her legs wouldn't take her weight, buckling at the knees.

Sabrina mimicked Ellie's voice. '*I thought we were friends but really you're after Rob.* You shouldn't make things up. It's pathetic.'

She felt so much worse than she had at the hospital, worse even than when she first woke up. That could not be right. Her head was spinning so badly she had to concentrate to not pass out.

'You really are gullible, aren't you?'

Had she heard wrong? 'I know you planted Hayley's necklace for me to discover.' It was the only explanation because Sabrina was here for Rob, not because of Hayley.

She tried to keep sitting upright but couldn't, slumping to the side. 'I know you're after my husband. Now get… out.'

Sabrina's voice was cold. 'Oh so you worked out I left the Celtic necklace for you to find? Then you're not such a sad case after all. The photograph of Hayley wearing the necklace was in the newspapers and when I did my planning a long time ago I bought one. I thought it might be fun to throw you off the trail.'

Fun? Was the woman deranged? A horrible sick feeling welled up and for a moment, Ellie thought she would vomit. 'I know you worked at The Grosvenor Club. Is that where you met?'

'Oooh you have been doing your homework. Clever girl.'

Her breathing was fast and shallow. What the hell was wrong with her? 'You met Rob- and- and you decided - you wanted him. Is that why - you dug around and found - out about my son? So you could use Jacob - against me?'

Sabrina made a huffing noise and examined her nails.

Ellie couldn't hold on much longer. She caught a waft of Sabrina's eau de cologne as the woman bent over her.

'Oh dear, oh dear, perhaps you'd better lie down.'

She was too weak to resist as Sabrina pushed her back onto the cushions.

The hatred in Sabrina's voice made her panic. Oh god what the hell was happening? Was the woman unstable? And why the hell did she feel so ill.

Ellie's vision blurred and then everything went black.

When Ellie came to, she felt as if she had been smacked into by a bus. Her head throbbed and her eyesight was off. She panicked. Then she got a grip and grabbed the edge of the cushions to haul herself up. How long had she been here and what the hell just happened? She panted, trying to get her bearings.

Think, Ellie. It was still pouring with rain and it was daylight but she had no idea how long she blacked out for. She edged her way off the sofa. She must get to the phone and call for help.

By the time she made her way to Rob's study, her head was spinning again and she had to prop herself against the wall. The surge of relief was physical as she picked up the receiver. Pressing the plastic to her ear, she waited. Silence. Where the hell was the dialling tone! She tried to connect again and again. Oh god. It was dead.

She clenched her teeth and tried not to lose it. She had a head injury and unexplained symptoms, possibly dangerous. In foul weather like this could she make it to Kath's house? Wait a minute – the internet. She must send an email. Logging on to Rob's computer, she checked she still had connection and thanked her lucky stars there was, sending a message to Kath and to Lian asking for help. Please be working on your blog, Kath, and check your inbox. Lian would be at the school and she must hope Lian checked her messages during her breaks.

Should she go to Kath's? It was as she was debating if she should risk landing face down in the mud, when a dossier on Rob's desk caught her eye. It had the logo of the lettings agency on the front.

She flipped it open. It was the original dossier on Sabrina and she was about to close it when three horrible things happened at the same time. First, she heard a sound from upstairs – meaning someone was in the house. Fear crawled up her back. Oh god, was it Sabrina? She had assumed the woman had left but what if she hadn't, what if she was still here wanting to make trouble. The woman was dangerous there was no doubt about it. Second, she remembered the scent of Sabrina's eau de cologne as Sabrina had bent over her on the sofa – musk and sandalwood – a scent so familiar because it was the favourite of Jacob's father, and third, she caught sight of Sabrina's name written at the bottom of a page. It wasn't written as Sabrina Gibson, but as *Sabrina Gibson (formerly Beaumont).*

The shock sliced through her, squeezing a cold hand around her heart. Beaumont. The same name as Jacob's late father, Olivier Beaumont, and suddenly it all made sense.

Chapter Fifty-five

Sabrina left Ellie comatose in the lounge and went upstairs. She wanted to know everything about Rob and Ellie's life, so why not start in their bedroom.

Ellie's beauty products and cosmetics were expensive ones. It was extremely satisfactory smearing in a finger here and there, mixing up and spoiling the colours, leaving off tops for them to dry out, spilling liquids and smashing the lipsticks to a pulp.

She poked around Ellie's drawers in the walk-in closet. The woman had a lot of outfits neatly arranged, and plenty of shoes. Sabrina broke stilettoes from a couple of expensive pairs. She tried on clothes and then discarded them, ripping a skirt that was too small for her as she forced her way into it. Six years ago she had lost a beloved husband and a child not yet born. It was Ellie who killed them.

There was a nice selection of jewellery. Posing in front of the mirror, she tried earrings and necklaces. After the shock of receiving the news of her husband's death Sabrina had refused help, despite being four months pregnant. She told the police she would phone her mother in the morning and then she sat up all night though at some point she must have felt drowsy, because she was startled awake by a sharp pain. Looking down, there had been a horrible red stain spreading out on the cushions. Sabrina remembered the terror she felt as she realised what it meant.

That night, Sabrina lost not only her husband but also one of her unborn babies, Maddy's fraternal twin. The doctors had battled to save the remaining twin, Maddy. To deter more disaster Sabrina had to spend the rest of her pregnancy in a hospital bed, dreading any moment losing her remaining baby. It was the reason she hated hospitals.

It was why she had post-traumatic stress and was terrified of losing her daughter.

Moving on to Ellie's perfumes, she sniffed the bottles and emptied a couple on the carpet, pouring them from a height. Ellie was a murderer. Why should Ellie have happiness when she had stolen Sabrina's.

She yanked out Ellie's drawers and was delighted to find a half-used pack of contraceptive pills stuffed down the back. Oh yes, this would send Rob ballistic. She sniggered as she took a photo and sent it to him. Of course it made sense Ellie would not risk another disaster after her son being so ill for so long.

Olivier's funeral had passed in a blur. Sabrina had been knocked sideways by the grief and had to rely on her friends. The doctors had not been happy about her attending the service and insisted she keep her time there to a minimum. Olivier had been popular and lots of his literary agency colleagues came. His extended family travelled over. Though they lived in France, both his parents were originally from Romania and Olivier looked just like his father.

Sabrina was glad her friends had picked out a wide brimmed hat with a veil for her and she hid behind it.

It was towards the end of the ceremony Sabrina noticed someone stealing away early. It was a woman, tall and with long dark hair, and she had been hanging at the back of the crowd. Sabrina wondered who she was and when she asked around, no one seemed to know. It was then she started to first have suspicions.

Hurling the wedding photo of Ellie and Rob to the floor and stamping on it, Sabrina raked her hair back from her face. She would not be the one getting out of the house and never coming back. No, it would be Ellie, but first, she must be snapped in half like a twig. Broken. Never to be repaired. Just like the bitch of a woman had done to Sabrina.

Chapter Fifty-six

Fear made Ellie shaky. There was someone else in the house and if it was Olivier's wife, Ellie was in trouble.

Cautiously, she made her way back to the lounge. Sabrina's piece of cake was sitting untouched. In a moment of clarity, she realised she had started feeling sick right after eating it. *Oh god, is that why I was so ill? Did Sabrina poison me*?

The woman was dangerous. Adrenalin flooded her system and it helped clear her head. Wow, that was a lot better, at least now she could think straight. If Sabrina had drugged her and then tampered with the phone, she must get out quickly.

Creeping as quietly as she could to the entrance, she grabbed the first coat that came to hand and jammed her feet into trainers. Rain hammered on the door. Sabrina's bag lay on the floor, the zip halfway, and a familiar green label peeked through the gap. Ellie took out the bottle of Olivier's favourite cologne. Taking off the cap, she sniffed. Then she noticed something else nestled in the bottom of Sabrina's bag. Reaching in, she pulled it out and stared, her blood running cold.

When Sabrina heard a noise, she raced downstairs. Dammit, Ellie must have recovered from the drugs. How inconvenient. She must have messed up the dosage or else the bitch had not eaten enough.

She found Ellie by the front door. Gosh, she had moved quickly for someone who was supposed to be fragile.

'Feeling better are we?' Sabrina said. 'What are you doing in my husband's coat?'

'Jesus, Sabrina, you need help. Rob isn't your husband.'

'He soon will be.'

'I know why you went after Rob,' Ellie said. 'It's because of Olivier, isn't it?'

Sabrina lashed out, sending letters and a paperweight flying off a side table. 'How dare you say his name!'

'I didn't mean for it to happen.'

'You're a goddam murderer and you got away with it! Now you're going to pay.'

Oh god, is that what Sabrina believed? Ellie wanted to deny it but she couldn't, could she? At least not entirely. She lost her balance, grabbing at the wall and landing with a thump which jarred her ribs and left her panting. Sabrina eyed her with distaste.

'You bitch. Rob is simply a convenient by-product. It's not him I've been after, it's you.'

Sabrina had discovered the truth little by little. After the funeral, she had questioned Olivier's colleagues, she had sifted his phone messages and his emails, and that's how she found out Olivier was having an affair with Ellie. Olivier was a literary agent and he had signed up Ellie with the publishing house. Sabrina found out her husband and Ellie had gone to Paris together when Sabrina had believed Olivier to be away at a Book Fair.

'It wasn't my fault. It was an accident,' Ellie said, inching herself into a sitting position.

'You murdered him.'

'That's not true.'

Sabrina flicked back her hair. Ellie had lured Olivier away with her money and her success. And when Sabrina learned where Ellie lived she realised Ellie had been responsible for his death because Olivier's car had been in a collision with a truck a few streets away from Ellie's house. He had been killed instantly.

'I never knew Olivier was married,' Ellie said. 'He lied to me. I would never had started a relationship if I'd known.'

Sabrina knew it was Ellie who had enticed him away and if he hadn't been on that road he would still be alive.

'I lost my baby because of you, Maddy's twin. And now you're going to pay.'

Ellie did not know what to say. Was there any point in explaining how Olivier had seduced her? That he told Ellie he was single. That they had spent a wonderful weekend in Paris and he told her he loved her and she believed him. When she found out after his death how Olivier was married, the betrayal had been total.

Then it got worse. She and Olivier had signed a contract for a new house and Ellie had put up the money. She had trusted him but when Olivier died, she discovered he had omitted her name from the papers and she had no rights to the property. She lost it all. But she had not known about the loss of Maddy's twin.

'I'm so sorry.'

'I'm so sorry.' Sabrina mimicked it. 'Bloody bitch. It was fun tracking your miserable life and while you were struggling with depression and with a sick, disabled son, I found it just punishment. But when you met Rob, that's when I started to get really angry.'

'I didn't know about your loss. I don't know what to say and I know there's nothing I *can* say, but Sabrina, Olivier fooled me. I had no idea he was married.'

'Oh yeah,' Sabrina came close. 'And did my husband drink at yours that last night? It's a question I've been wanting to ask for a long time.'

The post-mortem found Olivier had alcohol in his bloodstream, above the legal limit. He had been drinking before he came to Ellie's, and it wasn't long after he arrived Ellie realised why. Olivier had come to break up with her. It had been a cruel twist of fate he died straight after.

She didn't discover she was pregnant with Jacob until later. The night he died, when Olivier helped himself to spirits at hers and then walked out, she had known Olivier would be driving and she had not cared. Nor made any attempt to stop him.

'Yes he drank before he left.'

Ellie had hated Olivier's guts when he went out the door – for the betrayal, for dumping her with no explanation. That's why she let him leave with his car keys in his hand and it was a snap decision she regretted to this day. If she had intervened, Olivier would never have encountered that truck. And now she knew Sabrina would never have lost her baby.

Sabrina cut her an icy look. 'All Rob wants is a comfortable life and he's going to get one. With me. Did you know he's a gambler and he's led quite a playboy lifestyle? How do you think he's frittered away all of Hayley's money?'

Money – Ellie always wondered if it was what attracted Olivier to her. The weekend they spent in Paris had been a splurge on luxury hotels and restaurants and she had bought Olivier a ridiculously expensive watch. The novel she released with Olivier's publisher had been her first big hit and the Paris trip had been their celebration. Months later, after his death, when Ellie lost most of her earnings in the house deal, she realised how he had used her. It was one of the reasons she was so careful now with her finances.

'You went after Rob for revenge but I never went after Olivier. He came after me.'

Sabrina's look was pure hatred. 'When I learned you got married, I vowed to ruin it. I found out all about Rob and his habits, including the gambling and just to let you know it was easy to attract his attention at The Grosvenor Club. He was known as a man who liked the ladies and your husband didn't object when I was all over him. Why do you think he enjoys going to the casino? Sure, he's hooked but it's not only that. Rob likes sex. He didn't say no when I offered and he didn't say no to having me here, right under your nose.'

'How long have you been lovers?'

'Ages. Rob's promised me everything.'

Ellie shook her head. *You're welcome to him.*

'So your abusive ex was an elaborate hoax.' She gave a dry laugh. 'Was it really worth it?'

'Oh yes – very much. All the lives you've ruined. I guess you realise it was a mistake to come to my husband's funeral? I didn't have any suspicions until I spotted you there. The nerve of it, turning up in front of me, in front of his parents and family from Romania, who the hell do you think you are?'

'What about my son.'

'I tracked you and your life so of course I knew about Jacob right from the beginning, and your breakdown, and Clemence House, and then I learned you got engaged. I couldn't believe it! You don't deserve happiness. No, you deserve misery and suffering. Do you know, every morning I wake up and it's like part of me has been ripped away? My therapist says I'll always feel like that after losing my little boy.'

There was no way for her to make it right. She had made a mistake with a married man. One who had lied and used her. She also knew there was no point in telling Sabrina how she was living off Ellie's money.

'Rob started out as a means to an end, then again, I do enjoy your husband. We make a lovely couple, don't you think?'

'He doesn't care for you. It's just a convenience for you both.'

'Oh we're more solid than that. How else do you think we came up with such great ideas? It was Rob's brainwave to kill

Ishtar and mine to type the suicide note on your paper. Neat, huh? The funny thing is, Rob didn't flinch about it. Which makes you wonder what he really felt towards you, doesn't it? And I'm pretty certain that little accident of Hayley's wasn't an accident at all.'

Ellie tried to get her feet under her so she could stand up.

'Oh yes, and I found these upstairs.' Sabrina came close and jiggled the pack of contraceptives in Ellie's face. 'Since you were so reluctant to give up control of your finances, he's been working on getting an heir out of you so he can get his hands on your money. Now he knows about these he's lost the plot. And I can't wait to see his face when I finally tell him about Jacob.'

Sabrina grabbed her bag and groped around inside. 'Oh, and Rob provided me with a little gift. Don't worry you won't feel a thing.'

Ellie inched away until her back was to the wall. 'Are you looking for this.' She held up the syringe she had found in Sabrina's bag. Filled with a clear liquid, she dreaded to think what was in it. As a precaution, she had snapped off the needle so it couldn't be used.

Sabrina screamed and lunged. As she did, Ellie brought her other hand from behind her back and squirted Olivier's cologne straight into Sabrina's eyes. The woman shrieked and recoiled, covering her face with her hands. Ellie squirted again and again. Then she stumbled out the door into the pouring rain.

Chapter Fifty-seven

Rob was in a good mood because he had received great news about the malpractice case. The hospital had called in an outside expert who had scrutinised Rob's actions and laid the full blame on the robotic arms. Handsome, sharp as a knife and destined for greatness – he had it all – didn't that deserve a drink?

On his way home, he stopped by a wine bar and celebrated with champagne. An overdose had been a fitting end for Ishtar, after all, she had so pined after Zach, better for her to join him wasn't it? He took a slug from his glass and refilled it.

Sabrina had contacted Rob to tell him she had passed a pleasant hour chatting with Ellie and sharing cake.

It was a relief to hear Sabrina was sticking to the plan. Actually, he had been concerned she was becoming impatient, wanting to race ahead and get rid of Ellie too soon, whereas Rob was still in the process of transferring Ellie's funds from her account to his. He had logged on after his wife spilled her details but the banks were being cautious and taking time, given the amounts involved. Rebecca had cautioned him to be careful and to wait until the final transfer before taking any drastic action against Ellie. He had to admit he was looking forward to being rich again.

He was halfway through his second glass when Sabrina sent a text.

Found these hidden in Ellie's closet.

He stared at the photograph of a half empty pack of contraceptive pills.

Rob's chest went tight and he almost broke his glass as he slammed it onto the counter. She had been playing him all along! My god, she deserved everything she got.

He texted back *I'm on my way*

The bar man gave a wary look as Rob kicked a stool aside and stormed out. All he wanted to do was crush his wife's throat.

Ellie pulled the coat around her. *Get away. Get to safety.*

Kath's would be the quickest through the gardens. Her feet slipped as she splattered through the puddles. She was going around the side of the house, when the bushes brushed wetly against her cheek and a lost memory popped into her mind – of the rabbit going missing. She had been searching on her hands and knees when she caught sight of Rob returning from his Berlin trip, just before they learned of Ishtar's death.

Turning towards the honeysuckle, she clutched the coat tight at her throat. Rob scuffling in the dirt, that's what she had wanted to remember ever since the accident. Icy fear crept up her back as she realised what he had been doing. He had been burying something. And now she knew what it was. It was the missing piece of the puzzle.

She had to discover the truth.

Water ran across the drive and she sloshed through it, pushing foliage out of her way to get to the ground. How long would Sabrina stay blinded? *Long enough, Ellie, and you need to know.*

She scrabbled in the dirt digging deep with her hand. The soil clogged her nails as she threw aside sodden clumps. There was nothing here and she laughed out loud. So this *was* all made up. Rob was not a killer and Sabrina was mad. Then her fingers contacted something hard.

If this was what she thought it was, she needed to be clever. Using the hem of the coat, she pulled the object free. It was a bunch of keys attached to a dirt encrusted fob. These must be Zachary's. The ones DI Hunter had searched their house for. The ones Ishtar's murderer had used to let themselves in when they killed her. Oh god. It was him. Rob was a killer.

A crashing in the distance brought her to her senses. At first she thought it was thunder and then she realised in terror what it was. A car coming up the driveway. She saw her husband's outline through the windscreen.

Ellie ran for her life.

Chapter Fifty-eight

Ellie made for the gate in the corner of the garden, ignoring the pain in her ribs and forcing her legs to move. He must have seen what she was doing. If he caught her she was as good as dead.

The new latch was stiff and she had to work to get it loose, her hands clumsy. She could not stop snatching glances behind, terrified to see Rob or Sabrina coming to drag her back.

The child lock finally gave way and the gate banged her shins as she flung it open. Then she was crashing through the bushes at the end of Kath's garden. Get away. Escape. Survive.

The ground was sodden and the downpour blinding. Her feet slipped this way and that, her heart pounding and her breath ragged. Branches slapped her face as she pushed through the trees. Kath's house was ahead, obscured by the pouring rain but as she got closer she hesitated. An old lady and a little girl were inside. She would never forgive herself if she brought danger to their door.

No, she must lead Rob away and down to the river. Skirting the house, she carried on down the path.

When she heard a shout behind, she almost lost her footing. *Get up, go faster*. She was jogging now ignoring the pain in her ribs as the path took a turn, becoming steeper as it headed downwards. Suddenly she cleared the undergrowth and the river was in front of her.

The news said the banks had been breached in several places with the Ouse swollen to an enormous size. She stared at the brown swirling surface. Oh god, this was madness.

On this side she was a sitting duck. The other bank was crowded with residential streets which would make it difficult for Rob to follow her. Somebody would help her or she could find her way to Lian's.

She slowed as she approached the bridge. The river was dangerous and she could sense its power. The news had said the bridge was unsafe but she had no choice because it was the closest place to cross.

'Ellie!' Rob shouted.

He's catching up.

She staggered on. The police had erected metal barriers to stop cars and she pushed her hair out of her eyes as she skirted them. Stepping onto the bridge, her foot sank into water as deep as her knee. *Oh my god.* The flood had risen monstrously. *It's impossible. You can't make it.*

'Come back Ellie! We can keep the secret. No one need ever know.'

He had gained on her and he was lying.

The roar of the river filled her ears. Clenching her teeth, she waded into the icy water. *Come on Ellie, be brave.*

She clung to the stone wall at the side, making her way slowly by lifting one leg then putting it down and then the other leg and putting it down. The force pushing against her threatened to drag her over at every step. Three more strides and the water was to her thighs. She was almost in the middle.

I'll be swept away. I can't do it.

Grabbing the wall with both hands, she felt her left leg losing purchase and she pushed it down with all her strength. She risked a quick glance behind and saw Rob had crossed the barrier and was wading into the water.

If I turn back now I'm dead. One more step, keep going.

Lifting her foot, she felt the suck of the current as it pulled her over. She scrabbled madly for safety. Mixed in with the sound of the water coming over her head, she heard a high bright call.

'Mummy!'

She screamed as the river dragged her under.

Chapter Fifty-nine

Rob yelled in fury as Ellie waded across the bridge. The bitch. She had played him, cheating him out of an heir, trying to keep him from her money. Too bad, because now he had control of it he could do what he wanted with her.

He had seen her checking under the honeysuckle bush and it fuelled his rage and hatred. Ellie had found Zachary's keys. All the time he had wasted building up her confidence and grooming her and fucking her!

No, she would not escape, his wife would not get the better of him. He must get his hands on those keys and then he would deal with Ellie.

He followed her across the bridge.

Part of him knew this was crazy. The river was far too high and people had drowned in the past trying to cross here when the Ouse flooded but he had to stop her. Ellie would go to the police and then he would be finished.

The river roared in his ears as he took several strides. He ignored the freezing water. He must get to Ellie before she reached the other side. The best thing to do would be to finish it quickly and drown her, then he could pretend it was an accident.

His wife was making slow progress. She was weaker than him and lighter which meant the water was more dangerous for her. He grinned. This was going to be easy and he confidently forged ahead.

Though she had crossed the mid-way point she was struggling and Rob picked up his pace. He must grab her, push her head under and keep it there.

It was as he lifted his foot for a big stride the current took him by surprise. He tried to grab the wall and didn't make it, fighting with all his strength to stay on his feet.

Ellie had reached the other side and she dragged herself out, spewing water. She had swallowed what felt like gallons when the river sucked her under. On her hands and knees she heaved it up. It had been her son's voice which gave her the strength to hold on and not give up.

A bitter cold invaded her bones as she hauled herself to her feet. She turned as Rob shouted in fear, just in time to see her husband's arm flung into the air as the river engulfed him and swept him away.

Chapter Sixty

A member of the public called emergency services and it wasn't long before paramedics and uniformed police arrived.

Ellie's teeth chattered as she sat in the back of the ambulance. It seemed a witness had spotted her in the water and they had reported a man pursuing her and then that person being washed downstream. Ellie learned the police were organising a search and rescue for Rob. She hoped they would be too late.

Once a police officer had taken her name, Detective Inspector Hunter soon arrived on site.

'What's happened? Why were you crossing the river?' Hunter asked.

'My husband was chasing me and I feared for my life.'

'With the river so high you took a grave risk.'

'I know and I had no choice. He came after me because I found something.'

DI Hunter came to sit beside her.

'I think you'll want these.' Ellie held out the bunch of keys. 'When Rob came back from Berlin I saw him hide them in our garden. It was just before you first came to our house and I'm pretty certain they're the ones you're looking for from Ishtar's place. The concussion made me forget. That's why Rob chased me. It was because he realised I had found them.'

When she picked them out of the dirt Ellie had been careful, and she still was. 'I haven't touched them so there's no way my prints will be on them. I'm guessing Rob's will be.'

'I see. And you say you'd forgotten about them until now?'

'That's right.'

Hunter held out an evidence bag and then sealed up the keys. 'These will be sent to the lab for testing.'

'I know you're thinking Rob and I were in it together but we weren't. I had no part in Ishtar's murder.'

'The evidence will be the judge of that and once the ambulance crew have finished, I'm going to need a full statement from you.'

'Let me guess, down at the station?'

She pulled the hypothermia blanket closer around her shoulders. For sure, once Hunter dug into Rob's phone and financial records, she would discover all kinds of dark secrets, including the affair with Sabrina. Ellie fully intended to tell Hunter everything and would be giving the syringe too, which she still had in her pocket. The police would find traces of drugs in the cake Sabrina had given her. And the woman would certainly be implicated in Ishtar's murder.

After the paramedics were finished, Ellie was taken to the police station where Hunter grilled her. At the end of it, she realised her name would not be in the clear until lab results came back on Zachary's keys and corroborated her story. She just hoped to god Rob's prints were all over them.

Afterwards they learned Rob had not yet been found and teams would continue the search until nightfall. Rob was a poor swimmer.

'He'd better be bloody dead,' she muttered to herself.

Chapter Sixty-one

It was one o'clock in the morning and Ellie had just arrived home when she received DI Hunter's text.

Rob Mitchell's body has been found

She breathed a sigh of relief. He got what he deserved and now there was only one outstanding problem to deal with.

Ellie banged on Sabrina's door. It was a while before it opened.

'Rob's dead,' she said. 'He drowned in the river.'

'You killed him too!'

Ellie side-stepped as the woman lunged for her.

'Oh no, I wouldn't do that if I were you. He got what was coming to him and besides, you didn't mean anything to each other so no point in bothering about it.'

Sabrina seemed stunned by Ellie's confidence. Ellie was a bit surprised by it too.

Ellie marched into the kitchen. 'I want you out of here.'

'You wouldn't dare.'

'Try me. I've told Detective Inspector Hunter everything. About you and Rob and about your plot to kill Ishtar. How you threatened me and drugged me. She has the syringe and she'll get samples of the cake.' She casually glanced towards the window. 'I guess they'll be here any minute to arrest you.'

Sabrina stared at her in horror.

'Oh,' Ellie tapped her nails on the counter, 'and if anyone's to blame for Olivier's death, it was him. For drinking and driving.'

As police sirens sounded in the distance, the look on Sabrina's face gave Ellie so much satisfaction, her ribs hurt.

She stayed to watch Sabrina being led away and when the social worker took Maddy, Ellie made a promise to herself that she would keep in touch with the little girl. For certain, it would be much better for Maddy not to be raised solely by an unstable mother. With the authorities involved, Maddy had a chance.

Next, Ellie ran to the loft room and logged on, just to double check. Who would have thought she would have the presence of mind to set up a dummy account and a protocol with the bank, in order to set a trap for Rob? *Well done you.* She had held her ground despite the pressure the bastard was applying and it meant her finances were intact. Rob had gone straight to the dummy account and attempted to empty it entirely and the bank had stalled him.

With all the madness and the danger over, all Ellie could think about was Jacob. It was time to sweep away all the pretences. A few minutes later she took a cab to see her son.

Chapter Sixty-two

An hour later she arrived at Clemence House. It was her good fortune Daniel was on duty and though he was surprised to see her he gave Ellie another full briefing on Jacob. It was mostly a repeat of what Daniel had been telling her on the phone but hearing it in person was so much more comforting. She didn't wake her son but she sat in his room, lightly stroking his cheek as he lay sleeping.

As the hours passed and she sat by the bedside, her thoughts turned to Rob. She had been right not to trust him. There had been something fundamentally wrong with the man and her instincts had been correct to keep her secret to protect her son. But she had been wrong to not confide in her friends.

She could see things more clearly and looking at her marriage and the way she had fallen for Rob, she realised he had played a very clever game. He had also caught her at a low ebb, when she was desperately in need of support.

She dreaded to think what might have happened to her at her husband's hands and she sent a silent prayer of thanks both for Jacob being saved and for her lucky escape.

Chapter Sixty-three

At Kath's house, a teaspoon *chinked* on the saucer and liquid poured from on high as Kath prepared tea for them both.

'I'm so relieved it's all over,' Kath said. 'It's an incredible story.'

'You're telling me and I think I'm going to need several months to recover and without your support and Adam's help I don't know what I would have done. Adam checking on Sabrina for me was a life saver.'

'I know he's very pleased about that. There was no one more relieved than Adam that justice was served.'

The way Kath said it made the back of Ellie's neck tingle. She spoke carefully. 'Hmm, and he was right about the roses. The police found a stash of weedkiller at Sabrina's place.'

'She deserves to be punished,' Kath said. 'For trying to kill you and not to mention her part in the doctor's death.'

Ellie took her time sipping from her cup. 'You know I couldn't help thinking Adam must be a similar age to Christian and with his interest in roses and plants, it's as if he grew up in a house with a big garden, like Hayley's family used to have.'

What she didn't say was how she had also noticed Adam's emotion over all they learned about Rob. And when she herself went to visit Hayley's grave, there had been flowers placed there. Any local person might have brought them, but it had been such a pretty bouquet fresh from a garden and it had made her wonder.

Kath tutted. 'That's the trouble with you writers, you've got over-active imaginations.'

Yet Kath didn't quite meet her eye. Wouldn't it be curious if Christian really had come back to Lewes? She guessed she might never know for sure.

Kath passed over a plate of biscuits. 'It's going to be tough for Maddy.'

'I know and I'm hoping I can keep in touch with her. The social worker made positive noises about it, since Maddy and Jacob are related.'

And your son? How is he doing?'

'A lot better.'

'I'm so relieved to hear it and, you know I read a little about metachromic leukodystrophy. It said both parents need to be carriers for the child to develop the disease?'

'That's right. Both Olivier and I were carriers which is why Jacob has it. If it had been just one of us he would have been okay.'

'So I suppose that means Maddy is in the clear?'

'It would be a one in a million chance Sabrina was a carrier, and I'm sure she checked it out years ago when she found out about Jacob. So yes, Maddy must be okay. I'll make certain to raise it with the authorities, just to be sure.'

'I hope I can meet your son soon.'

'Me too and I was silly not to talk to you about him before, I hope you can forgive me.'

'I've told you already there's nothing to forgive, my dear.'

Ellie dabbed at her eyes. Her true friends had been so generous. Kath, Adam and Lian had showered her with care and kindness.

'You know it was the keys that saved me, because Rob's prints were all over them, whereas mine weren't. The police have dropped charges against me.'

Kath visibly shivered. 'Rob was such a wonderful boy. How can a life go so wrong?'

Hunter had told Ellie she had cast an eye over the death of Rob's previous wife. Hunter would not be re-opening Hayley's case, however, she had dug deep into Rob's finances and it seemed he had been very generous over the years sharing his wealth with his sister. After Rob's body was found, Rebecca refused to speak to Ellie which suited Ellie just fine because it looked as if Rebecca might have been involved in her brother's dark deeds all along.

Ellie had questioned herself about the very first meeting with Rob at the art gallery, set up by Rebecca. Kath wasn't the only one to shiver in the sunshine. It seemed Ellie had been manipulated by very clever people.

Chapter Sixty-four – many months later

'Pizza will be ready in five minutes,' Ellie shouted across the lawn. 'Did you hear me?'

'Yes, we heard,' called back one of Lian's boys.

Jacob glanced over his shoulder in Ellie's direction and he smiled. 'We got it Mum, don't worry.'

The three children – Jacob, and Lian's two, were playing together and Ellie watched as Jacob shuffled after the others.

'He's getting stronger every time I see him,' Lian said.

'I know his progress has been amazing. He's such a fighter.'

Lian smiled. 'Just like his mum.'

Perhaps Lian was right. After all, she had survived.

Ellie sat back and enjoyed the sunshine. It was her and Jacob's first summer in their new house. Actually, not just the two of them. They had brought Cleopatra with them because the rabbit had turned up in Ellie's garden a few days after Rob drowned.

It was strange to think how, without the horrible events, she would never have learned Jacob's father had ancestry in Romania.

Every moment of every day for months, Ellie had contacted as many companies as possible in Romania to ask their employees to volunteer to be donors. Not long after, like a miracle, a match had turned up.

Thanks to the donor, Jacob had received a bone marrow transplant. His regression had been stabilised and since then he had gone from strength to strength. Now he was on the register for a gene transfer with the hope of a true cure for the disease.

'Is Daniel calling by later?' Lian asked.

Ellie blushed. Her new place was not far from Clemence House. Jacob lived with her now but she had chosen the location to be near the facility, in case her son needed it, and also to be close to Daniel.

'He said he'd pop by.'

'I bet he did. How exciting.'

'We're not getting too ahead of ourselves,' Ellie said. 'Me and Daniel is just a casual relationship.'

'Of course it is and he is *so nice*.'

Ellie laughed. Daniel had been one of the saving graces and so had keeping her friendship with Lian.

Jacob was laughing at the top of his voice and Ellie so loved the sound of it. Doctor Venn had said the thing about remissions was you never knew how long they might last for – not all of them lasted forever. Ellie understood the transplant was a true blessing and from now on they would be making the most of every minute of every day. And they were both looking forward to the future.

*

You might also like…

Deadly Lies

When six-year-old Emily and four-year-old Lisa are abducted from their grandparent's house, Detective Grant and criminal profiler Ruby Silver race against time to find them.

The family have their fair share of enemies and when they receive a ransom demand from the kidnapper, secrets from the past come to light. Then a murder throws the investigation into turmoil as treachery and lies threaten to tear the family apart.

Who is responsible for the abduction and why?
And could the answers lie closer to home than anyone ever imagined?

What readers are saying –

'One of the best crime thrillers I have read this year!'

'...could not put this down and finally turned the last page in the wee hours. Yes this book is that good!'

'…lots of twists and turns...'

'A 100% must read'

Grab your copy today

A message from Ann Girdharry –

Hello and thank you so much for choosing The Couple Upstairs!

One of the things I love about being an author is hearing direct from readers.
So if you'd like to get in touch, please do. You might have a question about one of my books. Or maybe you have a general question about publishing. Or maybe you've spotted a typo or an error.
Whatever it is, feel free to send me an email. I'd be delighted to hear from you.

You might be interested to know I used to work in the quaint Sussex town of Lewes.

Like in this story, there was a huge flood in the town, in 2000. Barrels of beer went floating down the high street, when the local brewery was flooded out! I knew the brewery, because I used to collect used hops from Harvey's Brewery to put on my allotment. It was this flood which gave me inspiration for the ending of the story.

If you're an avid reader and you'd like to receive news and updates, you can join my Reader's Group. Don't worry, no spam. I'll only get in touch when I have something I think you might genuinely be interested in, like the release of a new book. I offer a free gift to new members and you can find details on my webpage – www.girdharry.com

Happy Reading,
Ann Girdharry
Email – ann@girdharry.com

Acknowledgements

A huge thank you to my wonderful early readers - Kat, Kate and Kath (yes, it was all K's on my beta team this time).

A very special thank you to Shalini at Digital Reads Library for her comments on the early draft of the story. Shalini did a wonderful job, as ever, getting it into shape. I know I can always count on her.

Special thanks also to Mark Romain for checking through the police procedural elements. Mark was a Metropolitan Police officer for thirty years. He spent two stints on homicide, the last one spanning ten years, and worked on a number of high-profile cases. It's always a pleasure to work with him.

Avid crime readers can be assured any mistakes in the storyline are entirely my own or included for dramatic effect!

Titles by this Author

Deadly Motives
Deadly Secrets
Deadly Lies

Good Girl Bad Girl
London Noir
The Beauty Killers

The Couple Upstairs

Printed in Great Britain
by Amazon

77616046R00163